I0780849

NYIF

For the readers.

CITY OF FIRE

I

HELL IN THERE

Adrian peeked through the gap between big wooden door and big wooden frame, with a light knock before entering his father's study.

"Come in," Eldon said.

Adrian came forward. He always did as he was told, unlike his brother. Ray, now twelve years old, was called into this room often. Adrian, the good son, almost never was. He didn't like it here. He didn't like the implication of reprimand that all wood-lined studies — like the principal's office at school — unfailingly implied.

The place was quiet, dominated by the barely-perceptible ticking of a clock. Adrian usually stayed out of Eldon's office on principle, entering only when he was sent for something or when his father called him. The clock unnerved him every time: water torture on the tympani of his eardrums. He hated its oppressive non-presence — its ubiquity of sound without apparent source. Adrian had looked, yet had no idea where the clock was. The sound might not even *be* a clock. For all he knew, his father had a metronome in his office: white noise more rhythmic than wind or static. It was the sound of tension to Adrian. He didn't know how his father could stand it. Every minute spent here felt like a countdown to something terrible.

"Your mother tells me you got into a fight."

Eldon didn't require his sons to call him "sir." He wasn't even that kind of man. But where he stood, feeling like he should be wringing a hat in his hand and saying *Yes, sir.*

Adrian was seldom punished. Seldom put himself in the position to *be* punished. Ray called him timid. Or, technically, Ray called him a pussy. Ray had no problem being called before his father. Why would he? They were exactly alike. Eldon was tall, brash, and manly — this fussy study notwithstanding. Ray was tall, brash, and on his way to being just as testosterone-filled. Adrian was quiet. It was ironic, the way the son who most needed discipline was the most comfortable, embracing punishments like a test of his mettle.

It wasn't that way for Adrian. Knowing how much Ray would mock him if he saw him now, he just looked at the floor and nodded. He was a beaten dog, afraid he'd displeased the master.

"Who did you fight, Adrian?"

"Cray James."

"I think I know his mother," Eldon said, nodding. "Big kid. Black hair. About yay tall?" Eldon held a hand up to indicate Cray's height. It was close to correct: a teenager's size, not an eight-year-old's.

Adrian nodded again.

"Hurt him pretty bad, I hear."

Now Adrian looked away.

"What did you hit him with?"

Adrian looked farther away.

"Adrian Marcus Porter? I asked you a question."

"It was a piece of metal."

Eldon nodded. He'd known; he just wanted Adrian to say it. "Rebar, to be specific. They make forms out of it before pouring concrete, to give it strength. Why did you hit that poor kid with a stick of rebar, Adrian?"

The clock ticked. "Dad, he was picking on Damon again! He was making fun of his clothes! Took his tablet and threw it in the fountain! He—"

Eldon held up a hand. It was covered in scars, front and back. A Legion's hand, forged in fire. Literally.

"I didn't ask what Cray did. I asked why you hit him."

"To make him stop!"

"Why not just talk to him? Why not use words instead of violence?"

"I tried! He wouldn't stop! He ..."

This time Adrian had trailed off on his own, because a strange look was on his father's face.

"Why not create a coherent argument and present it to him logically? Why not write up a proposal and present it to him?" Eldon sat one butt cheek on his desk, waving that scarred hand like a philosopher considering a koan. "*Why not* draft a treaty spelling out proper behavior and limits on bullying behavior, then get Cray to ratify it for you?"

Adrian's brow wrinkled. His father wore a cryptic expression. His eyes went to the still-ajar door. He got up and closed it.

"Let me show you something." He moved to a large, two-door cabinet in the room's corner. It looked like a wardrobe, but that was an assumption. Adrian realized as his father unlocked the thing that he'd never seen it open.

He'd never wondered what was inside.

The doors revealed a large space of shelves full of odd-looking items: all part of Eldon's research. He was known as a fighter, with another side the public didn't see and that Ray, who preferred acting rashly to thinking, refused to notice. The world believed Eldon was only a brute-force Legion. Secretly, he was curious, too.

Inside the cabinet was what looked like a small refrigerator. Eldon opened it and, after donning insulating gloves, removed two domed glass cylinders. White fog drifted from them as he crossed the room, then set them on a workbench in the corner that was stacked with papers and supplies for small experiments. So not a refrigerator. Adrian could feel cold air moving his way. It had to be a freezer.

"Look," he said.

Adrian did. Then he gasped.

"Are those ... Are those *fiends?*"

"Shh," Eldon said. "But yes. They're a subspecies the guys are calling 'sliders.' I shouldn't have them, but there's more research to be done than the lab is interested in doing right now."

To Adrian, they looked like worms. The bottoms of the two glass cylinders were about the diameter of a coffee mug. The worms-things were on these bottoms, with the glass domes rising four or so inches above them. Sealed. Frozen stiff. Already condensation had fogged the glass, freezing solid. Soon you'd have to wipe the ice away to see.

"So," Eldon said. "They're life, right? Even fiends are life."

Adrian wondered if that was a trick question. They were, though, in his opinion. Fiends were life in the way scorpions and deadly spiders were life. There were even weirdoes who didn't like the battle against the rifts, who protested the brigade for just that reason: Fiends were life, and Legions killed fiends. Never mind that all the fiends were trying to kill people. That they were tiny little hellspawn, bent on mayhem.

"I guess?"

Eldon smiled at Adrian's political answer. "They are. Just

take my word on that one. Sit here." He indicated a stool along the bench. He took one of the two fiend-domes and put it right in front of Adrian. The other stayed farther down the bench, behind him.

Eldon wiped the clear part to rid it of frost. As Adrian watched, the wormlike fiend in the container in front of him began to squirm very slowly.

"They're *alive?*"

His father nodded. "The cold makes them sleep. Look. Now that it's out of the deep-freeze, it's waking up."

The worm was still sluggish, only one end motile at all.

"They live in temperatures upwards of five or six hundred degrees Fahrenheit. That's what it's like in their domain." He tapped the container. "These little enclosures were made by our scientists. They're not glass. Glass would break, as cold and hot as these containers get. The environment inside is sealed. That's their air, not ours, inside."

Adrian looked inside with fascination. As the gas warmed, it took on a reddish tinge. His friend Matt would have said, *That's Hell in there.*

"The cold is terrible for them, Adrian. That's what you need to understand. They can *survive* it just fine, just like they can survive on our air, but it's agony. Our air isn't too big a deal, and normal temperatures like my office right now—" Eldon indicated the space around him. "—aren't too big a deal. But cold? *Actual cold,* like it's dealing with right now? Being frozen is incredibly, *incredibly* painful for them, according to the scientists."

Adrian kept watching. It was hard to feel sympathy for the thing, seeing as it was a worm. And a fiend.

"I could help it, though. Because it's life, and because I want to be kind, and because I have a heart and don't want anything to suffer, I could give it a hand."

Eldon pushed some glassware away: beakers, tubes through rubber stoppers, a rack of empty test tubes. He pulled a stand forward, then put the dome containing the fiend in a mounted ring clamp. He pulled a small bunsen burner forward, turned on its gas, and used a sparker to light the flame.

The blue-gas jet was right under the fiend container. It warmed fast, ice melting and the tinged air inside becoming noticeably red.

As the container heated up, the fiend inside began to move with more animation. It was soon climbing its containment's walls. Then it began to grow, at least quadrupling in size until it was a big fat maggot, a tiny toothed mouth on the underside trying to chomp the glass.

"See? Now it's happy. Now I've helped it. And that's good, right? To be kind. To do no harm, because it's like us; it's life and it deserves to live. I didn't have to keep it frozen. I didn't have to kill it. I didn't even—" He looked meaningfully at Adrian. "—have to beat it with rebar so badly that it had to go to the hospital."

Adrian's eyes flicked to his father. He hadn't known that. Cray went to the hospital? Adrian had only hit him three times. Okay, four. Once in the face. It'd taken that much, though! Cray was a real ass, unwilling to back down.

"I'm sorry, Dad."

"For what?"

"For hitting Cray. You're right. I know better."

"So you agree." Eldon was nodding slightly.

"Yes."

"You agree that there's always a better way. That the correct course of action was to find a teacher, not deal with that bully yourself. That you should always try to do the right thing first. What's right is always right. Good is good, and a moral person knows the difference. Compassion first, correct? Violence only as the very last resort. *That's* what your mother taught you, Adrian. What the school taught you. What the entirety of society — the same society that falls apart if people can't agree on a code of conduct, doing good for each other — has taught you. Is that about right, Adrian?"

This time he *did* say it, with head hung: "Yes, sir."

"Look behind you."

Adrian looked over his shoulder. The sight startled him so badly, he nearly fell off his stool and hit the ground.

The fiend inside the second container — the one Eldon had left down the bench — now completely filled its prison. It was easily ten times the size of the fiend inside container atop the bunsen burner. The glass was still flecked with frost, thawing only because warm flesh was pressed against it from the inside. Its tiny legs were thrashing, trying to reach Adrian through the glass. Its mouth, much larger than the other one's, was biting the walls, trying to reach its victim and tear it apart.

Adrian staggered as he moved away. He backed into his father, who caught him and turned him around.

"I didn't call you in here to yell at you, Adrian. I called you in here to say I'm proud of you." He pointed. "Those fiends? They're connected to one another. I think all of them probably are. They're not like us. I have *one* body. *You* have one body. But I think the fiends have *many* bodies. That's why they keep coming no matter how many we kill: because to them, it's like losing a fingernail here, a strand of hair there. We don't kill individuals. Not really — not in any way that matters. We're only killing smaller parts of a larger whole."

Eldon squatted, eye to eye with his son. "I was just trying to do a good thing, warming up that poor cold creature. That poor, cold *living thing.*" He laughed. "But was I really just helping it get by?"

He shook his head. "I applied heat to one of them. It sent the vitality I was giving it through their bond to its buddy instead of keeping it for itself, though. It did it even though that meant continuing to suffer. So you see? I tried to throw a lifeline. But it didn't want a lifeline so much as it wanted to use the rope I threw to tie a noose. A noose for you."

He pointed at Adrian. "It wanted to kill you more than it wanted to be comfortable. That's how people can be sometimes, kid. If you'd just told on Cray or if you'd tried to fight him fair, what would he have done with your compassion? Would he have thanked you for it? Or would he have seen it as weakness, and made you pay?"

"Are you saying you want me to act first and think second, like Ray?"

Eldon laughed a little. "You're not like your brother. You're not even that much like me. I don't want you to stop being who you are, Adrian. The world needs thinkers. It needs people who are compassionate and patient. But only up to a limit."

He pointed at the tubes with the fiends inside. "The lesson of what I just showed you is that you can't always do 'the right thing.' Sometimes, even though everything inside you says you shouldn't, you have to do the *wrong* thing. Because the real world isn't black and white. Not everyone and everything plays by the rules."

Eldon opened a container covered in warning stickers at his feet. Its contents fogged, its label declaring it to be liquid nitrogen. Then, using tongs, he took the tube from the burner and dropped it into the nitrogen.

A cloud boiled out, the fiend flash freezing. As it did, the fiend inside the second tube, nowhere near the nitrogen, shrunk and froze as well.

"Sometimes you have to do the *wrong* thing, because real life is filled with grays, and sometimes there's a lot more to things than anyone else sees." He looked direly at his son. "Always do the greatest good. Even if it means doing bad now. Even if it means everyone hates you and thinks you did something wrong. Even if you end up taking punishment for it."

"Punishment?" Adrian asked.

"You're grounded. You did the wrong thing today … and don't tell your mother, but I'm proud of you for it."

2
DREAMS

Adrian jerked awake hard enough to sit fully, racking his skull against the underside of the bunk above him. Up there, Harrison Kim was still snoring. The dream was still with him. He had to look down to verify that he still had adult legs. He had to look at his hands in the dim of the bunkhouse: adult hands. Yet he could still feel Eldon's hand on his shoulder. Seconds ago, he'd been alive again.

"Ade?"

He looked over. Ray.

Dee Scott, who slept above him, breathed as soundly as Harrison. Only Adrian and Ray were awake. The Porter brothers had always had a bond, always a little able to feel what the other was feeling. Ever since the bottom almost fell out of the world six months ago, that bond had at least tripled.

Erika Dale, before she'd halfway transformed into a fiend and died, had told them that the fiends communicated telepathically, *feeling* into each other more than using actual words. It hadn't turned out to be entirely accurate, what their father said about all fiends being parts of a single whole. It was halfway true, but not all the way. Some were individuals, the scientists at GEN thought now. Some were small collectives — groups that might number in the hundreds of bodies, but really only followed one mind.

The official line still said those minds, small or large, were ultimately mindless. Adrian and Ray knew otherwise. They had spoken, through mental impressions and feelings, to one of them on the day the mother of all rifts nearly opened.

That's how they'd made the bargain that saved the world.

That's how Adrian, without meaning to, had traded his girlfriend for the city of Fortune. Maybe for the entire world.

Somehow Adrian's mind had found the trick of talking to the enormous red demon's mind. Ray, after it was over and the rifts closed, told Adrian that his mind had done the same. The after-effect of that bond had been interesting, if sometimes disturbing: These days, they could damn near feel into each other.

"Dreams?" Ray asked.

The thump of Adrian's head must have woken him. Or maybe it was feeling Adrian's pain, which followed the thump. It was subtle. Nothing useful, like everything that had happened since.

Adrian nodded.

"Laurel?"

No. Thank God. If there *was* a God. Adrian was no longer sure if he believed or not. Genuinely; he did not know. He'd once been devout. Riftfare had made that devotion practical, literally a job to do.

Was "the fiend plane" another word for Hell? If it was, shouldn't there also be a Heaven? It felt more and more like semantics. As confused as the issue had been in riftfare's prime, it was even more bewildering now.

Ray and Adrian used to look demons in the eye. Now more

often than not, it felt to Adrian like even all that past had to be taken on faith.

"This was about Dad."

"In Hell?" Dreams of Laurel were always in Hell, because that's where Adrian's own instructions had dragged her.

"No. It was a memory." He rubbed his head, feeling his eyes wide in the darkness, the bunkroom lit only wanly by the cool light of a gibbous moon. "It was so real. I was *there*, Ray."

"What memory?"

Adrian shook his head, hoping it was answer enough to stop Ray from asking again. He didn't want to relive it for Ray, their father's favorite. There were many times when it'd just been the two of them, just Eldon and Adrian, but the dream he'd had was the most intimate. With Adrian, Eldon liked to talk theory. Only that one time had he taught Adrian something in the go-hard way he'd have taught it to Ray.

Only that one time, in Adrian's memory, had his father said he was proud.

"It's the dreadnought," Ray said.

"You think?"

Ray nodded. "They're holding it just two blocks down. I saw them bring it in. And *Jesus* on that, by the way."

Adrian laid back on his pillow, unable to hear Harrison's snores as different from the incessant ticking of his father's clock. He'd heard that happened to some people — the foggy thoughts the dreadnought caused — but he hadn't thought he'd be among them.

Something about the big thing's energy made radios go on the fritz, too.

Denny Brennan said it generated a "distinct electrical disturbance" not unlike the massive disturbance that had shut Fortune down before Matt Baker and Erika Dale's so-called "sundering" almost occurred. Adrian tended to think of it in less scientific terms: It was bad juju that fucked with your head, plain and simple. And maybe it went double for heads that had already been demon-fucked, like those of the Porters.

As if he'd heard Adrian's thoughts (and who knew? Maybe he had), Ray tapped his head and said. "Me too."

"What do you dream of?"

"Mom. Dying. Over and over and over. *Screaming*, Adrian. I've started taking pills Kaur gave me. Herbs of some sort. They keep it at bay. Keep me from dreaming."

Adrian wondered if he should take heart from what Ray was saying. Ray's dreams of Mom dying weren't real, obviously, because Mom wasn't dead. She'd responded so incredibly well to the new Zen Scan treatment that even doctors who used to only say "remission" were starting to use the word "cured."

Maybe if Ray's dreams were just that — only dreams — then so were his. Maybe Laurel wasn't being pulled apart over and over again. Maybe she still had her skin; maybe she hadn't been flayed. Maybe she wasn't in constant, screaming agony the way he dreamed of her — and not just screaming, but screaming his name because the fiends who'd taken her in the devil's bargain Adrian hadn't meant to make had told her *Adrian* was the reason she'd gone.

It was hard to believe. The dreams were so real. He could feel the furnace-heat of the other plane, which increasingly he had to recall from deep down because it'd been so long since he'd felt it in life.

In those dreams, he couldn't breathe because he wore no rebreather. His eyes dried out, crusted over, and yet kept right on seeing. He heard the hellscape: the rolling of cogs, the boiling of brimstone, the clanking of unseen chains, and of course the symphony of misery that came from everywhere at once. The scent was odious, like a world full of rotting eggs.

Sometimes, when he woke from those dreams, his tongue could still taste the sulfur.

And the dream with his father. *That* had been real. So which should he believe? That the dreams showed him the truth of Laurel's whereabouts? Or that those horrors were his own book of invented lies?

"It felt …" Adrian stalled out, then tried again. "It felt like the dream was some part of myself trying to—"

The muster bell rang. The lights, tied to it, came on. The bunkroom roused, but sleepily so. What time was it? Adrian hadn't checked. He wanted to check. He *shouldn't* want to check anything other than himself, though, because his mind should be on one and only one thing when that bell rang: rousing, hitting the locker room, and suiting up.

But he wasn't the only one. There was a day not long ago when the ringing of the bell would turn the stationhouse from slumber to muster in a blink, but it felt like a distant memory. To just about everyone.

Harrison sat up above Adrian, creaking the bunk. Adrian heard him yawn. He saw an arm past the bunk's edge, lazily stretching.

Above Ray, Dee was sitting up, her massive black hair flat on one side. Nobody was hopping down. Nobody was running.

"The hell?" said Harrison.

Then the PA came on, and Darren Kaur's voice boomed through it. There was a camera in the corner. Adrian was drawn to it, feeling like he was looking directly into the captain's eye.

"Get the fuck up, you assholes!" Kaur boomed. "Are you waiting for an invitation?"

They moved sluggishly even then by brigade standards, though it was lethargic with a purpose this time. The recess housing the Porters, Harrison, and Dee was one of the first to empty and reach their gear, but the rest of the old Stitchers and Legions came soon after.

Adrian pulled on his boots and, because had no idea what this could possibly be, donned his asbestos pants as well. It felt like putting on a Halloween costume. Beside him, Stitcher Shannon Holt looked like she felt the same way.

"Pants too?" She looked at Adrian.

It was strange, having any amount of conversation. Six months ago, they'd be in the vehicles by now, screaming toward the scene of some big rift, some demonic incursion. Now, in the same amount of time, nobody was even dressed. They weren't used to being woken in the middle of the night anymore. Or being called. Or rifts. Or dressing quickly, let alone donning gear.

The joke lately had been that the station was the world's worst hotel. You could sleep all night with a dozen other people in rooms that smelled like feet instead of sleeping at home a few nights a week ... but at least there were no wake-up calls.

Until now. Until today.

"I don't know," Adrian told Shannon. "I used to just do the jacket 99 percent of the time, but I figured it was best to be prepared."

"What's going on?" she asked, going for the pants.

"I don't know."

"Is it a rift? Has there been a rift?"

"*Shannon.*" Adrian pointed at his head, which was a mess. "Look at my hair. Do you seriously think someone with this hair knows more than you do?"

Chatter was everywhere. Could it be a rift? Anything was possible, but to Adrian his entire past career had started to feel like a dream, and it was a much less realistic than those of Laurel, those of his father.

Had it all really happened? Did they really used to rush to enormous flaming gashes in the fabric of the universe, wielding bulky backpack gear like some poor man's Ghostbusters? It was so strange to think about, now that they all had distance.

They were night watchmen now. They were mall cops. It was only a matter of time before they became a line item on some politician's budget: an easy *Yes* to be stricken. You save a lot of money when you stop paying so many people to do so little.

Kaur burst into the locker room, screaming and making big circles with one arm.

"Go! Go! Go!"

So they went. All of them. The Legions geared up with Rollards and the new GEN multifunction weapons. The Stitchers took their welders, their extra filler rods, and the M9 sidearms they all wore just in case ... and they went.

The only questions were: *Where?* And *Why?*

3

NO MAN'S LAND

Ollie Davis and Jacqui Keogh, both Legions, struck Adrian as two adults playing dress-up as they sat across from him in the deployment truck. He looked like an action hero and she looked like Tomb Raider. Their gear was brand new: shiny black flak shirts still with creases where they'd been folded, Ollie with his overcoat in his lap, forearms the diameter of bowling balls crossed on his chest in a way that implied this mission had better impress him. Their weapons were mostly unused. Nothing they held or wore was marred with scorch marks or bore the telltale streaks of Zen corrosion — a curious thing that happened when unrefined Element interacted with aerosolized metals from their side in the presence of blast gasses from ours.

The weapons' matte-black perfection made them look like toys to Adrian. The people holding them looked like poseurs. The Brigade's old gear had projected a very different atmosphere than the one in the truck right now. That gear had been honest, having gone to Hell and back. Now, though, even their Rollards were clean. That was just wrong. Pristine Rollards were like a gleaming Jeep. In a rational world, neither was supposed to happen.

The wheels on the road made a steady, soporific drone. The men and women inside were human metronomes, rocking back and forth. The clatter of their gear, one shoulder against the next and rack to rack, counted the beats.

"So," said Ollie.

"Nobody knows, Ollie," said Ray.

"Nobody?"

"Nobody," Ray echoed.

Ollie looked at Adrian. He was a mountain of a man, probably Samoan. "Adrian?"

"I don't know either, Ollie. The call rang. We scrambled. We'll find out when we get there."

But there was a lot about their interaction that didn't quite work. The first question was why Ollie, after getting nothing from Ray or anyone else who might have spoken up, had specifically addressed Adrian. It couldn't be because they thought he was a rat for working with Special Agent J. Dixon in Spread and Containment. The Porter boys' "save the city" move when the shit went down had erased most of that. It wasn't long ago that every Legion and Stitcher in the city had been lured to Matt Baker's cabin up at Devil's Castle, stripped naked, and held in a corral like pigs for the slaughter, leaving only the Porters to enter the last rift Fortune might have ever seen. The fact that Adrian worked with Dixon (who was building a case against Brigade One for Zen theft) had stopped mattering when he and Ray prevented the sunder. It was because of Ray and Adrian that the final hole hadn't opened. It was because of what they did that day that rifts, practically speaking, never really opened again.

"I don't get this shit," Ollie said, apparently not finished. He didn't mean the situation; he meant the gun-thing on his lap. They'd all been trained with the new gear, but only Ray had used anything like it in battle. A Legion never trusted a weapon until they'd covered it in blood. "First wave we face is just gonna laugh at me. Paulson rifles and the stuff we used to use at least looked intimidating. But I mean, look at *this.*"

He hoisted it. It was too light, made of a rock-hard polymer that resembled plastic. "Shit was made by Hasbro."

"It's the most advanced weapon you've ever held," Ray said. "Don't knock it 'til you've tried it."

Ollie looked doubtful but said nothing else.

When Ray and Adrian had started fighting small rifts on their own last year — without a brigade's worth of Legions to hold the incursion back while the class was determined and the right weapons selected — GEN had given Ray a dinky version of what they all held now. Just six months ago, the idea of packing all necessary weapons into a single unit meant sacrificing power for versatility. It had been more important for Ray to have every option at his disposal than for any one of those options to be terribly strong.

After the crisis, fear loosened purse strings and development money flowed into GEN like presents at Christmas. Funds were all it'd required to take that first multi-function and ramp it up — to make each selectable weapon as powerful as the old stack of separate weapons used to be.

Thinking this gave Adrian vertigo. He was looking at a brigade's worth of spectacularly-equipped newbies — the most-ever expenditure in service of nothing. How much time had passed between the Federal endowment and the effective end of riftfare? Maybe two months before things had ended on their own? All this shiny new gear only arrived *after* it was needed. Until tonight's deployment, the best gear they'd ever had was sitting in boxes and hanging on racks. Most of it even smelled new.

"It's not a weapon," said Lee Barnes. "It's a noose."

No one replied. Lee was an academic sort, big on saying weighty things just so he'd sound smart. The others usually mocked him. This time, not so much. Because the weapon in every Legion's lap right now *was* a noose, same as the improved Stitching gear in their laps. Same as the protective gear was a noose and the scoop gear used by the rendering crews (or actually, *not* used).

Billions upon billions of dollars had been spent because the near-apocalypse had finally scared the wider world into paying attention to the Gore Point again. That's why, unused, it'd become a liability now.

Ironically, the politicians who'd voted for those dollars would be happier if Hell was still on the world's doorstep. At least that way, they'd feel like their money was well spent. As things had shaken out, the rift problem seemed to have solved itself. One last push by Fortune's riftfare brigades after the big incursion — using the old gear, before the new shit was ready — had apparently closed things for good. Just as almost happened on the day Eldon Porter died, the final rifts had been closed and kept closed. GEN thought the planes were healing, now that weak spots had stopped appearing.

It was at that point — after *problem solved; nothing to see here* — that the new gear had arrived. All that expense for nothing; that's the way Washington saw things. What followed was nationwide buyers' remorse. The foul taste of it, in political circles, had put a big red X over every brigade. Ironically, having spending money just might end up being what killed them for good.

They had blown their wad too early. Or too late. They'd needed a big budget before Hell arrived or a smaller one after it left. Instead, it seemed more likely each day that almost all of riftfare would get the axe in an attempt to retroactively stop the financial bleeding — a move like closing the gate after the cows were all gone.

How many Legions, Stitchers, renderers, and scientists would be allowed to survive? Adrian pictured one bored watchman on a stool: the only thing standing between Earth and ruin, if it ever started up again.

Maybe, he thought as the truck rattled on, *this call is a good thing.* Middle-of-the-night. Energy in the air. Peril was back and they'd be in danger. For now the camera crews were still on call, still eager to watch them fight.

Good. Let the world see that there are still rifts. That the Gore Point hasn't gone quiet after all. That there's still a need for brigades, so they'd better not close them down.

The game had changed, not ended. Now back after a short intermission. That's what Adrian hoped as they barreled toward the unknown, unsure it'd make a difference.

"My dick's rock hard," Ollie announced. "That feels like a good sign."

The truck drove. No one replied.

"Prison break," Harrison Kim purred, hoisting his weapon. He said it in testosterone fashion. If the weapon had a slide like a shotgun, he absolutely would have racked it.

"No," said Kaur, arriving in the second truck. "Just a prison."

Adrian looked up. With no rear windows in the truck, they'd had no idea where they were headed. There would usually be a briefing along the way: whatever it took to get the Legions ready to fight the rift ahead and the Stitchers ready to close it.

The lack of a briefing this time had dampened his hope. All the new gear had made the department cocky — no briefing needed because the job was so *done* — or what was actually true: There *was* no rift. Nothing to fight at all.

Adrian didn't know that for sure, but it felt right. The facility they'd reached wasn't truly a prison in the normal sense, but instead a holding place for expelled fiends. That's how fucked things had gotten in the last half-year: Instead of killing fiends out of hand, the flow had slowed enough that the last ones through were captured instead.

It happened because during the big cleanup, some asshole had gotten hold of Erika Dale's private notes and shared them with the internet. Nothing too confidential, just some things the brigade had learned the hard way.

Specifically, the world now knew that beings from the other plane weren't as dumb as they pretended to be. There was a lot that used to be common knowledge about riftfare: rifts only opened inside the Gore Point inside the city of Fortune; only one class of fiends came from any given rift; only one rift opened at a time.

Eldon Porter had suspected those things weren't necessarily true, Erika had learned it by collaborating with the other side, and everyone around Adrian now had found it out when one by one, those rules had been broken. Now the Brigade knew it'd been one long con — a ploy the fiends had made so they could build up to the sundering that never ended up happening.

Unfortunately, the internet knew it, too, though thankfully they didn't know the next thing: that the fiends hadn't been *defeated* that day so much as *decided* not to rip the world a new bleeding asshole — that a deal had been struck, and Adrian alone knew why.

Laurel for the world, if indeed that wasn't yet another deception.

The internet had many opinions on things they had nothing to do with, after seeing Erika's findings about the fiends. One of those opinions was that if fiends could run cons, they obviously weren't as mindless as people used to think.

If they weren't mindless, they possessed intelligence ... and, hey — you couldn't just *murder* things that had intelligence. Especially because Erika's notes had also told them another thing: She'd believed the fiends didn't want to conquer us. What we'd done to them, in harvesting their Zen, was at least as bad as what they'd done to us.

That made them feel like less of a threat. Like maybe they shouldn't be slaughtered, but reasoned with instead.

So said all the keyboard jockeys out there. All the people who had the luxury of living far from Fortune, out where the notion of capturing instead of killing fiends made perfect sense.

"We're here to burn it down. *Tell* me we're here to burn it, Cap."

Kaur didn't dignify Ray with a response. He took the front of the gathering and the cameras turned his way. They were the same cameras that used to cheer for Ray's gory fiend kills. That felt like a forever ago.

"Ladies and gentlemen. What we have here is what GEN calls an 'energetic disturbance.'"

Groans percolated. If a rift existed, they wouldn't be standing out here, cool as a press conference. Which Kaur's gathering sort of was, in addition to being informative to the people here to do their jobs. All the new attention on Fortune had put everything under a spotlight. "Transparency" had become an obnoxious new watchword.

Now that Adrian had "press conference" in his head, he could hear the delicacy in the captain's words: the precision he was exhibiting to make this a properly informative performance, not just what his soldiers needed to know.

"GEN alerted me this morning that Zen Element sensors monitoring this holding facility seemed to be showing rift-like activity. Personnel inside says they've seen flashes coming from some of the containment environments — flashes that sound a lot like rift aurora. That gives us a fair degree of confidence that there are, in fact, incursions happening inside."

That seemed to lift the brigade's mood a little — hesitant cheers replaced the groans — but Adrian withheld judgment. He'd been looking up at the building since they arrived. It had many windows, mostly for watchdog reasons: wouldn't want anyone accusing the state of abusing the otherworldly prisoners. The windows showed no flashes. No aurora. In the old days, they could feel rift energetics from a mile away. The hot breath of its expulsion had a distinct feel and an unfortunate, unforgettable smell.

There was none of that here. It was civilized enough that Adrian felt out of place with a stitching rig on his back. He should be wearing a suit. Shaking hands. Maybe kissing babies.

"What magnitude?" Ray asked.

Kaur exhaled. He seemed to have wanted to not address that one aloud. "Nothing for the public to worry about. So far they're also exhibiting a shorter-than-usual period. Remember, that's good. It means the work we do is effectively preventative, necessitating less—"

"Okay," Ray said. "What *period?*"

Kaur looked at Ray for a full second before answering.

There had been something between them for weeks. Ray *needed* fighting. It's what defined him. Without rifts, Ray had no adrenaline, excitement, or way to measure his own worth and strength against the world at large. Adrian's burden was guilt, with a much heavier weight.

"Seconds," Kaur answered.

The group chattered. Heads turned. Annoyance percolated.

"Okay, listen," he said, and hearing him Adrian actually felt heartened. Before now, they'd been hearing from Kaur the politician, determined to say the right things and not come off like the showboats a lot of public opinion felt rift-workers to be. Forced into a public corner by Ray, Kaur had become a captain again. "You assholes get paid to do a job. So you know what? Now you're gonna fuckin' do it. A hell-bringer comes out of a Wal-Mart, that's on us. But this? This shit's on us, too. I don't care if you think you're too good for it. You hear?"

Ray was still stone-faced, but at least respect for the captain was back.

"Seconds-long periods," Kaur repeated. "Most of what's going on there will close before you get a chance to pull up your pants. To me, the video they sent me looks like it could be salt and pepper. Or maybe it's nothing. I could care less."

Salt and pepper. Was that really possible? That was how it all began.

They hadn't seen the little bang-pop of pre-rifts attempting to open in all the time any of them had been fighting, but everyone present knew what it was. Supposedly the name came from a Legion on Eldon's brigade who'd once been a hibachi chef. He said the tiny flashing light show the other plane put on in the old days, when it was first trying to break through, looked like when he sprinkled pepper into flames to wow his dinner audiences.

"As to magnitude, it's what you'd expect to go with the light show. These are zero-fives."

"What's a zero-five even look like?" Shannon said to nobody in particular.

"Size of a baseball," Ray replied. "My dad called them puppet-box rifts. They were just big enough to stick your arm through. If, you know, anyone would do that."

"That's right." Kaur nodded. "I'd say the average rift in what I saw is maybe four inches long and lasts two or three seconds before closing on its own. Intel can't say why they started. That's part of what we're here for: to find out."

"And the rest of why we're here?" someone asked.

"Transport and relocation. Surveil and respond."

"You're kidding."

"I'm not kidding," Kaur replied. "Let's go."

ONCE OUT OF the camera's eye, Kaur spoke even more plainly after pulling Adrian aside. "There's more."

"Cap?"

They'd just entered the facility. It was technically a prison because it contained beings and didn't plan to let them go, but there was another institution that matched that definition that Adrian for one found more fitting: a zoo.

The building was only two floors, open in the middle and strewn with catwalks and metal staircases. Around the perimeter were sealed, environmentally-controlled chambers containing up to a dozen fiends each, sorted by size. It was supposedly fantastically expensive to maintain and, in Adrian's opinion, a far greater waste of taxpayer dollars than making sure the brigade was prepared for incursions that had yet to come.

Kaur had Adrian in a recess, away from the others.

Including Ray. "You're the only one here other than me who knows everything that happened at the GEN warehouse last year."

He was talking about their final showdown with Erika Dale, when a black portal opened and the entire place filled — quite literally — with every class of fiend ever discovered. The showpiece had been a demon so large and so apparently intelligent, in charge of it all, that it officially hadn't been there at all. Special Agent Dixon had heard their report, then told them to tell no one, under any circumstances.

Kaur only thought he knew everything. In truth, he knew only a little more than everyone else.

"Ray's report mentioned something a lot like what's happening here. Like salt and pepper."

"It did?"

Kaur nodded, surprised that Adrian didn't know. His attention had been on Erika as she transformed from human to fiend so she could live among them when the bottom fell out of forever.

"I didn't notice. Maybe you should talk to Ray."

"I'm talking to you. Spread and Containment never gave Ray official clearance. I know you two talk. Obviously. But it's off-books enough that ..."

He didn't need to finish.

Adrian looked beyond Kaur to see the brigade, under the leadership of its lieutenants, spreading out and climbing the stairs. It was repugnant, what they had to do next. Instead of slaughtering the things up there — things that, unlike the giant beast that hadn't officially existed, really *were* just mindless, no more important to their collective than fallen-out hairs and certainly without feelings to hurt — they'd get the honor of putting them in restraints and moving them around.

It was janitor duty. One by one, they'd open each environment, clear out the sulfur, and look for popping rifts that didn't need their attention anyway. It was solid proof that Fortune had stopped looking to Brigade One for salvation and had started looking for things for it to do while soaking up the budget.

They were fully isolated. Kaur really didn't want to be overheard. Or seen talking to Adrian, who S&C would never want him talking to in private.

"I don't know what to tell you, Cap. There was a lot happening. There was a whirlpool that looked like black ink in the floor and nightmares kept coming out. We had one Rollard and one beta-era multifunction weapon. I was too preoccupied with ..."

Damn. Adrian liked Kaur and really, now of all times, wanted his thoughts on this. But he couldn't mention the enormous red demon or the fact that Erika had figured out how to become one of them. Those things were Top Secret, for GEN, S&C, and the Feds' eyes only.

"With all the other stuff that was going on," Adrian finished.

"Tell you something, Porter," Kaur said, moving a fractional inch closer to him. "I think there's something we're not being told."

"About this deployment?"

"About everything."

Kaur's eyes were dark brown. Hard. It was difficult not to flinch away from them.

There was no question of *I think* in Kaur's mind; Adrian understood that now. Kaur didn't *think*; he *knew*. He *knew* there was something the grunts weren't being told about the state of planar warfare, if it was indeed still warfare. He also knew that Adrian knew what it was, and didn't like it one damned bit.

"Anything you can tell me will help," he told Adrian.

"I honestly don't remember salt and pepper."

He remembered killing Erika by blowing the dust of one highly allergenic peanut into her face.

He remembered how, once Erika was dead, the big demon's desire for the Porters to join their Hell-on-Earth campaign had only increased, wanting them even more than before.

He remembered his own cowardly insistence that they take Denny Brennan instead, because Brennan knew how to refine Zen to give them the energy they'd been losing and sorely needed.

He remembered how, instead of suggesting Brennan, his shoddy psychic impression had suggested they take Laurel instead.

He remembered his nightmares since. His need to find her, and his willingness to charge into the first rift he saw afterward to do so. The only problem was, there'd never been a chance. Outlying brigades had handled the first post-near-sundering repairs, and by the time they were done, rifts had stopped opening. None to run into, foolhardy as Adrian wished to be.

Adrian remembered being willing to die if it meant getting her back. Truth be told, he remembered wishing for it.

But he didn't remember salt and pepper. That was the truth.

"Because," Kaur continued, "the official line here is that this is just some sort of equalization discharge. They tell me all these fiends in here are just sort of sparking off in harmony with the other plane as it repairs ... blah blah blah; it's all very condescending and sciencesplained. And, okay, maybe that's the truth. God knows I wouldn't have a clue one way or the other. But if that's *not* what it is — if there's even a small chance that this might be micro-incursions in advance of another entry like happened at the beginning instead of little equalization bubbles — that means my people are in danger. *Your* people, Adrian."

This was no-man's land. Kaur could be right. *Might* be right. But it remained true that Adrian had no clue. It didn't mean he couldn't find out.

"I don't know, sir."

Kaur watched Adrian for another few seconds, then dropped his eyes and let him go. "All right. Then *fall in.*"

4

INHALE

Adrian fell in with the others. He climbed the first metal staircase he found, joining the Stitchers up top rather than looking for Ray among the Legions below.

The job was already proving to be as menial and thankless as they'd feared: Legions assigned to opening cells, corralling the occupants, then holding them using a repellant field GEN originally built for the fiend version of crowd control. After Ray and Adrian's report, the entire field of Zen Element weapons development changed. It had to. It was clear now that there had only ever been one class of fiend in a given rift because the fiends did it on purpose — to give humans the illusion of an ongoing battle instead of one they should have lost long ago.

The fiends wouldn't sandbag in the same way now; that was the thinking. Thus the development of multi-use weaponry, able to select for different classes on the fly because Legions could no longer count on predictable opponents coming one-by-one in orderly fashion. Thus the need for better blunt-force weaponry, seeing as only blunt force — in the form of Rollards — had the ability to kill anything. And thus the development of a sub-field GEN called "control weapons," like the repelling field. That way, Legions could push back the fiends they didn't have time to fight.

In this case, it was more like fire hoses, plastic cuffs, and rubber bullets meant to keep mobs from getting out of hand. Inmate relocation for cell cleaning: That's what Legionry had been reduced to.

The Stitchers on the second floor, on the other hand, were doing work closer to what they'd been trained for. It was *less* undignified. There were still no rifts big enough to step into, no need for oxygen or rebreathers or even heat suits, no need for finding midlines and using rigs to fire Zen epoxy meant to seal a breach. Things were as Kaur described: many small rifts popping into and out of existence on their own. They happened mostly off the floor, at chest or head height, and even calling them 0.5 magnitude seemed to Adrian like a stretch.

The rifts were tiny. Open and closed. Numerous. Sparking with aurora for only a few seconds, closed without intervention almost immediately after. They reminded Adrian of pop-bang firecrackers. Or, yes, as salt and pepper.

His father's voice, as they ate around the dinner table: *It's like there's a whole other dimension behind the things. Peeking in. Testing us.*

Of course he'd been drunk. Mom hadn't liked it when he talked about the rifts even before the very first fiend crossed over — before there had been a proper rift or the word to go with it — but the boys hadn't been afraid of talk of another dimension: not Adrian, certainly not Ray.

Eldon Porter became the world's first Legion, but before that he'd been a curious man willing to take risks when scientists weren't. The thing about little rifts being just big enough to stick your arm through? Eldon, foolhardy as he was, had bragged about doing just that.

But mostly it was his father's idea about the other dimension "peeking in" that recurred to Adrian now. The little rifts felt experimental to him. And they were odd, too. Big rifts blew outward like a blast furnace. Standing near the huge downtown slash rift last year — the one that tore open from the top floor of a hospital to the lower floor of an apartment building down the block — had felt like entering a furnace.

These little popcorn rifts should feel like breathers playing peek-a-boo: a hot breath on the back of your neck, but when you turn around, the rift that blew it was already gone. That wasn't always happening, though. Some never exhaled at all.

Abid Sher was elbowing past him, micro-stitcher at the ready. Nobody knew what to do with these things. Should they try to close them or not? As far as Adrian could tell, not one of them had persisted.

"Abid," Adrian said. "Give me a cigarette."

"Ah. Now Hell has truly frozen over."

He laughed, but Adrian didn't. Things were far from Hell freezing, but he wished he didn't know as much as he did about thermodynamics and entropy. Living with Laurel and liaising with Danny (not to mention speaking a bunch to Erika Dale, before he knew her as a traitor) had given him a kind of scientific contact high. He didn't know all the details of their work, but he'd absorbed enough to feel it when something was wrong.

Hell wasn't freezing over, but what bugged him now did have to do with heat. Or at least with energy, which seemed to be moving in the wrong direction.

"You are serious," said Abid.

"Come on. My mom got rid of her cancer. I miss it. I want some of my own."

Shrugging, Abid handed him a cigarette. Adrian used Abid's lighter to light it, coughing for a full minute when the ignition inhale hit his lungs. The other Stitchers in the room laughed, but they were all watching. Adrian didn't smoke. This was something else.

He dragged on the thing, careful to only take smoke into his mouth. Then he waited for a rift to open nearby and blew a plume at it. What happened next was just as he'd suspected.

The popcorn rifts hopping up inside the fiend containment facility weren't neutral, breathing out only a little bit of super-heated breath. They were actively *inhaling*.

"Woah," said Shannon, coming alongside. "That's weird."

But it wasn't just *weird*. It was *wrong*. The coolest parts of the other plane were still over five hundred degrees Fahrenheit, whereas the room they were in was sixty-five at most. Thermodynamics said heat should move air *out* of the rift, not *into* it.

It made Adrian think of something Erika had said while she was monologuing, about how people talk like Zen Element violates the laws of thermodynamics because it produces more energy than it consumes. About how that's not actually true. About how that energy has to come from somewhere. About how all the energy humanity harvested from the stuff wasn't free after all.

They had been stealing without knowing it — taking all that bounty from the fiends' plane, and draining it dry.

What did it mean? His gut called back to Erika's words, not his brain. Adrian was smart, but he was no Laurel. If Laurel were here, she'd be able to tell him what the hot rift's inhaling meant. If Laurel were here, she'd be able to put words to the creeping feeling he had right now — this sense that as innocent as all of this tiny-rift-popping seemed, it was far from harmless.

It's hot there and cold here ... and yet air's moving from cold to hot, not from hot to cold like it should.

It meant some sort of energy imbalance. Where thermodynamics were concerned, there was no such thing as a free lunch.

He thumbed his radio, tuning in to Kaur's private channel. "Captain, there's something you should—"

He stopped when the complex around him erupted in a fusillade of loud snapping sounds — as the whole place seemed to fill with unseen firecrackers, exploding like wood knots in a fire.

5
EMPTY

When Adrian exited the cell he'd been in (dutifully evacuated of its occupants by Legions so the more-relevant-for-once Stitchers could do their work), he entered the most chaotic scene he'd seen since the big perforation, the electromagnetic pulse, and the bargain that had nearly ended this part of the world.

It took a second before he thought to be bothered. His first reaction, right from the gut, was relief. The way things had been in Fortune lately — no rifts, no incursions, just the handful of fiends in facilities like this one that needed to be rounded up — was wrong.

Adrian couldn't explain why, but it was. The public was happy. The people of Fortune were happy. The country was happy and the government, despite bitching about all the money spent in Fortune for no results, was quietly happy. No news was good news, right?

Adrian's senses had told him from the start that it wasn't. Not in riftfare. Not even after the big fiend told him that the human plane would be safe as long as the fiends kept the scientist who'd teach them to refine Zen and save their world.

The big fiend didn't mean this, Adrian kept thinking. *It meant we'd be safe in that bargain ... but it didn't mean this.*

All this silence. All this non-activity. All this normality. It was wrong. Something more was going on, just as Kaur suspected.

Chaos on the prison's lower level burst that abnormality, and for the first few seconds Adrian believed the false peace had ended; a rift had finally opened and the world made sense again. Atop that shallow relief was a deeper kind specific to Adrian: Rifts were doorways; they knew that now.

Common sense once said it was death to enter rifts for longer than the minute it took to stitch their insides, but last year Matt Baker, Ray, and Adrian had crossed a hundred or more yards of hellscape. They'd used a pair of rifts like a wormhole to shortcut all the way across town. The geography wasn't one to one and the rules were different, but in the end he'd come to think of the fiend plane as just another place. He'd survived it for a while. With the right equipment, he could survive for longer.

Long enough to enter. To walk around in their homeworld the way he'd walk anywhere else. To do whatever it took — whatever was required to hunt down Laurel and bring her home.

Yeah, said a sinister voice inside, laughing at his naïveté. *Whatever's left of her.*

But Adrian had no time for the macabre. No time for pessimism. No time, even, for optimism. Because his first impression turned out to be wrong about what was happening on the prison's lower floor.

It wasn't a rift. It wasn't an expulsion and there were no new fiends. No Hellbringer had arrived unexpectedly to slaughter his friends like one ended his father. The scene below was exactly the opposite.

Movement flashed in the corner of Adrian's eye. His head jerked, not seeing whatever-it-was in time. He'd spotted a flash, heard a gasp, but now all he saw was Dee Scott staring at nothing with her eyes wide. She had her weapon raised, the repulsion nozzle out and extended. Her thumb released the trigger and what had looked like heat-haze in front of the muzzle (actually the repulsion field, meant to drive Element-filled beings away from the weapon) disappeared.

A pair of fiend restraints — this one for quadrupeds; Adrian thought her group had been relocating halfskulls — lay on the concrete floor looking lonely. As Adrian watched, Dee looked to someone in the cell beside her that he couldn't see, her mouth open.

She mouthed something that looked to him like *What. The. Fuck.*

Another pop, again like a knot in a fire. Adrian jumped and so did Lee Barnes, who'd come up to stand on the metal catwalk beside him. He must have seen what made the sound, though Adrian again had missed it. His face looked like Dee's had.

"What is this, Adrian?" he asked.

More shouts. More pops. Someone, maybe Kaur, was yelling for a report, barking for calm. Nobody was hurt; Adrian couldn't even spot many fiends below. It was chaos of confusion, not battle. Whatever he'd yet to pin down was incomprehensible more than threatening.

To Lee, Adrian said, "What was it? What did you—?"

But then he stopped, because he finally saw.

In the middle of the open area below, some of the Legions had corralled twenty or so fiends they'd taken out of one of the units so Stitchers could check it out — and do exactly the same kind of nothing with the salt and pepper rifts down there that Adrian and the others had been doing up top.

It had been a pointless exercise until now, but all that was changing.

The fiends were surrounded by guarding Legions, each one restrained with bindings suitable to their class. They were well-behaved: quiescent and not causing trouble. That in itself was strange by last year's standards, but that particular thing had been odd for a while.

Used to be, fiends charged from rifts with intent to kill. After the sundering was called off, though, the fiends that came out of the remaining rifts had been almost docile. Stripped of their mission to murder the humans in front of them (which, Adrian sometimes thought, might have been put on for show anyway), they simply allowed themselves to be captured. And it was a good thing, too, because by then the know-it-alls from the internet had begun showing up on every rift-fighting scene like watchdogs, making sure the "visitors from the other plane" weren't mistreated. Killing them like the old days would have been ... What was the term Kaur used?

Politically problematic.

That's how things had been on the lower floor before all the noise and commotion began: fiends out of their cells, held in the middle of the floor so their areas could be inspected. Legions surrounded them, repulsion weapons deployed.

But now the fiends were exploding one by one.

There would be one of those jarring, fire-knot pops followed by a cloud of gray dust in place of a fiend. Restraints would hit the floor. The Legions would gape in confusion. Dust would settle, maybe half as much in volume as an urn of human cremains.

"Adrian?" Lee again.

Everyone these days asked Adrian for answers that he had no way of knowing.

"I don't know, Lee. Nothing I've heard even—"

Another fiend burst. Adrian stopped talking as he startled. This was like inflating balloons to their limits and waiting for one to pop.

But in truth Lee wasn't totally off base, asking Adrian what he knew. It wasn't *nothing*, the way he'd said. He didn't know anything useful, but he *had* seen dust like the kind coming from the popping fiends before. It'd been at GEN, with Laurel, in the lab of a rendering specialist. She and the renderer had shown him the process used to extract Zen Element, starting with the intact body of a dead fiend. It'd taken hours for the process to remove every bit of moisture (including but not limited to Zen) from the body. When it was over, all that remained of the creature was dust.

This reminded Adrian of that — like some sort of instant rendering. One quick pop, and the fiend could fit into a Big Gulp cup. The rest of it disappeared, same as anyone who hopped into a rift.

Adrian scampered down the stairs, stopping beside Ollie Davis. He didn't seem to notice. None of the Legions were really guarding the fiends anymore. One by one the fiends were leaving the inner circle anyway — through death or whatever it was, if not by escape.

Everyone was muttering, jumping a little each time a new one exploded to come down like dirty confetti. Now that Kaur had joined the circle, he'd stopped demanding information nobody could offer and instead stood like the others with nothing to say. Everyone who'd come to the job, including the captain, was in the containment building's center now, watching its prisoners vanish one at a time.

The last fiend popped. The circle was empty. Heads turned

without purpose, as if seeking further instructions. There was perhaps a full minute of silence, then the same commotion spilled from the facility's other long hallways: bangs and cracks echoing all up and down the cell rows.

Most of the Legions and Stitchers ran toward the new round of sounds, but Adrian stayed put, looking at the central area where the fiends had been corralled. He knelt and tentatively touched the dust. If it was just dried-out fiend-corpse like his instruments said, it wouldn't hurt him. There was no Zen anymore. Nobody had thought to don masks while all those fiends were exploding, and Zen Element was highly toxic. They could easily have been standing around slack-jawed, breathing it in. But no. It was only dust. It was safe.

Adrian ran his fingers over the ground. A rough circle of floor was covered in what looked like fine ash, like hard dirt topped with a skim of powder. He could use his finger to draw a circle, maybe get some other kids and play a game of Marbles.

A boot stepped into his peripheral vision. He looked up to see his brother.

"Tell me you have some idea what's going on," Ray said.

Adrian stood. "Why does everyone assume I know more than the rest of you?"

"*Because*, Ade." Ray said it kindly, as if Adrian was too stupid to understand. "Because you talk to Brennan. Because Brennan talks to Spread and Containment. Because most of these guys spent half of last year wondering … well, wondering about what you did there."

"You mean wondering if I was a rat."

Ray shrugged. It wasn't fair. In the end, Ray had been just as isolated from the rest of the brigade as Adrian, but Ray was Eldon's favorite son and above suspicion. Even though information gleaned from Adrian's "special mission" had saved every man and woman in Fortune's riftfare brigades.

They all knew it. In the end, they even knew that Adrian was fully aware the Legions had been pilfering raw Zen Element and selling it to make up for cuts in their pay … but that despite knowing, he hadn't once opened his mouth to the brass.

"I don't have any idea, Ray. I don't know anything that you don't know."

Again, technically untrue. He knew because he'd spent years living with Laurel. Because although he actually didn't talk to Denny Brennan much these days (why would he? The saboteur had been caught and Adrian was just another grunt again), he'd spoken to Denny enough in the past to absorb nuance that most people didn't have.

Most of all he knew because he'd spent his life studying the nuances of what the rest of them thought *had* no nuance.

Ray hadn't even been curious about the circumstances of their father's death: the only time in history that two classes of fiend had come out of a single rift, just in time to kill Eldon Porter. To Ray and most of the others, up until everyone learned the fiends had been soft-balling their human exterminators on purpose, it wasn't worth thinking about. Shit happened.

Chaos happened.

Only Adrian had been curious enough to keep wondering. To keep asking questions. All the others had given him, for what turned out to be world-saving curiosity, had been mockery and grief.

Ray knew all of that, but shut his mouth.

Adrian pulled out his rift energy detector. He held it up and began to walk the area, looking like a man waving his phone around to find a signal.

"What are you doing?"

"Shh."

"We already know there's rift energy here. From all the salt and pepper."

"So it *is* salt and pepper? You think this is what Dad said happened before the first rift opened?"

"I didn't mean literally. What should I say instead? 'Popcorn rifts'?"

Adrian didn't answer. He kept thinking that Ray's slip of terms felt a little too accurate. Despite its pedestrian name, 'salt and pepper' had a specific meaning in rift research, referring to small, experimental, possibly advance-recon rifts formed without a pre-existing energy differential between local areas of the planes. For decades there had only *been* differential: huge disparities between the Zen energy lost on the fiend plane and gained on the human plane. Supposedly, now that new rifts weren't forming, the energetics had begun to equalize again: no big imbalance at all. That was what the Feds said, but from what he could get out of Brennan these days, GEN suspected otherwise. How could both be true?

Salt and pepper rifts. Hallmarks of equilibrium and a new beginning.

From what Adrian had seen, neither shoe fit. The energy still struck him as imbalanced, as if more rifts were open than ever even though he knew that wasn't true. At the same time, these weren't ordinary popcorn rifts. They inhaled, for one; he'd almost forgotten about that.

On the screen of his detector, the needle jumped all the way to the right and stayed there. His head came up, immediately on a swivel.

"What?" Ray asked.

"Oh, shit. *Ray.* A rift is coming."

"What?"

"A rift! A rift! You remember rifts, don't you?"

"Where?" Ray's eyes were darting around, his body language somewhere between excitement and panic.

Adrian thought fast. He was working on gut, not protocol or habit or even logic. Here and now, there wasn't time for any of those things. The system used to be a well-oiled machine, precision to the second. Energetic detection was someone else's job within that system, not Legions' or Stitchers'. That's the way it was supposed to work: An indicator somewhere told someone that shit was about to go down, at which point that someone called someone else. Only after that happened did the brigade respond.

But Adrian didn't know the department's protocol above brigade level. He wasn't a detection specialist. He might be reading this wrong ... or he might be reading it right but with no clue what to do next.

There might even be something he *needed* to do next. How did the monitoring team localize the rifts? Was there prep they usually rolled through, to make the forthcoming rift ready for fighting? Was there intel the brigade needed, other than location, that it didn't currently have?

For all Adrian knew, the first step of any repellence might be a call placed to Captain Kaur, providing him with vital, life-saving information.

Adrian knew none of it. He didn't even know if he was *supposed to* know, and already the clock was ticking.

He'd get no support on this one. Whatever came next was happening regardless. Even if the monitoring team was on the job, the energies were building too fast for their warning to do much good now.

Adrian had already learned what they'd tell him, more or less. All that mattered was that the rift would open in seconds. Minutes at most. Hell didn't wait for them anymore.

All the punches the fiends used to pull as part of their decades-long con? Adrian missed them. This was so much easier with their handicap.

The world itself opened top to bottom: a reality behind pulling down a zipper.

The air shimmered with blue and green aurora. The aurora was some kind of spectral signature; he knew that much: Laurel used to watch recordings of repellences through a GEN lens that told her all sorts of things about it.

Before now, Adrian had never paid enough attention to know what green meant, what blue meant, what any of it might mean. It used to be Legions up front, then a second line of Legions behind. Far back, called in only once the way was clear, were his corps of Stitchers.

The thing seemed to breathe into him with that rotten egg aroma. He wasn't used to rift discharge; the sheer heat of the thing knocked him back.

Ray caught him, both brothers staggering away. For a few moments, he seemed confused. Then the past clicked back into place and he became Famous Ray Porter again, Rollard high with handsome face stern and camera-ready.

But nothing came. Nothing exited.

They waited, waited, and waited some more.

Adrian kept checking the count-up timer on his wrist, automatically activated the second it detected enough rift effluence.

How long did it take, before the first wave of fiends came? Did the old rules even apply? Would there even *be* a wait? He thought the last bit automatically, well after the wait was already too long, nerves akimbo from all of today's strangeness.

In the old way, the rifts waited until the brigade was ready before they opened at all, then waited for the Legions to hoist their Rollards before the fiends emerged. Only looking back was the convenience of those things obvious. They used to be fools. Used to believe it was all just luck — or skill — that made the timing so perfect.

How would they come? Would they lead with big bosses, instead of easier-to-dispatch soldier demons? Would they emerge as multiple classes, impossible to fight efficiently even with the new weapons?

The game had changed and the gloves were off. Anything might happen now.

But nothing did. Even after Ray yelled into his comm mic and called the other Legions and Stitchers back ASAP, nothing came from the rift. It just floated in the middle of the room, breathing its noxious breath.

"Close it," Ray said.

"I don't understand. Where are they?"

"I don't know. I don't like it." He swallowed, then looked down the main corridor, where the rest of the brigade was still sprinting toward them. "Just do it."

"But what if—?"

"Adrian."

Adrian looked at his brother. It was a rare thing to see Ray Porter frightened.

"Please," Ray said.

Adrian's paralysis broke. He squinted against the heat and light, trying to peer across the boundary into the other world. They'd never figured out how things really worked over there; rift incursions had stopped too quickly for GEN to digest the new info and find out. They now knew, thanks to Eldon Porter's theories and Erika Dale's firsthand report, that Primordial Form was true.

Fiends took form only in the presence of humans — mostly

just before exiting a rift. Before that, they might be anything. They might exist naturally as something more like goo.

Adrian looked for anything at all. Any fully-formed fiends, any primordial substrate that could become fiends the second he stepped up, weaponless, to stitch the rift. This wasn't how it was supposed to work. First the fiends were dispatched, and only *then* did Stitchers get this close.

Maybe nothing was coming. Or maybe they hadn't come *yet* ... but would, as soon as Adrian was within striking distance.

Ray stood at his brother's side, too close, Rollard ready to make mincemeat.

But he wasn't needed. Nothing came.

Adrian determined the rift's topology, then raised his rig. Good; he wouldn't have to enter this one to close its far side. He could do it from here.

He pulled the actuator and braced, but the nozzle just sputtered.

"What's going on?" Ray asked.

"I don't know. My ..." He shook the nozzle, pulled the actuator again, then slapped the nozzle like a black and white television with bad reception. "Something must be clogged!"

But that wasn't it. One glance at his status screen revealed the problem plain as day.

The rig was empty. All of the filler rod bays were occupied, and the resin reservoir was intact ... but there was no epoxy in the filler rods. No resin in the reservoir.

It was all just ... *gone.*

He'd checked the levels before heading out, but now the rig was bone dry.

Activity swirled on the rift's other side. Adrian could see it: whorls like strange red clouds. A fog bank seemed to form, and soon that fog sprouted legs, horns, heads. Was this what it looked like up close, when fiends took form?

"ADRIAN!"

"I'm out! I can't make a weld!"

"What do you mean, 'You're *out*'?"

"I mean I'm out, goddammit!"

The first fiend came. Ray swung hard, cutting it in half. Two more were behind it. Ray broke the barrier, this time swinging more on the other side than on the human plane.

The Rollard's tines came back red hot, as if pulled from a blacksmith's forge.

"Hurry! They're coming!"

"*I'm empty,* Ray! Didn't you fucking hear me?"

The brigade arrived, a score of boots stomping as they hit the brakes. Dee came up beside Ray, both improvising, both swinging without technique or protocol. And that was all right. *Protocol* had been a product of the old way: the way where the fiends played soft, letting humanity win every battle as part of their decades-long con. The worst thing anyone could do, if they were playing for real this time, was embrace *protocol.*

A voice, calm but insistent, spoke in Adrian's ear: "On your left."

Adrian looked. It was Lee Barnes. Unlike Adrian, all of Lee's indicators were full.

"Lee, I can't close it. My supplies. They're ..." He shook his rig uselessly.

Despite the urgency, Lee paused long enough to look Adrian's way. He gave a polite smile that reminded Adrian of down-home hospitality, a meal cooked for family with love.

"No worries, bud. I got you."

There was a whoosh of gasses as the lines wrapping Lee's

rig flash-froze the air around them, making frost. Adrian, lost and confused, could only watch it happen.

The other Stitchers joined Lee, their bulk squeezing Adrian out of line.

They worked fast. Inside of two minutes, the opening was closed.

After the dust settled, it occurred to an unknown voice in the huddle that the prison complex had gone silent. The popcorn rifts had stopped opening and closing. No more bangs or bursting fiends, exploding into dust.

It was over.

And the entire population of the containment facility was gone.

6
DELIRIUM

A hand fell on Adrian's shoulder, stopping him as he marched toward the equipment room.

He hadn't seen it coming. Hadn't noticed Captain Kaur when he passed Adrian going the opposite direction, hadn't heard the squeak of his shoes as he button-hooked behind Adrian and looped back to follow, hadn't noticed when Kaur called his name.

He'd been inside his own head, only aware enough of the outside world in the way autodrive was aware of its surroundings.

Adrian spun so fast, Kaur flinched like Adrian might hit him.

"Captain?"

Kaur's mouth had been set with grim purpose. Now that he saw Adrian's face, he seemed to relax, realizing Adrian hadn't been ignoring him. He'd just been somewhere else, marching through another plane of existence.

"You okay?" Kaur asked.

"Fine."

"You don't *look* fine." Kaur seemed to be deciding this now, taking clues from Adrian's appearance and manner. "You look like a panda."

"What?"

"*A panda.* Rings around the eyes? Because you're tired and look like shit?"

"I'm okay, Cap. Just a hard night. I ... don't sleep as well as I used to. Especially here."

Instead of chastising Adrian for his lack of grit, Kaur surprised him with a nod. "Tell me about it," he muttered while rubbing his face. "I guess it could be worse. You could have just called someone a panda."

Adrian saw fatigue in the captain's eyes, too. They'd all slept better when they'd spent their days fighting right versus wrong, Earth versus Hell. This abnormal normal — always waiting, always sure things weren't as over as the rest of the planet pretended they were — felt a thousand times harder.

"You getting on?" He asked with one raised eyebrow, surely meaning Laurel.

"Yeah." Adrian forced himself to add, "Thanks."

Everyone tiptoed around the topic of Laurel Gantry these days, conspicuously avoiding her name and raising it in equal measure. Before she was taken, Stitchers talked about new GEN tech and Legions talked about new GEN weapons. Both development lines tended to go through Laurel in one way or another — either because it was her work that made them possible or because she was closest to the brigade and always went out of her way to be the person to brief them, the person to explain how new things worked.

Talk of their jobs had always been peppered with mentions of Laurel because GEN was tied to the work and Laurel was Brigade One's personification of GEN.

Without her, GEN was faceless. It felt like government.

Denny Brennan was a friend, yes, but Denny was as charismatic as a stack of crackers. Laurel, on the other hand, had been everyone's smartest buddy. Now it was like she'd never existed ... except when she was all the others would talk about, which happened when people were unlucky enough to find themselves alone with Adrian.

Her absence, in a way, made her specter more present around the brigadehouse than ever. Nobody knew quite how to handle it. Would Adrian rather never hear her name or would he rather hear it all the time?

The awkwardness of it all had driven a wedge between Adrian and pretty much everyone else. Maybe that was why he got so many questions now: He'd become the expert on things he knew nothing about. Maybe because he was the new surrogate for questions that used to be his girlfriend's. Or maybe it was simply the only way anyone knew to interact with him anymore: at arm's length, without risk of emotion.

"Adrian ..."

He braced himself. Kaur tended to only use first names when he was trying for compassion, which after so much exposure had come to feel more to Adrian like pity. "I can't begin to know what it's like for you. Laurel's death ..."

"She's not dead."

Kaur waited.

"Laurel's not dead, Cap. She's missing."

"Sure. But I'm starting to worry about you."

"I'm fine. Really."

"I'm willing to give you all the slack you need to move on. There's lots to do that's not out in the field, if that's easier for you to focus on. If it's less stress. What you and Ray did that day ... Well, let's just say that in my mind you've done a lifetime of Stitching already. If it were up to me, I'd let you retire with a full pension."

"What's this about?"

Kaur sighed — a movement that rose tall, then sagged with chest and shoulders. "We were *all* rusty today. Nothing works the way it used to, and that rift caught us by surprise. Every one of us."

"Yeah. Weird day." But Kaur was stalling. *"What's this about,* Captain?"

"You froze, Adrian. I understand it, and I get it, but facts are facts."

"Froze?"

"It's like I said. You and Ray? Full honors. If they come at us again with budget cuts, I'll throw myself on their swords to keep you drawing a salary. There are a lot of ways you can help us. You know more about what's happening — and what *might* be happening — than anyone in the brigade. I'd rather go to you with questions than Brennan. Brennan's ..."

Kaur made a strange expression and shook his head. "I just don't know where his loyalties are, now that so much of GEN's budget is Federal. I like him. I trust him. I *want* to trust him. But money talks, and I don't understand why they're doing so much work in containment and weapons development given that ... What? Maybe *five* rifts have opened in the past three-four months? Tiny ones? I get the feeling there's more happening with GEN than we know. Brennan used to talk to us. Now, it's like he knows who the new boss is, and we're just cleanup."

"I didn't 'freeze' today, Cap."

"Adrian. You didn't make a single suture. Your rig didn't record even *one* drop of expelled resin. I saw you back there, lost trying to find the midline. You looked like a deer in the headlights."

"Didn't make ... For fuck's sake, Cap — my rig was empty!"

"When?"

"At the job! At the repellence!"

Kaur looked puzzled. "It showed as full when you pulled it off the rack."

"But it was all red bars when I needed it! Ray saw; ask him!"

"You're saying the reason you didn't stitch the rift was ... *because you didn't have any compound?* No resin?"

"Yes!" Adrian was more frustrated than angry. He'd told the equipment chief about it right away, as well as complaining to anyone who'd listen on the ride back to HQ. Why was Kaur only hearing about it now?

"But your rig was *checked in* full, too."

"*What?* No it wasn't!"

Kaur sighed again, and Adrian felt a shift in their conversation. This had begun as a discussion between a capable fighter and his CO, but now it was a careful explanation Kaur was making to someone delicate and dumb.

"Don't look at me like that! If you don't believe me, go check my rig!"

"I checked it. Just now. Gert checked it, too."

"Before recharge," Adrian clarified.

"Before recharge," Kaur echoed.

"Then Gert didn't hear me. She was busy. Didn't hear what I said about the fault in my rig."

Kaur took a small tablet from his pocket, then pulled up the brigadehouse status. He navigated through a rank gate, entering the officers-only menu. Once he'd found what he wanted, he showed Adrian.

Things were just as he'd said: At 4:04am, Adrian was logged as checking out a fully-charged rig. At 7:12am, he'd returned a fully-charged rig. The Zen usage stats agreed, showing no Element moving from the station stores to Adrian's recharge bay, which is what would happen if it'd been low on return.

Adrian gaped. "Something's wrong with the system."

"Nothing's wrong with the system."

"Cap, I'm telling you …"

Kaur put his hand back on Adrian's shoulder. It took all Adrian had not to slap it off.

"Stress can do weird things. So can sleep deprivation. It's called delirium, and it's legit. Sane people get sick, or end up in the hospital on an upside-down sleep schedule, and end up telling you that a cult came when nobody was looking and took them away. They'll say it with a straight face, like it's sensible as anything. Nobody believes it can happen to them, but it can. It *does*. You're confused, Adrian. There's no shame in it. After all you've been through? You've got all the reason in the world."

"But—!"

"I'm putting you on paid leave through the weekend. It's not a punishment. Look me in the eyes, Porter. I need you to look me in the eyes."

"I'm not—!"

"Porter!"

Adrian stopped.

"Look me in the eyes."

Furious, Adrian did.

"This is not a punishment. Do you hear me? I'm not doing this as your CO. I'm doing it as a friend. A friend who can force you to do it because I'm *also* your CO. Now do you hear me?"

Adrian tried to reply but found he couldn't. He nodded instead. In truth, Kaur wasn't entirely wrong. He'd had all those nightmares. So many clear visions of Heaven and Hell.

"Good," Kaur said. "Now get the fuck out of here."

7

FOLLOW IT HOME

The bunk room. His car. Laurel's apartment.

The scenery around Adrian seemed to change without his volition or say-so. He'd become a passenger to whatever-this-was, only now seeing the fog his life had become for what it was instead of fighting his way through. For months the ground beneath his feet had seemed to lose its solidity, becoming a boggy mire that took him wherever he wanted to go. He was a passenger. A witness to everyday's unfolding.

When he raised his hand toward the locked door, the hand did not seem to be his own. When he pushed the key past the tumblers, his muscles did not guide it. He saw the apartment's interior as if through the wide window of an observation booth.

Whoever lived here was a slob. He did laundry only when necessary, and even then he did it poorly and never put it away. The trash can was several days past due for emptying. When Laurel lived here, the air was perfumed with incense and a floral aroma he'd never understood, because there weren't always flowers. Now it smelled like a locker room and looked like a flophouse.

Was Adrian squatting, living here without her? Laurel owned the place, but it was as he'd told the captain: she wasn't dead. At least not *officially*. Laurel was just one of the missing, and on that day so many people had disappeared. The sundering had never happened, but chasms had opened all over as the planes weakened. So many were just … gone.

On the books, that was what happened to Laurel. Adrian sometimes wondered if fiends had come for her like a squad of Nazis. Maybe she simply disappeared.

He'd kept paying the rent on her behalf. Fortune's infrastructure still hadn't settled, so nobody had connected the Case of the Missing Scientist with the Case of the Boyfriend Who Still Lived in Her Home. Maybe he was illegal. Maybe he should go and live with Ray.

His brother had certainly offered. *Begged*, practically. It was like Ray expected his baby brother to kill himself if left alone.

And who knew? Now that he no longer had the distraction of work, he just might.

He took a shower and changed his clothes, half to get rid of the sulfur reek and half to convince himself he wasn't entirely off the deep end yet. He treated himself to a clean towel from the linen closet, stopping as he dried his face to inhale deeply.

So much here still reminded him of Laurel. So much still had her verdant scent. That wouldn't be true at Ray's place.

Inhale.

Inhale.

In his mind's eye he saw her face. He told himself the towel was not the towel, but was instead clothing she was wearing now. It was her hair. The furnace draft on the exposed skin of his neck? That was Laurel's breath, as her head rested on his shoulder.

Without warning, his legs gave out. Adrian sat hard on the closed toilet seat, naked, and began to sob.

He thought of *Laurel. Laurel. Laurel.*

His mind spun memories from deep cuts, presenting him with moments he'd forgotten. He was betraying his pride, becoming exactly the mess that Kaur had put him on leave for being.

His thoughts became a reaching hand, stretching toward wherever she was as if he might somehow bring her back. But gone was gone. Fantasy was fantasy.

Maybe he should move on.

A squeaking sound returned his mind to the present.

Adrian looked up, the towel still cupped in both hands in case he decided to return his face to it. He squinted. Looked around. He was more than alone and had heard every sound this suite of rooms and neighborhood had to offer. The noise he'd just heard was new.

He stood, wrapping the towel around his waist as he went to the window. Nothing had brushed against it. He put a finger to it, feeling its cold, then dragged his finger down through the condensation. It squeaked, but he'd see streaks in the fog if the window was the sound's source.

Nothing was outside either.

He turned to the shower. Again, Adrian dragged his finger along the glass enclosure, then the plastic shower wall inside. Yes, it made about the same sound.

But again, it hadn't come from here.

So fucking what, Adrian? Stop wallowing and let it go.

He wasn't thinking straight. That's what Kaur said and (let's be honest), it's what everyone had been thinking about Adrian for a while. A promising mind and a famous Stitcher was losing himself after losing his girl. Such a tragedy. Such unnecessary suffering.

He shook it off, then turned to the mirror to finish the shaving job he'd roughly began under the shower head. That's when he saw what'd made the sound and realized:

Someone had written on his mirror, apparently using a finger as the brush. The message was in red paint. Or ketchup. Or blood.

Come get me.

Frowning and aware he was less freaked-out than he should be, Adrian rubbed his own finger through the words. The writing looked wet but wouldn't come off. He licked his finger and tried again.

No big deal. So someone wrote on the mirror while you were head-down on the toilet, naked, crying your eyes out. Happens to the best of us.

But a saner voice spoke up inside Adrian when the first voice was finished, eager to raise the alarm.

Listen, buddy boy, and listen real close. You're losing your mind, you hear me? Might be temporary. Might be fixable. So what you're going to do is, you're going to turn away from that mirror right now and you're going to walk into the bedroom and pretend you didn't see a thing. You'll dry off and get dressed. Then you'll call Ray, swallow your pride and ask him to come get you. You will not drive yourself. You will not lose your cool. You will not pass Go or collect two hundred dollars. Once you're at Ray's, you will calmly tell him that you're experiencing waking nightmares. Delirium. It's scary, but with sleep and rest and maybe some therapy, it'll all go away. As long as you don't buy into it. As long as you know that none of it's real.

But Adrian didn't move. He saw now what the problem was — why he couldn't wipe the words away. Viewed up close, he could tell his finger was against the glass but the message was maybe a sixteenth of an inch farther back, where the mirror's silver backing had been painted.

The message had been written from the other side of the mirror.

The room around Adrian seemed to darken. He could see something deep inside the reflection now, as if a distant thing far behind it was lighting up. A funhouse trick in action: a normal mirror revealed as just glass once the lighting changed.

You should be afraid right now, he thought.

Strangely, he wasn't. The lights in the bathroom had all but snuffed, but Adrian wasn't scared. None of it felt unusual. The growing something inside the mirror was perfectly normal.

Adrian was both in and above the moment: participant and objective observer. He was able to dissect the moment's oddity in an academic sense, but it came with no emotion.

Why?

Because your connection provides the passage.

Not Adrian's voice this time. He'd heard that almost as clearly as if the words had been spoken aloud. It didn't really mean much to him ... but at the same time, he understood it perfectly.

Connection.

Passage.

You have to feel it, not think in words.

That last one almost rang a bell, but Adrian had no idea from where. He wasn't thinking clearly; he was quite sure about that. He accepted all he saw as if agreeing to the facts of a dream.

He leaned in. He wanted to see what it was in the distance, growing brighter. It looked like a person, curled up like a sleeping dog, glowing from within. He could almost see what was around them: a fireplace, walls, books in bookcases on those walls. A desk to one side. An office? A study? It made no sense.

The person on the floor was large. Tall. Male. Narrow

through the shoulders, sort of like Ray but not. He was nude. On a rug. And the fireplace was lit, but the flames were more red than the usual yellow and orange.

Adrian leaned in. And in. And in.

His feet left the floor. He tumbled forward without actual motion, the physics happening inside his mind. A moment later he felt pressure on one side. Cold to the front, heat behind him, something soft below. He opened eyes that weren't precisely his normal eyes and saw that he was now the man on the rug.

He'd become that person. A moment ago, he'd been seeing himself.

"Like a dog."

Adrian lifted his head. Whatever had still seemed strange about this no longer seemed odd at all. He was here and was meant to be here, in the way of dreams. And visions. And intrusions of the mind.

"Is that really how you see yourself, now that I'm gone?"

Adrian rolled over. Laurel was sitting in an armchair behind him.

"I'm naked," he said.

"As I like it."

"Why am I naked?"

The thought dressed him. Now he was in his Stitching gear, minus the big asbestos coat. He was sitting in a second armchair, like Laurel, both of them watching the fire.

It wasn't an ordinary fire. When Adrian looked close, he could see creatures inside the flames, capering across the burning logs. They were tiny fiends of many different classes, above the planes, looking down.

The fireplace Hell was all red rocks, no logs, smelling of brimstone and sulfur.

"Now ask if it's really me," Laurel said.

"Is it really you?"

"Good. Now it's out of your system."

"But is it?"

It was *and* it wasn't. It was so strange, the way that part of him understood exactly what was happening here ... but it was a deep, ancient part of his mind that his modern lobes could no longer fathom. This was something old. Something inborn. Something those on the mortal plane had long ago forgotten how to do.

"Gone," Laurel said.

"What?"

"Gone," she repeated.

He looked toward the fire, following his intuition. That's what she half was, after all: his instincts personified. The other parts were somehow her mind. Filtered. Changed. Subconscious. It was impossible to grasp or articulate.

But part of him knew what "gone" meant, because as he looked into the fire, he watched new fiends pop into existence: not *gone*, but *arrived*.

They were somehow spectral — not corporeal like the fiends already in existence. It was because they didn't have bodies. Or skin. They were only blood. Only the Zen Element that gave them life, somehow propped up to stand on its own.

Then there was a great inhale and the Zen ghosts vanished, the fire with it, sucked backward instead of blown forward. The fireplace went missing and now they were his father's study, from all those years ago.

"Where did the fire go?" Adrian asked.

"Find out," Laurel said, "and then follow it home."

"Laurel! Are you really here? Are you safe?"

The dreamlike part of whatever-this-was had started to wear off, bringing clear-minded cognition with it. Yes, he'd fallen into the bathroom mirror, but Laurel was here, and she needed help!

She turned to him. For a moment, Adrian thought she'd answer.

But then she opened her mouth. Faced him. And until his last breath of this place finally gave out, she belted an inhuman scream.

8

FINE

Adrian woke with one side of his face against the porcelain feel of the bathroom floor. He was cold, not hot. Naked again, with only a towel beside him.

He was in Hell all right, but this was the one of everyday existence. The Hell in which he'd betrayed the woman he loved, failed his brother and brigade, shamed his family legacy, and gotten himself put on leave. The last was its own compound folly: a little on-leave because he was incompetent, a little on-leave because he was crazy.

Well. Let them see me now. I'm not crazy. I passed out in the bathroom after Laurel sent me a message, finger-written in blood. It wasn't my imagination. I saw her with my own eyes. She was deep in the mirror, inside damnation made just for me.

"Adrian? Ade." It was Ray, lifting his head a little, slapping his cheeks. "Come back to me, Ade."

He sounded worried. Genuinely *worried*.

Adrian had been on the receiving end of many emotions from his brother over the year, but they usually sifted into two piles: hate and love; they were brothers, after all. Hate took many forms, from aggressive to innocuous. Often he was irritated. Annoyed. Usually he complained about Adrian's lack of guts or his infuriating over-analysis of everything. This, here, went in a third pile: closest to love, but with loss baked in.

His little brother was falling apart, obviously and demonstrably no longer the man their father wanted them both to be.

A coward. A victim. No longer a fighter — instead, just another spineless civilian.

Adrian made himself get up onto his elbows and pull the towel over his nudity. He would not be propped up by his brother. Ray had forcibly made himself Adrian's backbone too many times in the past.

"I'm okay," Adrian said, a little more roughly than he'd intended.

"Just take it easy." Ray had his hand behind Adrian's back, helping him sit without falling.

With the bathroom door open, the apartment's geography betrayed them. Adrian could see a straight shot through the bedroom corner, through the living room, and all the way to the front door. He could see Ray's keys still in the lock, the door neglected and open because he'd seen Adrian the second he entered.

Poor Adrian. Always needing Big Brother's help to get by.

His head was already clear, the dream taking its proper place in his memory. Outside, Geoffrey Day from down the hall lingered as he passed, looking in with concern that Adrian wanted not at all. He resisted the urge to yell across the apartment at him, suggesting that Geoffrey mind his own goddamn business.

He slapped Ray's hand away. "I said I'm okay."

Still Ray lingered, eyes wide with concern that made Adrian furious. He could see what must have happened here. It couldn't have been long after Captain Kaur sent Adrian home that Ray learned about it. He'd probably texted and called, and when he couldn't reach his brother, he'd swung by and used his emergency key.

Five, ten minutes later and Adrian probably would have woken on his own. He could have told Ray that he could handle a little layoff when he arrived. He was a big kid now, in need of nobody's defense.

Ray was still looking at him with wide eyes, full of worry.

"Why are you here?' Adrian demanded.

"I wanted to check on you."

"That key was for emergencies. Laurel told you to never, *ever* use it unless there was a really good reason."

Ray hesitated before responding. He was probably considering pointing out that before he entered, Adrian's non-responsiveness had given him a good reason.

Or was it something else Ray was thinking: perhaps that Laurel's rules didn't apply anymore? The way everyone saw it, this was Adrian's place now. They'd all humor him a little longer if he wished, playing along and pretending she might return ... but the adults all knew full well she never would.

They took her, Ray, Adrian had said that day. He'd known it before they even started searching. Every time they looked for Laurel somewhere else in all that post-rift chaos, Adrian went in knowing they wouldn't find her. Ray had tried to be optimistic for both of them.

You don't know that for sure, he'd say. So every single time, against his better judgment, Adrian would allow himself to believe a little that they'd find her. And every time, confirming what he'd already known was like a dagger in his heart.

How many times had Laurel asked to leave this forsaken city? Even at their worst, she'd refused to go without him. It was because of Adrian — his stubborn, feet-dragging inability

to break free of his brother and his dead father's shadow —
that she'd been here in the end.

In Fortune for him.

Gone from Fortune because of him.

"Adrian, I ..."

"I don't need your help." He stood, grabbing the towel. "I
didn't ask you to come here."

"You were out cold. Ade? I think you hit your head. You
should see a doctor."

"You can go now, Ray."

Adrian marched into the bedroom. He was trying to be
indignant and angry, but for some reason that wasn't how he
felt. His insides were boiling. He wanted Ray gone so that he
could assimilate the experience he'd just had without courting
more unwanted sympathy. It was only a dream.

A dream while you were awake.

A dream that came without warning.

A dream so real, you could feel the flames.

Ray put his hand on Adrian's shoulder.

Adrian slapped it away.

"Adrian! You need to sit down!"

"Don't tell me what to do." He'd doffed his towel and was
pulling on clothes. He wasn't even dry yet. His hair was dripping. But that didn't matter. Things were normal here, and
when things were normal and you were feeling okay and you
weren't pathetic or incompetent or crazy, you got dressed after
a shower. That's what independent people did when they were
just fine, when they didn't need their superior brother to pave
the way.

"Did you pass out?" Ray asked, following him.

"I slipped."

"Well? *Did* you hit your head?"

"It's fine."

"You're not answering my question. Adrian? *Ade!*"

They'd devolved to an adult game of tag. Adrian was now moving just to move, to stay ahead of Ray's assistance and insistence. If Ray would stop following him around like he thought Adrian might collapse at any second, Adrian would stop moving around just so he could stay away. They'd become a self-contained system, one brother's need to escape driving the other to chase him.

"Adrian! Listen to me!"

Adrian spun and stared. "You're not Mom, Ray. And you're for *damn* sure not Dad."

Ray's jaw firmed. "Then I guess you're welcome."

"For what?"

"For finding your ass after you got fucked up on the floor. Literally. *Your ass.*"

"Look at me. I'm up. I'm fine. I slipped; so what? I don't need your help, Ray."

"I'm worried about you. Everyone is."

"I don't need your fucking worry either!"

Ray nodded slowly, controllling himself. Adrian didn't like that, either: his brother's clear effort to rise above his instincts and not jump down Adrian's throat like usual. Ray never threw softballs — not unless he thought Adrian was already too far down, that he'd had enough of a beating. How many knock-down, drag-out fights had they had in their lifetimes? It was how their relationship worked. Adrian didn't want sympathy. He didn't want pity.

"Then I guess I'll go."

"Good idea."

"We'll talk about this later."

"It's done," Adrian said. "There's nothing to talk about."

"You were talking. Muttering. About Laurel."

"Well, she's on my mind."

"You said you had to find her. You said you had to save her."

"Obviously I can't do that, now can I?" Adrian stepped closer, daring Ray to meet his challenge. "She's fucking *dead*, right? That's what you say. That's another thing *everyone says.*"

"Look ... Adrian ..."

"I know how people talk about me," Adrian said, still holding himself firm. "'Poor Adrian. Lost his girl. But he can't accept it, can he? *So many* people died. *So many* went missing when the rifts opened.' It's poetic, isn't it? Here I am: The Stitcher who, for once, found a hole he can't close. I guess that makes today a fucking sonnet. 'Couldn't close the rift could he? *Now* look at poor Adrian! First he was just delusional, but now, it's affecting his work. And he had so much promise, didn't he? Or did he? Let's not kid ourselves. *Ray's* the strong Porter boy. Adrian was always just along for the ride.'"

"Nobody says that."

"Fuck off, Ray."

"What do you want me to do here? What's my role?" Ray spread his arms wide in a picture of exasperation. "I'll do whatever you want, Ade. You want my help in any way? I'm there. You want to do it alone? I'm gone. I'm *sorry* I was concerned you might be fucked up or pissed off over the thing with Kaur. I thought you might want to grab a drink. Bitch about the captain a little. I'm on your side, Ade."

"Because you believe me? Because you were there, and know my tanks were empty?"

Ray hesitated. It was a bad move.

"Go," Adrian said. "Just leave."

"YOU'RE NOT IN THIS ALONE, GODDAMMIT!"

Adrian walked away. Ray stood where he was for a moment, then huffed, grabbed the bag he'd dropped on his rush to the bathroom, and yanked his keys from the apartment's front door.

Adrian stewed. The place was too quiet. He had nowhere for this sudden, largely baseless feeling of anger to go. He'd just have to wait for it to vanish bit by bit, like waiting for boiled water to cool.

There was a knock on the door.

"What."

The knock repeated.

"WHAT?"

And then a third time, now rapping.

Adrian yanked it open. "For fuck's sake, Ray, if you want so badly to—!"

He stopped, because it wasn't Ray standing in the carpeted hallway. It was Laurel. Her eyes focused far past Adrian in a thousand-yard stare. She seemed to have been doused with blood: Stephen King's Carrie, fresh from the prom.

"Find the heat," she said, her voice a gurgle as if blood had found its way into her throat as well, "and follow it home."

Adrian froze. He blinked. Was this a dream again? He could smell her rot — the blood not just dumped, but curdled and gone-over. She was radiating heat, like a coal.

"Laurel? Laurel, are you—?"

She burst into flame all at once. Her legs gave out and she fell to the floor, igniting patches all around her. He watched her eyes pop like squeezed grapes. Her tongue blackened, shriveling to jerky. She curled up, writhing, screaming with agony.

Adrian snatched an afghan from the chair beside the door and fell on her with it. The flames were too hot, and impervious to smothering. Soon the afghan was aflame, and Adrian's sleeves, then his jeans and hair. The scent of roasting flesh plumed into his nostrils before his face began to burn, and his throat filled with licking flame, and—

"Adrian?"

Ray was standing over him, looking down. Adrian was on the hallway floor, yelling and crying, using an unburned afghan to smother nothing at all. Down the hall, two neighbors had poked out of their doors and were watching, too aghast for retreat even when Adrian, completely broken, raised his head to look them in the eye.

"Come on," Ray said, helping his brother to stand.

This time, Adrian didn't protest at all.

9
FAR FROM TRUE

Adrian waited. And waited. And waited.

The room was small but pleasant. A short couch sat against one wall and an enormous plush armchair — big like an Alice in Wonderland prop, wide enough for two adults side by side — sat opposite. Between the two was a coffee table topped with fidget toys, a metronome, a Newton's cradle, and of course a box of tissues. For crying. Because after patients were done fidgeting and looking down at their hands, they always ended up in tears.

Ray was probably still in the waiting room. *Good job, Adrian — you've gone from brotherly pity to brotherly custodianship.* Of course Adrian told Ray to leave him: He could talk to the damn departmental shrink on his own. Of course Ray wouldn't. Adrian had gotten Ray to leave him alone once today, but he wouldn't be that lucky again.

He yawned, feeling fatigue like a weighted blanket. It had been a very long day. He'd started during what was still effectively nighttime, witnessed incomprehensible fiend behavior, battled a rift with no Stitching resin in the tank, found out everyone thought he was insane when it turned out there *was* resin in his tank, was put on leave, and then had some sort of a breakdown in front of Ray. Twice.

Now Ray would *never* leave. Adrian would be lucky if Ray ever left him alone again. So what was next? Ray feeding him? Ray wiping his ass? Once he was in a straightjacket, he for damn sure wouldn't be able to do it himself.

There was a knock on the small room's second door — the one that didn't lead into the foyer. The therapist didn't pause after knocking, entering without waiting for Adrian's okay.

But it was Special Agent J. Dixon, from the department's version of Internal Affairs: Spread and Containment.

"Dixon?" Adrian was gobsmacked and had no idea what else to say.

"Please. Please. Call me *Special Agent* Dixon." Dixon's manner was bustling and impatient, as if annoyed to have been bothered. He looked around the room, then sat in the big chair when nowhere else seemed more appropriate. "Jesus. This thing's big enough for me to have five asses."

"Um ..."

"Tell me about your mother."

"Sir?"

"Or don't. I don't fucking care. But seriously. How is she? I hear she beat the big C."

Adrian could only wait, staring.

"Relax," Dixon said, dropping his shrink act. "I don't believe in this shit." He looked around the room, annoyed by it and everything it contained. Apparently *this shit* referred to psychiatry, or mental health in general. "You want to believe you're the queen? I don't care. No offense."

Dixon seemed amped-up on caffeine. He'd been that way last year, when Adrian was working for his department behind Kaur's back: always talking with quick and brutal authority, as if it was his way or the highway ... but everyone could still think his bone-dry jokes were funny if they cared to. Dixon had disarmed Adrian back then and he was definitely disarming him now.

Adrian sent his mind back, scrambling to adjust to this latest development. He couldn't remember the last time he'd seen Dixon. There were unresolved gripes between them, weren't there? The way Dixon was assuming command right now seemed to push past that, but Adrian was still pretty sure he'd ended the year hating Dixon.

The man was a user: always willing to lie and cheat so long as he got what he wanted — which, to be fair, usually meant catching his version of the bad guy. The only problem was that last year, Adrian's entire brigade had been in his crosshairs. Turned out their petty theft wasn't the worst crime in town, though, so Brigade One ended up escaping the broadsword. S&C had let them off the hook in the end, but it's not like Dixon had ever made amends.

"Apologies for the switcharoo," he said, indicating the therapist's office around them. "Frankly it's much better for me if people think you're fucked up. Officially, you're talking to Gloria Dunham today. She's been briefed. Fortunately confidentiality works in our favor. Gloria's not allowed to tell anyone what you talked about with her today."

"But I didn't talk with her at all," Adrian said.

"That leaves you, champ," Dixon continued, ignoring him. "I'm going to need you to toe that same line. Anyone asks, you went in to talk about your feelings today. It's not really a request. You don't get to sign a confidentiality agreement. How about we all be adults and you just do what I fucking say? Good? Good. Now: *Ray.*"

"What?"

"Ray," he repeated.

"What about Ray?"

Dixon sighed. He seemed unable to believe Adrian hadn't yet let the whole "fake therapy appointment ambush" thing go. It'd been upwards of thirty seconds since Dixon entered, and there was *still* confusion?

"Ray. *Ray.* Your brother Ray."

"Again: What about him?"

"Can I trust him?"

Adrian couldn't keep up. He saw the issue now. Last year, Dixon's impatient energy had apparently been blunted by the presence of Denny Brennan, who'd been adjunct to the confidential saboteur investigation to which Adrian had been assigned. Right now, though, Adrian was seeing Dixon unleashed. This was what it was like to work with him directly, when there were no competing authorities around to order him around.

Dixon snapped his fingers several times.

"Um ... *Yes?*" Adrian answered. "I guess you can trust him?"

He actually wasn't sure. Ray had never worked with Dixon — only with Adrian, who'd broken confidentiality to eventually tell Ray everything. S&C (and Dixon in particular, as S&C's face around Brigade One) was generally seen as the enemy. The brigades fought rifts, but S&C was always suspicious of the brigades. Adrian thought it'd be okay, though: If Adrian told Ray to trust Dixon, he supposed Ray would — and that would make Ray worthy of Dixon's trust in return. The only question was whether *Adrian* trusted Dixon. He'd technically betrayed Adrian a few different times, but in the end they'd shared a mutual goal.

Dixon had wanted the saboteur and so had Adrian. The saboteur (technically plural: Matt and Erika) had been caught and now both were dead. The fact that Dixon didn't go after the brigades *anyway, after* it was all over, was probably as close as the man got to keeping his word.

Dixon struck Adrian as a by-any-means-necessary sort of guy. The trick was to chase the heart of what he wanted rather than its specifics, then stay out of the way.

"Good. Call him. Tell him to get his ass over here. Dunham's office. ASAP." Dixon said *a-sap* instead of the four individual letters.

"I don't need to call him. He's out in the lobby right now."

Dixon looked like he might laugh. "What, like your babysitter?"

Adrian wouldn't answer that.

Dixon took his silence as confirmation and went for the foyer door himself.

Ray entered when he was called, looking as confused as Adrian still felt. This was supposed to be a psychological intervention for his mentally disturbed brother, but now it looked like an IA investigation all over again — this time with both brothers in the loop instead of just one.

Dixon bustled through the confusion, answering only enough baffled and annoyed questions to get Ray seated on the couch beside his brother. Then, before beginning business in earnest, he picked up a teddy bear that had been left on the floor with other comfort objects. He threw it onto a shelf, where it somehow landed sitting up.

"I don't have to tell you two that nobody can know we met," Dixon said.

The brothers nodded. They knew now.

Adrian was trying to get the temperature of this thing, still feeling six steps behind. Direct explaining was probably already over, knowing Dixon. At this point, Adrian could only connect the dots.

If he'd been sent for a psych evaluation but ended up with

Dixon instead, that meant two things. First, Adrian didn't actually need the therapy appointment — and second, Dixon saw him as sane enough to meet with in the first place.

Did that mean the weird things Adrian had seen had actually happened? Was it possible the oddities were real, instead of signs he was losing his mind? Dixon wouldn't approach an insane man for ... for whatever new secret what-the-fuck this turned out to be.

"First let's get something out of the way," Dixon said. "Your dog tags? They're chipped."

Adrian looked down. He couldn't see his tags because they were under his shirt, but he supposed that was exactly the point. Nobody was required to wear their tags off duty, but everybody did. You just got used to the feel of them against your skin, and it was a lot worse to forget to wear them than to wear them too much.

Sometimes accidents happened. Sometimes people got killed when fighting fiends, even today. When scenes went bad — though it was rare — they went *very* bad. After fire rolled through a unit, brigade dog tags made it possible to identify the remains.

"'Chipped'?"

"GEN tech," Dixon said, nodding. "And no, Brennan doesn't know. About any of this. Nobody does other than me, you two, and the pair of ladies I report to. No I'm not going to tell you who they are. It's need-to-know, and that need does not include you."

He shifted in the chair as if uncomfortable with its breadth, unsure where he should be sitting.

"Chipped," Dixon repeated. "I swapped them out myself last month during your med scan. Since then, your tags have measured the psionic energy you've been exposed to, plus your movements, what's been said around you, and a few other things. Bottom line is I know everything that you've been up to. What did you tell your brother happened today?"

"I ran out of Stitching resin. I couldn't close the rift."

"After that." Dixon waved this answer away. "I've got fifty other ways to know what happened at the fiend containment facility. We'll get to that shortly. I'm talking about when you went home. I'm asking about whatever made *you*—" He looked at Ray. "—send *you* here."

Now he looked at Adrian, waiting to hear what made one brother think the other was crazy.

"I passed out. Hit my head."

Dixon scoffed. "I'm asking what *really* happened."

But Adrian was stuck on something else. "You said the chip in my dog tags measures 'psionic energy.' Isn't that like *psychic* energy?"

"It's Brennan's term," Dixon said, and Adrian understood that things must be as they'd always been: Brennan working, Dixon's people siphoning off his knowledge without bothering to bring the man in on it. "Obviously it's not 'psychic' in the usual sense. It's kin to rift energy. Frankly the whole thing is above your pay grade." Which meant: *Stop trying to understand what's none of your concern and just answer my question.*

"Why are you monitoring me for rift energy? Without my consent?"

Dixon made a face. "Oh, I'm sorry. Am I stomping on your rights? *Fuck* your rights. My concerns are a little bigger than your illusion of independence. We weren't monitoring *you* so much as what happened *around* you."

"Why me?"

"Because of Laurel Gantry. Because she was closest with you."

That was the last thing Adrian expected. He could only blink.

"We don't have time for you to be coy and try to preserve your dignity. In front of your brother, especially. So here's the deal." Dixon leaned forward and put his elbows on his knees, hands clasped with fingers interlaced. "The things that happened today at the facility? Those things surprised *you*, but they didn't surprise *us* in S&C at all. Adrian, your rig really *did* go empty. You didn't imagine that. We even thought something like that might happen. So yes. You checked it out full and you returned it full, but for a while in the middle, when you stepped up to close that rift, you *were* in fact empty."

"How's that possible?" Ray asked.

Dixon shot eyes toward Ray's question, but right now he was talking to Adrian.

"Kaur has no idea. To him, you're just not thinking straight. To Kaur, you *needed* to be put on leave because you're unstable, and that instability made you unreliable. That's not accurate, though. I know because I've been watching you, listening in. After the chip in your tags heard Kaur send you home today — after the tracker registered you as being at Ms. Gantry's place — the psionic sensor detected a major incursion. I *know* something happened in that bathroom, Adrian. And more importantly for you, I'll believe what you say, no matter how weird it strikes you. So." He spread his hands on his knees like granting a favor. "How about we stop pulling each other's dicks and you just *tell me what happened* before Ray found you?"

Adrian looked at Ray, who had no answers. He replayed the scene in his head. Ray said he'd been muttering about Laurel when he woke up, so for all Adrian knew, everything in his dream had been said aloud. If the chip contained a microphone, those mutterings were all Dixon knew.

He was starting to think that none of it had been a dream. He *wasn't* crazy. Something actually *had* happened when he stared into the bathroom mirror. Dixon knew it, and in some strange way almost seemed to have been expecting something like this.

Across from Adrian, Dixon nodded encouragement.

There was no point to evasion — not if Dixon stood ready to believe him — so Adrian told his story without pulling punches. Ray hadn't heard it before. Judging by his reaction, Ray was less than convinced, still afraid for his brother's sanity. But it didn't end there. Dixon kept asking even after the bathroom tale was finished, encouraging him to plumb deeper into his mind for further oddities.

Adrian did as he was asked, finding confession a relief. Within fifteen minutes, he was empty. He'd told the agent about his dreams of Laurel in Hell. About the ultra-realistic memories of time with his father. Of the way the two bled together: his first lessons in riftfare intermingled with the guilt and loss and pain of unintentionally sending Laurel from one plane to another. He couldn't take it back, and now Hell itself wouldn't stop taunting.

Dixon sat back when it was over. He nodded to himself, slotting Adrian's insane verbal diarrhea into orderly cubbies inside his mind. Somehow, all that wackiness worked for him. Somehow, it made all the sense in the world.

"*'The famous Porter brothers,'*" he said after a long, digestive pause. "Had a nice ring to it, once upon a time. Feels forever ago that Gilette plastered your faces on every commercial. That you couldn't go anywhere without being stopped for autographs. Wasn't that long ago that everyone who was paying attention owed you a debt of gratitude. Even if it wasn't widely known, wasn't that long ago that the two of you *saved the world.*"

Then he said, "Bet you miss it. What about you, Ray? Would you be interested, if I said there are still fiends left to battle?"

Ray looked at Adrian. Riftfare was a lost art, and today's rift didn't count. The report had already come back: What happened at the prison was equalization in action — an energetic counter-reaction of interplanar physics brought on by whatever zapped all those fiends into dust. The brains at GEN said that'd been the other plane's last gasp. Most of the fiends were now gone. The rifts would supposedly never return. In all the ways that mattered, the long dance between Earth and Hell was finally over.

Except for the dreadnought. The dreadnought — a lieutenant to them, and a summoner of others — was still being held in magnetic containment, its deadly influence still present to irradiate Adrian's dreams. What did it mean? Adrian's eyebrow was raising at Dixon already, before Ray said what they'd both believed aloud.

"But the department's already being dismantled," Ray said. "There aren't any more incursions. No more rifts. There's nothing left for someone like me to do."

Dixon shrugged, his head tipping side to side. "Technically, that's far from true."

IO

FAMILIAR TERRITORY

Sunlight was like the blast of a furnace when the rear doors opened.

Adrian and Ray had been in the dark rear of an anonymous box truck for perhaps forty-five minutes with only the glow sticks from Ray's pack for light. Their eyes had adjusted. Seeing day again was an assault, like being born.

It wasn't Dixon who opened the rear. It was a soldier in camouflage wearing shiny black boots and carrying an automatic rifle. An officer came up beside him. This was the first the Porters had seen of either of them. Dixon had had the truck backed up to the rear door of the building in which Gloria Dunham, PhD had her therapy office, hustling them into it out of sight. Dixon had closed the door. Adrian just assumed he'd been the one who'd then started their pitch black ride, the one who drove them across bumpy roads to wherever this was.

The officer gave a respectful nod, just short of a salute. Then she extended a hand, which they shook.

"Colonel Priya Patel. Apologies for the blackout, gentlemen. Brass wants a low profile on this one. A troop carrier would have been more comfortable, but these were my orders."

They looked down the truck's side, bearing the logo of a furniture company. Above, they could hear the buzzing of drones.

"You're invisible here," Patel continued, indicating the drones. "Those are ours. Watching for others. Obviously no-fly all the way up. I won't bore you with the details, but suffice to say no one knows, or will know, you're here. You're already cleared for entry. If you don't mind, it's best we get started. Agent Dixon preceded your arrival and is already inside. If you'll follow me this way."

Patel turned toward the corrugated side of a huge, silent, run-down building. There were no vehicles except for theirs. The place looked abandoned. And familiar. Adrian was far too close to the building to identify it as more than a big metal wall, but there was a tip-of-the-tongue feeling about everything.

They neared what seemed to be a massive hangar door, tall and broad enough to accomodate a blimp. The colonel put a hand on it as if she thought she could move such a massive thing without mechanical help.

The uniformed soldier with the gun spoke up. He looked about sixteen, baby-faced with a look like someone eager to prove himself.

"Do either of you have metallic objects inside you? Implants, surgical pins ... an artificial hip or knee?"

They shook their heads.

"Old fillings? Silver, maybe gold?"

"No."

"What about dental implants? Even if the crown is porcelain or resin, the abutments and fixtures are usually metallic."

They shook their heads again, but now Adrian was starting

to feel like he might forget something and suffer for his negligence. He didn't know why the soldier was asking, but the questions sounded serious.

"All right, gentlemen." He reached through the door itself, as if it wasn't there, and pulled a pair of plastic trays from nowhere. They looked like the kind of thing airports used at security to pass small objects through the scanner. "Anything metallic you have on you, drop it in here. Rings. Pens. Belt buckles. Any piercings. I see metal snaps on your coats. Better take those off as well." He looked down. "Are there steel toes in your boots?"

"There's steel in my zipper."

Ray had been joking, but Patel nodded as if he hadn't. "Of course. We don't get visitors often. Our uniforms all use soft fasteners. That might have been unpleasant." She was looking now, scanning Ray's pants. "I see metal rivets as well. You'll need to take the trousers off as well, I'm afraid. If you'd prefer, I can provide a modesty tent for—"

Ray was doffing his pants, revealing plain black boxer briefs. Of course he looked good in them. Adrian was closer to chicken legs and would have accepted the modesty tent, but now Ray would ridicule him if he did.

The soldier took all of their offered items, including the airport small-item dishes, and set them inside of a latching black case. Then he moved farther down the building's side, where Adrian saw only more corrugated metal, and pushed it through.

There was no door or passage. As happened when the soldier removed the dishes, the object went right through the door like it wasn't there.

"Are you sure you're clear of all metal, sirs?" the kid asked.

"I guess we'll find out," Ray said.

"Fair enough," said Colonel Patel. "If you'll follow me."

This said, she walked directly through the wall.

Ray looked back at Adrian, half amused and half disbelieving. He reached out, touched the door, and found it insubstantial. He then walked through it as Patel had. Adrian, unsure, went last.

The inside of the building was nothing at all like the exterior. Outside had been bucolic silence and dust: the true meaning of "nothing to see here." The building's interior, however, was an assault to every one of the senses.

The ceiling was high, visible as metal framework far above. The floorspace was covered with enormous clanging machines that filled that height at least halfway, every one of them crawling with workers, technicians, and milling military personnel, both officers and those in camouflage. It was impossibly loud — all churning and banging and grinding. Something acrid had burned; the air reeked of melted plastic, and Adrian found himself tasting it as well as scenting it.

"APOLOGIES AGAIN! Patel shout-said, extending two pairs of over-ear headphones: hearing protection, Adrian assumed. "LIKE I SAID, WE DON'T GET VISITORS!"

Adrian took the offered headphones, noticing a rubber gasket that extended around the soft parts that pressed against the wearer's head. Only, it wasn't quite rubber. It was *like* rubber, but definitely something else.

He put them on and all sound ceased. If Adrian closed his eyes, he could have believed he was in a library. It was surreal. The context of the scene changed entirely: all these people rushing around and busy, the works clashing with utter silence.

Patel too sounded like someone in a library. Adrian almost wanted to cringe: Her normal speaking voice would surely disturb all these quietly-working people.

"I don't know the science," she said, tapping her own

headphones. "From what I hear, it's not like the normal kind of science anyway. Usually there's no way to block out all sound. You don't just hear through your ear canal under normal circumstances. Loud enough sounds make their way to your inner ear right through your skull. On top of that, you'll get what's called 'bone conductance.' Somehow these cancel that out. It'll be easier on your brain if you don't ask."

"I can hear you," Adrian said.

"Oh, sure. You'll hear anyone talking to you. You can also hear anything you make an effort to hear." She pointed, meaning a pair of techs nearby. "Try paying attention to those two."

They did. At first, there was nothing. But then Adrian could hear them too, perfectly clear.

"The technology is intentional," the colonel said, meaning whatever ran the headphones. "It works as if it reads your mind, knows who you want to talk to or hear from, then pulls out just that voice so you can hear it. The dampening works the same way: blocks the sound at the level of your nerves, not a physical block of the sound itself."

"But how—?"

"I'm afraid I'm going to have to ask you to just roll with it, gentlemen," she said, kindly but firmly. "The hearing protection and our illusory entrance—" She nodded to the door-but-not-actually-a-door they'd walked through like a hologram. "—are some of the *least* impressive things I daresay you'll see today. I'm afraid I won't have the luxury of explaining it all. Time is a factor. We need to keep moving. Your belongings."

Adrian looked. The soldier had opened the black case, which seemed to have gone through yet another unknown mechanism down the line. They re-donned their pants and re-fitted their loose ends.

"Metal is okay inside?" It was a relief; Adrian had assumed he'd have to walk around the entire time half naked.

"It's just the barrier that's a problem, sir."

"Why don't you send people through inside one of those cases, then, so they don't risk forgetting some random piece of metal?"

"That's what we do with people who have metal inside their bodies, sir. We don't like to do it more than we have to, though. Sometimes the protective cases disrupt nerve conduction. Entirely. If that happens, it can be fatal."

"Well, what if—?"

"I'm sorry, Mr. Porter. We really do need to be moving on."

Patel walked up a short set of metal stairs, then along a catwalk that ran three feet above the ground. Beneath, lines of multicolored light shot between emitters and sensors hooked to unfamiliar machines, like lasers.

"Zen Element," Adrian whispered to Ray. It was surreal to whisper, knowing how loud it was in here. "It's Zen that runs these." Like Patel, he tapped the headphones.

"Why do you say that?"

"Laurel described tech like this under development at GEN. GEN's never had a shortage for ideas of how to use Element to do all sorts of impossible things. It's anti-entropic, creating energy and order instead of dissipating energy and disordering like every other fuel. The problem was always getting enough to work with. She said the brigades used almost eighty percent of all the refined Element harvested when we were stitching at our peak. The rigs, the fillers, the weapons ..."

He shook his head, looking across the massive space: a hangar indeed, or maybe two tied together. "But even the Zen we're *not* using recently doesn't explain this. We've almost entirely stopped fiend rendering now that the rifts are closed. Where's it all coming from?"

"But she said it's 'intentional,'" Ray said.

"Exactly. It's not passive. It knows what you're thinking. Or, maybe more accurately, what you're feeling. What you *intend* to happen. Sound familiar?"

It took a moment, but Ray nodded. That's how Erika Dale described the fiends' language. You didn't actually have to know their words; you could just sort of know what you meant to say and make a few sounds. Thanks to interplanar voodoo, everyone understood everyone else with a bit of practice.

There was another thing, too: the way the dreadnought's energy poked its way into Adrian's dreams. That felt like lubricating real communication more than his own mind inventing fantasy. He never felt like he was dreaming about Laurel so much as receiving messages from her.

They seemed to be headed toward what looked like a windowed office at the catwalk's end, but there was something interesting to look at every step along the way. Adrian was taking it all in when Ray spoke.

"Ade. Do you know what this place is?"

"What?"

"It's the warehouse. Erika's warehouse."

Adrian scoped the place with new eyes, seeing easily enough that Ray was correct. They hadn't known where their little rift-through-rift jump would take them on the day of the near-sundering, so even then it'd taken time for Adrian to ID it. Laurel had brought him here in the early days, when GEN was using it mostly for storage. The place was abandoned by the time they found themselves inside it again, chosen by Matt Baker as the ideal location to detonate his psionic bomb because it was more or less in the center of the perforated rifts when viewed from the fiend plane.

Adrian's head completed his nostalgic tour: Six months ago, he and Ray had battled endless waves of fiends over *there*, as part of a test. Matt Baker had died *there*; maybe there was still a stain on the concrete where the fiends disemboweled him. Erika had mostly blown up: anaphylaxis combined with whatever errant biology had been in the process of turning her from a human into a fiend. That, he thought, had happened over *there*.

And that corner? Under the massive I-beam? That's where the original dreadnought had sat, deciding the fates of worlds. That's where the massive, horned red thing had been when Adrian thought at it, accidentally trading Laurel's expertise for the mortal plane's salvation.

Was the one he'd spoken with the same dreadnought they'd captured? Adrian had never thought about it before, only now wondering why he hadn't considered it.

Could there be many fiends that big? GEN thought now that primordial form didn't apply to what they jokingly called the "boss caste." The hellbringer that slaughtered their father might always be a hellbringer, but that thinking went 10x for anything as massive as a dreadnought.

Was it their king? Was there only one?

Those aren't the questions you should be asking yourself, buddy boy, Adrian thought. *You're wondering what they want you to wonder — what it makes sense to wonder, because those are the questions that matter to you, to your mortality, to the safety of the planes. But have you ever wondered how they captured it in the first place? Halfskulls can be caught with tackles and shackles. But what had it taken to make a boss of bosses submit?*

"This is us." The colonel opened the door, where the Porters found Dixon surrounded by charts, sketches, and sheets full of numbers.

He wasn't wearing hearing protection, speaking at the top of his already-formidable voice to hear himself speak.

"WELCOME TO THE NEW HOME OF SPREAD AND

CONTAINMENT." Then the door closed and he spoke in a normal voice. "Although these days, we don't worry much about either."

II

TWO BEACONS

"You can take those off." Dixon pointed at Adrian's headphones.

Patel had already set hers aside. Ray and Adrian followed suit. The office was as stone-quiet as it had been, now that the door was closed.

"Dampening field," he said, waving a finger around. "Kind of like we're all inside one big set of headphones. It's the same tech used on the outer walls to hide the noise. And to hide the grounds. That's another thing. This entire patch of land is covered in vehicles and aircraft. The field is tied to the building. They had to bring planes and helicopters here in pieces."

"What the hell's going on here?" Ray asked.

"Right to the point. I like you." Dixon stood. "Well, then. Let's just get something out in the open, in case it's not already." He turned to Adrian. "The other side liked you. It liked you very much. The tech developed since Sundering Day can see interplanar attachments, and they've never stopped reaching out to you. To your mind. Following me so far?"

"Not at all," Adrian replied.

"We know you learned the trick of communicating with them," Dixon said. "We had to reverse-engineer some stuff to figure it out, but ... Well, it's tricky to explain by the usual rules of physics and time and space and all that bullshit, but one of the reasons Zen Element seems to defy our usual science is because it's cheating energy across a time differential. Let's just say we're able to look back. Maybe a little bit forward, but that's more like good guessing for now. What you did left a trace that people a lot smarter than me can read, so what happened in here that day? We know all about it. Play by play. We're talking the most-reviewed bit of game footage in the history of GEN.

"That day, Ms. Dale explained to you how they communicate in a way you might call 'psychic,' but we prefer to call 'non-locally.' The interpretation part, we don't understand because our brains aren't wired like theirs, if they even have brains. But we do understand how it works across distance. I think Ms. Dale explained *that* to you, too."

Adrian nodded. That was the quasi-wormhole phenomenon. Places that seemed far apart sometimes were actually very close together when viewed from the other plane.

"I mentioned 'psionic energy' earlier. Again, feels like a misnomer, but jokes made between scientists tend to stick. So, okay. Let's pretend it's psychic. Psychic phenomena, even if they're not technically psychic, leave traces that the people here can see. You've been like a beacon since Sundering Day. But you're not the only one."

"Ray," Adrian said.

"Laurel," Dixon countered.

Adrian started to open his mouth, but Colonel Patel cut him off.

"Maybe it's Ms. Gantry and maybe it's not," she said, eyeing Dixon. "We just know that your 'taste' of the dreadnought's energy seems to have primed your system. Think about it like riding a bike. Talking once allowed a part of you to know how to talk to it — and the rest of them, and the plane itself — forever. When they took Ms. Gantry, the process probably—"

"You know about that? You know they took Laurel that day?"

"And that your mind basically sent her," Dixon said. "Let's move on."

Patel continued. She didn't talk like military. It made Adrian think that maybe she was two things: a scientist on one hand, a military leader on the other. They'd need people like that, for whatever was happening here.

"When they took Ms. Gantry, the process probably gave her the same knowledge you had. But it's like I said, we can't be sure it's her on the other end. They operate as a semi-collective. Some beings are in charge. We think of them as a 'brain caste.' That caste is definitely not collective. The lower fiends are, though, just like they tend to be primordial before they emerge from a rift. It's entirely possible that whatever Laurel learned when she crossed over, the fiends picked up."

"Why?" Adrian asked.

"As a lure," said Dixon.

Patel nodded as if that was half-true, or true but not the whole picture. "It's commonly believed that riftfare is ending. It is not. We have reason to believe that there is some degree of strategy and consolidation happening on the other plane. Simply put, they may not be quiet after all. They may be planning an attack."

"What's that got to do with me and Laurel?"

"One of two things is happening, and this is straight from the acknowledged branch of S&C," Dixon said. "As I mentioned, we've been watching you because of the tie you seem to have to the other plane. One thing that might be happening is that you're *intending* so hard, it's like your yearning itself keeps reaching across the planes."

That felt true. Adrian had done little else over the past months than yearn for Laurel's return — to regret, with every waking moment, his role in her vanishment.

"But the other option," said Patel, picking up Dixon's baton, "is that communication is happening in the opposite direction. Maybe you're seeking Laurel, and I suppose it's even possible that somewhere over there Laurel is seeking you, assuming they found a way to keep her alive, which they'd have to do if they wanted her knowledge. But it's equally possible that you're not calling out, but are instead being drawn. Something — and in this case, maybe not Laurel at all — is using your beacon to gather information."

"You think I'm a spy," Adrian said.

It was nothing new. That's what the brigade thought, the last time he worked with Dixon.

"Not intentionally," Patel replied. "You give them a tendril in our world, is all. If you're curious, there's a report I could show you that explains the phenomenon. We first noticed cross-plane 'signaling' after a Russian civilian went through a rift deep inside a Zen Element mine in Fortune and came out in Moscow. It's classified, but we stole it from the Kremlin after the Cuban Missile Crisis — so what the hell; it was never ours to begin with."

"Jesus," Ray muttered to Adrian. "Cuban Missile Crisis? That'd be ... what? 1962?"

"Technically re-dated by the CIA as March 30, 1963. You want to read it?" She began waving vaguely to someone deeper in the room.

"Not even a little," said Adrian.

Patel shrugged and lowered her arm. "The point is: Yes, the

other plane is able to see into you, and that means they can to some degree see through to us. But that's okay. We can flip it around: back-trace the signal like a homing beacon."

"A homing beacon?" Ray asked. "What exactly do you plan to home in on?"

"We'll get to that." Patel's tone permitted no discussion.

Adrian was catching up at lighting speed, and didn't like where this was headed. "My nightmares. My 'visions.'" He eyed Dixon and added, "The shit I saw in the mirror. You think it's a message, don't you? Someone is trying to reach me — trying to tell me something from the other side — and you want to back-trace it? You want to use my 'beacon' to send some sort of a bomb?"

Patel and Dixon traded a look, as good as a *yes*.

Adrian found himself thinking of the way the military ran this place. How Dixon had said there were planes and helicopters out there, though without rifts that didn't make much sense. Either way it spoke of hegemony. It spoke of destruction. Spread and Containment had never been friendly to the brigades, but before now they'd still been public servants. They were still curious, wanting to understand.

Dixon was an ass, but his intentions, before now, had always been pure: *Find the problem. Contain it.* Like GEN, and like Adrian and Ray's father, they'd always wanted to understand instead of wantonly destroy.

Apparently modern times made new and terrible bedfellows.

Adrian didn't like it one bit. To Patel, the mainline of thought he had into the fiend plane could be tied to anything on the other end. To Adrian, however, the sender was clear. Now that he knew he wasn't going crazy — that these happenings were coming from the Hell plane and not his imagination — he was positive it was Laurel speaking to him.

He'd seen her face. He'd heard her suffering. He'd taken her pleas for help ... and he'd be damned if, in reply, he'd help Dixon send a nuke to kill her.

Find the heat, and follow it home.

The fiends had her gagged. She couldn't speak freely. His own mind was in the mix of their communication, filtering everything she thought and sent to him through his own confused brain. He was seeing her using an unpracticed mode of contact, for a human. She couldn't just talk to him; something on her end or on his was in the way. He had dreams. Hunches. Hints. Intuition.

Adrian didn't know what *find the heat* meant, but he could easily interpret *follow it home.*

Follow it to me. Come find me, Adrian.

That's what Laurel had been trying to tell him. And they wanted him to turn that channel traitor, use it to deliver a virus?

Over his dead body.

"It's coming from Laurel," Adrian said.

"You can't know that. They're consolidating. If we wait to find out what you're speaking with, it could be too late."

"You don't need to wait," Adrian told Patel. "I already know who I'm speaking with. I can feel it. I can feel *her.*"

Adrian was staring at Dixon, trying to appeal to him as a fellow civilian.

But Patel's gaze warned him off as she answered his non-question. "You can't make that call. It's too big a risk to take."

"I won't help you," Adrian said. "It's about intention? I'll *intend* that you never see what I see."

Patel looked confused, then amused. To Dixon she said, "You didn't tell them?"

"Tell us what?" Ray asked.

"Why do you think we brought both of you? You're the only

living humans who've ever crossed from rift to rift. Every time we try to do the same, people burn." Her face grew serious. "From the start, the other side has always been interested in both of you."

It was true. Erika basically said as much. Ever since they were boys, the fiends had always been interested in the sons of Eldon Porter, a man they had killed without wanting to. Ray and Adrian were legacies. If Erika's original plan had held, they'd already have joined the other side, having been tested and determined worthy.

"We don't want you to *talk* to them," Patel said. "We need you to lead an expedition. To *guide us to them.*"

Adrian looked at Ray.

Ray looked at Adrian.

Then Ray said, "How? There are no more rifts."

Patel rose. She put on her hearing protection, and soon enough the other three in the room did the same. "One more stop on the tour. And it's a doozy."

12

MAGNITUDE 35

They could only gape. The spectacle in front of them was equal parts beautiful and horrible.

One warehouse over, the old GEN facility's reconstruction had removed the entire concrete floor and then excavated down far enough that the place now went down into the earth twice as far as it used to go up. The warehouse was already doubled-up to the one next to it: a tandem job, once upon a time meant for GEN's most ambitious experiments. The new owners had doubled it up again, using that same obscuring field to hide the remainder from outside eyes.

The final building was two warehouses wide, two warehouses long, and three warehouses high with two thirds of that height below deck. A titanic space, and it seemed one entire end was dominated by a flaming eye the size of a stadium.

Adrian had never seen a rift so big. It was hard to look at for long. Some trick of its emissions was unsettling in a way nobody on-base had been able to articulate — a phenomenon Colonel Patel compared to subsonic sound used as a weapon.

There's no fabled "brown note" able to make the enemy crap their pants, she'd told them back in the factory office. *We'd know; our weapons people tried to find it. There is a "disturbing note," though. Sit too long in front of speakers at certain hertz and you'll start to feel like dying might not be so bad. I guess the same kind of thing can happen with their aurora,* she added, *with something close to light — some frequency we can feel in our guts, but cannot see.*

To Adrian, the "thing we cannot see" felt like dispair. He tried to be awed while standing on the catwalk before the rift. He tried to be angry that this had been kept from the world. He even tried to be inspired: He was a Stitcher; this would be the ultimate Stitch. Instead he felt hollow, like there might never be joy again.

But at the same time, it was beautiful, in the way death can be. Patel had said the room was six hundred feet wide, six hundred feet tall, and nearly a quarter mile long, yet the rift almost filled its far end.

A hundred Adrians could stand inside it if they stood on each other's heads. He wanted to watch it forever while wishing he'd never seen it at all.

"We should be dead just standing here," said Ray.

"Another Zen containment field," Patel explained. "Don't go past the big red signs at the end. With raw exposure, twenty heat suits piled on top of one another wouldn't keep you safe."

They hadn't even been able to build structures that far down. The machinery, ladders, and walkways all stopped short of huge red signage anchored directly into the rock, warning personnel not to go farther. It was rock and dirt down there — nothing man-made except for what looked like a flagpole-diameter rod running along the floor and angling up into the rift's lower third. It was the only thing ruining the view.

The aurora here was substantial enough to rain in curtains

that extended into the human-filled safe area, undulating just like the borealis.

"We estimate it as a magnitude thirty-four, thirty-five," Patel said.

Adrian was sure he'd heard wrong. On a logarithmic scale, magnitude 35 would make this rift 10^{25th} times larger than the biggest rift he'd previously been able to imagine: a magnitude ten multiplied by a one followed by 25 zeroes. Even the enormous downtown rift last year (so large it was more commonly called a *rip)* wasn't quite a 10.0. This was a billion billion million times that.

They were wearing their magical Zen Element headphones. Without hearing protection, the blast from this rift would obliterate their eardrums. The field between it and them must do more than hold back the heat and brimstone odor because even the force coming from it would be strong enough to shatter concrete.

Small rifts exhaled. Big rifts blew a gale. This would be all the world's air at once, stronger than the solar wind.

"You can't close it," Ray said. "That's it, isn't it?"

"We opened it," Patel replied.

Ray could only stare. "Why?"

"To the average person, the sundering that almost happened was the barely-averted end of the world. To you, it was the job of a lifetime. It was something like an act of war to most human leaders of this world. I believe you know the history."

They knew the first so-called fiend to cross the first rift had been an explorer. They knew a human contingent, including their own father, had met that explorer. They knew it hadn't taken humans long to realize how precious the materials from the other side were: how their new friend's doorway exhaled an infinite energy source and how his blood was filled with a substance more precious than diamonds. They knew the early humans' "counter-explorations" had actually been mining operations. How very quickly, humans had lost interest in the other beings and instead grew interested in the potential of refined Zen Element.

A race to open doors, take what came out, then battle back fiends as if they were the enemy. Soon they became just that. The brothers knew that for five long decades, the fiends had let humans believe they were winning riftfare because by then their only way out of the energy crisis it caused on their plane was to push the whole thing forward. Fiends couldn't seal rifts larger than a certain magnitude. The only option had been to orchestrate the mother of all rifts: the sundering, which would intermingle the planes for once and for all.

Adrian and Ray knew the history, all right. They knew that the sundering, while it would have destroyed Earth as people knew it, was the fiends' only possible endgame.

Act of war, *yes*. The only way to save their world? That was also *yes*.

"At first we thought the failure of the sundering would mean their plane's collapse," Dixon explained. "Every model we used at S&C predicted that. There's only so much energy in the world — worlds, I suppose — and the first law of thermodynamics says it can't be created or destroyed, just changed from one form into another. The Element that'd spilled into our plane, especially after the near-sundering and all the rifts it entailed, should have left them barren. We allowed one small rift to stay open, here in an earlier version of this room and extremely well-guarded, so we could monitor the other side. But energy over there did a strange thing. For a while, it declined, before ramping back up. Spectral analysis detected the presence of both raw and refined Element. That was supposedly impossible on their plane. So we went to someone who had looked into that specific problem — how to refine Element in their atmosphere — and guess what we found."

Adrian wouldn't answer that. The question was rhetorical. They'd gone to Laurel, found her gone, and used that belated spy tech mentioned earlier to determine where she'd gone and how she'd gotten there. He couldn't help but feel some pride. Laurel had done it. No matter what else had happened, she'd found a way to accomplish the impossible, for the fiends, on the other side.

"The discovery was alarming," Patel explained. "S&C's calculations, before we knew the other plane could refine Zen Element, made it clear that they'd never be able to launch another attack of any substance. Our detection tech had improved, and their ability to open rifts had diminished. Any rifts they opened could easily be dealt with once we developed better multi-weapons and trained Legions to use them. You dealt with many of those early post-sundering rifts yourselves, in the weeks after things began to settle. Soon enough the fiends realized the futility of it all and ceased ingress. Because they couldn't close most of the rifts they opened (they needed our Stitchers to do that) they were just wasting their limited cache of global energy, opening new holes in a leaky system. But after we discovered they could refine Element? After their energetics started to rise again?"

Patel shook her head. "It didn't feel like recovery. It felt like re-armament. We nearly got burned once. We couldn't give them a second chance to try again."

"Recently, strange things are starting to happen. 'Strange' if you don't have all the information, but perfectly sensible if you do." Dixon pointed at the big rift. "The Army Corps of Engineers devoted millions of man-hours to opening a rift large enough to siphon back some of their stockpile. It was supposed to be like bombing an enemy fuel depot. It worked a little too well. Once the rift was a certain size, it was like its own new perforation. The planes around it weakened and for a while they thought it might spin out of control — might just sunder after all."

"Salt and pepper," Adrian said. "All those little inhaling rifts."

"You'd think," Dixon replied. "But no, the energetics you've seen are evidence of something else. This rift was stabilized months ago. All the Zen flowing out of this one sort of sucked the others closed. It allowed the rest of the plane to heal. *This?*"

He again pointed at the rift. "This, gentlemen, is the reason rifts no longer open. We used to think a weak area would stay that way forever. Instead, this single point became the pressure valve. Its expulsions were so enormous, all the other old rifts were able to seal completely. In one sense, it did your jobs for you. Forever."

Adrian wasn't seeing it that way. What had been done here was the opposite of solving things. It was an abomination, the equivalent of curing a roach infestation by burning down the house.

"How much Element does this rift expel?" Adrian asked.

"That's classified!" Patel snapped.

He looked to Dixon, but Dixon wouldn't even look back. Their interplay gave Adrian all the answer he needed.

How much Element came out of the monster rift?

Why, plenty to line all the government coffers, of course.

It explained all the new weapons. All the new defensive technology and GEN's recent burst of innovation. The impervious rod he'd seen that led from the machinery into the rift's center? That must be a harvester: a straw they'd stuck into the other side's Zen to turn it into a second Alaska Pipeline. The entire infrastructure was robbing Peter to pay Paul in the most stunning display of shortsightedness the world had ever seen.

The war machine seemed to see no downside here. All the other rifts had closed and the world was rich with more energy and weapons and technology and (let's face it) cold, hard cash than it would ever need. Zen Element was flowing through the streets like gold, and the only catch was this mall-sized gateway to Hell.

What could possibly go wrong?

"The micro-rifts you saw at the containment facility weren't genuine salt and pepper rifts," Dixon said. "We saw openings like them not long after this building was expanded and excavated to uncover enough area around the rift, once it finally stopped growing. There were a few, then they stopped. Some of the GEN people thought they were just equalization ripples, but the rest of your adventure yesterday proves they're not. As you said, the rifts you found *inhaled* instead of *exhaling* like most rifts. Then your filler rods emptied. Emptied of what, Porter? Not stitching resin. Not really."

"Zen," Adrian said. "They emptied of Zen."

Dixon nodded. "The fiends know what we're doing here. They know we're keeping a wound open so they can't consolidate the resources they have left and come after us again."

Keeping a wound open ... and collecting its precious, precious blood, Adrian thought.

"They know what we're doing, and they can't fool us in the same way they did last time. Last time they let us think we had them beat, then lured vulnerable minds like Erika Dale and Matt Baker into helping them open new rifts we *couldn't* best. We think your experience yesterday proves they've taken on a new tack — a new offensive against us."

"Why?"

Patel answered. "They're testing. The small rifts are trials, maybe to map our topology. They inhale because they've found a way to invert pressure on their end, effectively pulling

Zen expulsions inward so they aren't lost outward. Your rig emptied, most likely, because micro-rifts opened inside the rods themselves. But it was just a test, to see if they can open rifts with pinpoint accuracy, then steal refined Zen directly from our store. We've witnessed the same thing in several of our stockpiles: supplies diminishing, then rising again when the test is complete."

"Why would they give it back?" Ray asked.

"Who knows? Maybe they don't have holding technology perfected yet. Maybe they're just finding out where everything is, collecting coordinates so that at some future point, they can reach back in and take all of it at once. For all we know, they'll find a way to turn even this big rift around on us. Right now, it's one big deflating balloon. They might turn it into a vacuum instead. What we do know is that they're not being as coy with body-resident Element. *That*, they're already taking for keeps."

"The fiends you saw 'disappearing,'" Dixon explained. "They didn't really disappear. The Zen was sucked out of them all at once. And yes, we're sure. The rendering crews who followed you found absolutely no blood — no raw Zen — in the remains. It was just dry carbon and other trace elements. They sucked every one of those prisoners dry, pulling the Element inside them back to the other side."

"You can't know that."

"We do know that," Patel disagreed. "This is classified, but what happened at the B1 facility happened elsewhere at the same time."

"Where else?"

"*Everywhere* else. There are no prisoners anymore. They're all gone. Their biomass was significant. A substantial loss of Element from our side, pulled back to theirs."

Adrian found himself thinking of what the Laurel dreams had told him — not really dreams anymore, but instead genuine messages filtered through the confusing miasma of his own sleepy subconscious.

Find the heat, and follow it home.

Thermodynamics. That's what she'd been trying to tell him. The tiny rifts had sucked heat back instead of blowing it forward. Zen was flowing back, not forward. Where Dixon and Patel saw the consolidation of a vital resource, Adrian saw a path. At the end of that path — wherever all that heat and Zen and energy had its focal point — that's where Laurel called home.

Follow it home.

Which, through the lens of Adrian's dreams, became: *Follow it back to me.*

She'd been calling him for help. Telling him how to find her. He just needed to hitch a ride on a breath of hot air, ride on a backdraft of Zen Element returning to its source. If he could enter the blistering, suffocating world beyond a rift, chasing the streams that Patel found so sinister, he could find her again.

It's not that simple. It could be a trap.

But Adrian wouldn't even look that thought in the eye. Instead he stared at the rift. It was a broiling doorway, his deadly ticket to undoing the harm he'd done — maybe not to the world, but to Laurel at least.

"Make no mistake," Patel said. "This is an arms race. They struck first with their sundering. We struck back, opening this rift to keep them disarmed. Now we think they've found a way around the leakage, using tiny rifts to rip refined Zen back to us so they can use it. Done right, it could give them the final strike — the definitive blow, making the sundering look like child's play. As of right now, we have no viable way to pre-detect rifts as small and with such short periods as you saw. If they can pinpoint a location as specific as the filler rods inside one

Stitcher's rig, what's to stop them from opening one in the Oval Office? On the Senate floor? They might be able to develop their own multi-weapon, slashing through us the way we slashed through them. They wouldn't even have to get close. Just open a tiny rift inside your skull. My skull. One tick and lesions start to form in the cerebellum. You stop breathing. The autopsy would show surgical precision, as if a neurosurgeon magician did no-touch brain surgery on you, cauterizing the muscles that keep you breathing from an actual world away."

"And now you want us to go in," Ray said. "To strike back one last time."

"Correct," Patel nodded.

"And do what?"

"The streams leaking from our world seem to be converging somewhere on the other side. Our readings suggest is that the convergence point is some sort of a nest."

"You want us to destroy a *nest?*"

Patel nodded. "And if we're lucky, we believe that nest is home to a queen. Maybe *the* queen."

While they'd been talking, a group of soldiers wearing special insignia on their shoulders had begun to assemble just on the safe side of the field protecting the room from the rift. At first there had only been a few, but now those few had become ranks, standing at-ease with hands folded behind their backs. Facing the catwalk. At the front was a man with a jaw like an action figure, scarred from eyebrow to chin.

"Who are they?" Ray asked.

"Your crew," Patel replied. "Now let's get started."

13

FUCKED

There was very little prep. The Army — or whoever this group was, that Patel led — had already put everything in perfect order. The mission had been mapped out. Equipment specific to the mission had been developed, modified, and custom-fitted.

As far as armament went, they saw the truth now: the multi-weapons used by the brigades for rifts that never opened were really just live-action placebos: weapons that worked, yes, but had only been distributed to keep the public from looking in all the wrong directions. Only riftfighters fought rifts.

That was the official line, so of course in all the post-sundering melee, Legions and Stitchers had been abundantly armed. It didn't matter that they had nothing to fight. It only mattered that people felt safe. That they saw no threat and yet knew that if threats came, the brigades still stood ready to address them. Believing all those outdated things kept people quiescent. Nobody asked about riftfare these days.

In truth, all those new weapons and defenses had been

built for this specific mission. The multi-weapons were better here than they were at the brigade. And there were weapons that the Porters had never seen: a hand cannon that shot a beam of what looked like pure white light but in fact it was an extravagant waste of pure Element: the equivalent of rabbit hunting with a bazooka. A modified grenade launcher shot pewter-headed harpoons that swelled once they hit home, sizzling with a deadly chemical reaction nobody bothered to explain.

Perhaps most impressive of all were the blunt-force weapons. They weren't sexy like Zen weapons, but their ingenious brutality rivaled torture devices from the Middle Ages. Fiends could be destroyed with enough physical force. That was the reason the first line of Legions always swung Rollards: cutting and slashing wasn't class-dependent and worked on everything a Legion could strike before it struck them. The new weapons had taken that thinking to absurd, evil-genius heights. Force killed all fiends? Well, then all they needed was to increase the force, and ideally make it possible from a distance.

Thus the flying impact hammers.

Thus the razor-bladed rotor drones.

Thus the so-called multipliers, which shot rounds that shot rounds that shot rounds. The final rounds reminded Adrian of an old horror movie called Phantasm, where baseball-sized orbs deployed blades to spear, slash, and maim. The multipliers ended in thousands of such balls. They were either AI-driven or driven by Zen Element, able to chase their prey, deploy different blades depending on circumstance ... or, if nothing else worked, to simply pummel even the largest fiends into tenderized meat paste.

There was almost nothing for Ray and Adrian to do but go along. About which they were technically given no choice.

There was never talk of permission. Never talk of agreeing. They were both guests of honor and prisoners. Adrian never once considered refusing. It was too obvious how *No* would be received.

"This situation is fucked," Ray said.

"And?"

"And *fucked,*" he repeated.

Of course it was fucked. If the compound itself had been wearing a name tag, that's the way it'd introduce itself: HELLO, I'M FUCKED.

"We need to get out of here, Ade. These people are psychotic."

Adrian agreed. He also wasn't quite sure leaving was a good idea. Or even possible. The idea that two brigade workers would be useful to this team of superbly equipped born killers was tenuous at best.

Yes, Ray and Adrian had crossed a rift. Once. Yes, they'd known more about the true nature of the other plane than even GEN, even this whole warehouse full of dorks. Sort of. But did any of that matter? Finesse didn't strike Adrian as high-priority here. This supposed mission to invade a nest of fiends and maybe find a queen did not sound surgical in nature.

If the Porters were willing to lend their expertise, awesome. Knowing more about what they might face would save some time, maybe save some lives. But if the Porters weren't interested? That didn't seem like a very big deal.

The scar-faced platoon leader was a hard-edged asshole of premium caliber who obviously resented their presence. *He* was the badass; *they* needed no one's help. The man's name was Graves, and Adrian got the distinct impression that the loss of the Porter boys would be a benefit to him, not an inconvenience.

"How?"

"I don't know," Ray said. "You're smart. You figure it out."

But Adrian was busy figuring out something else. Ever since their tour had begun, he'd been feeling Laurel's presence inside his mind growing like a benevolent tumor.

After meeting Graves and his troops, Adrian excused himself and went to the restroom. Two of Graves's men followed him and stood guard just in case he decided to skedaddle. It was surrounded by twelve inches of concrete on all sides as if people here were in the habit of taking radioactive shits that required containment.

In the bathroom, the last of Adrian's certainty evaporated. In the stall, he found Laurel's decapitated head floating in blood in the toilet's bowl. This time, her message — still not entirely literal, still fighting its way through Adrian's psychology as required by their psychic bond — was different.

Find the heat, and follow it home, she'd said before.

This time, though, she rolled in her rotting water until her eyes found Adrian's. And added, "Nothing is what you think it is."

"*Nothing is what you think it is?*" Ray repeated after Adrian told him. "What the fuck does that mean?"

Adrian had managed to shake his guards and they'd met behind a machine that made what looked like hockey pucks, only they were glowing and made both men feel sick to look at. They could hear the grunts trying to find them.

Adrian was still trying to decide what he'd say when they eventually did. So far, the best excuse he could come up with was a joke about hide and seek. "I think it means there's more going on than we know."

"That's not helpful. Ask her what specifically she's talking about."

"It doesn't work that way."

"What the fuck do you know about how it works?"

"More than you," Adrian said. "You thought I was crazy, seeing visions."

"There's nothing here that's not crazy. These people are psychotic. We need to get out of here."

"You said that already, Ray."

"It's still true."

"I don't know how to get out. And if we got out, I don't know where we'd go, or what we'd do. This is bigger than Captain Kaur. A lot bigger."

"What, then?" Ray asked. "We can't just go along with it. Let's just pretend they know how to enter a rift of that size. Let's pretend they know a way to survive over there. Let's say they have inexhaustible rebreathers. Heat protection like nothing we've ever seen, to withstand it long enough to do a damn thing. Let's pretend they've got it all worked out, and they know how a bunch of soft, burnable, oxygen-needing humans are supposed to cross their plane in search of some sort of holy grail."

Adrian nodded. He'd already pretended those things. It took no effort. As impossible as all the things Ray had just said sounded, Adrian had no doubt the military complex had addressed it all. A machine like this did nothing without planning. And planning. And planning. The true movers of this world were never surprised or half-baked. They were too paranoid, and paranoia was kin to preparation.

"Let's just suppose all of that's possible. Even so, I don't think what they're planning is a good idea. You want to know what I think?" Ray pointed at the rift. Even though they were hidden, there was nowhere in the complex from which you couldn't see the monstrosity. "I think we should be focusing on closing that rift. *The rift* is what's pissing the fiends off. *The rift* is what's making them desperate. Close the rift and they'll stop losing Element. Close the rift, and maybe they'll leave us alone."

"Just close the rift," Adrian said.

But Ray didn't hear the sarcasm. "You've got a line to Laurel. I believe that now. Okay, Adrian? I'm sorry I doubted you. She's gone, and you can still talk to her, and that gives us a line to the other side. So tell her we don't want this, this thing they have planned. Ask her what we should do. She's smart as hell, Ade. We should be using her, if she's gone out of her way to talk to you."

"It's not idle chat, Ray. You act like we're on walkie-talkies. These visions? They're more like trying to manipulate a dream. For both of us. She can't speak clearly and I haven't figured out how to speak back to her at all. She might not even know I'm getting what she's sending. There's no help there. We have to find another way."

Ray seemed to resent this answer. He repeated Laurel's message with rolled eyes, as if he was angry with her for saying something so unhelpful: *"Nothing is what you think it is."* He scoffed. "Hey, ass — how about you tell us what it *actually is?*"

A uniformed soldier with a buzz cut came around the machine. He already had his sidearm out and pointed at the brothers. "You."

Adrian raised his hands. After a virtual dick-measuring, Ray raised his as well.

"We got lost," Adrian said.

"Sure you did."

"Think we haven't heard about you two? Think it's a big mystery who you are? Tell me you're on board with the rest of us. Tell me you aren't already wondering if you can do it better."

"Look. You don't need the gun," Adrian said. It was alarming that the soldier hadn't drawn because Ray grabbed a big heavy wrench or anything else aggressive. No, he'd come around the corner this way. Not just *considering* shooting them, but seemingly with that as the primary goal.

"What isn't what we think it is?" the soldier asked.

"What?" Ray wasn't making the connection.

Adrian did right away. Those were the words Laurel used. It meant the soldier hadn't just popped up. He'd been listening. He'd overheard them. The question was, *how much* had he heard?

Had he heard them talking about wanting to close the rift instead of obeying orders? Had he heard them talking about involving Kaur?

"It's nothing," Adrian told the man.

"Rockstars, aren't you? Will you bring your TV cameras? What about sponsors? Is that what this carefully planned mission — the one that suddenly detoured at the last minute to involve the Fabulous Porter Brothers — is going to be? You shine a spotlight on this, those fiend-protection shitbags will be all up our asses. Sharing our plans with the media. Exposing our strategies. I said it from the start: Bring in those two glory hogs and the mission ends."

"Listen ..." Adrian said.

But the soldier had been thinking. Now he shook his head slowly, making up his mind. It was just the three of them. Maybe he'd have to disobey in service of what he saw as the greater good.

"On your knees."

"Excuse me?" Ray asked.

The soldier hauled back and hit Ray hard with his pistol.

Ray tottered, then flexed to fight. He stopped when he saw the muzzle was still trained squarely on him.

"On your knees!" the soldier repeated.

"Why?"

"Because I shot you trying to escape. Our unit is ready. *Been* ready. We're a finely tuned group with a plan that will work. You're putting it all in jeopardy. You're in our way."

"You can't just shoot us," Adrian said.

"Let's find out."

"Graves's orders say—"

"Let's find out if Graves gives half a shit. Let's find out if he wouldn't do the exact same thing."

"Now wait just a goddamn—!"

"Problem here?"

Adrian spun. Dixon's bald head was right behind them, not looking particularly perturbed by the scene.

"Agent Dixon," the soldier said.

"*Special* Agent Dixon," Dixon corrected.

"I thought you'd gone."

"I'm not going anywhere."

"Maybe that's okay." The soldier hadn't really lowered his weapon.

Adrian could see cogs turning in the man's head. He was trying to decide who was actually in charge here. Technically, Dixon's bosses were, but also technically, technicalities didn't really matter. They'd never find another group of people willing to enter a rift that size, and that made the soldiers — even the grunts among them — a lot more important than Dixon.

"Shoot them and you'll have to shoot me," Dixon said.

"Understood."

"Shoot me, and you'll hit the stockpiler behind me." He jerked a thumb over his shoulder. "Hit the stockpiler and the field falls. How's that strike you, soldier? Bake everyone in your 'elite unit' before they have a chance to suit up, present company included?"

The soldier's jaw worked.

"Kill us some other time," Dixon said. "For now, why don't you go home to daddy."

The soldier looked furious, but accepting of what Dixon said. He wasn't leadership. Right now, the worst thing Dixon could threaten him with was dishonor in the eyes of his commanding officer. Hit anything vital and Graves might disapprove. Kill Dixon, and the mission, somehow, might fall into jeopardy.

"They come with me," the man said, meaning Adrian and Ray.

"Of course. But first, they come with me."

"Why?"

Dixon stepped closer, near enough that if the soldier pulled his trigger, the bullet would go straight through.

"Because what I want more than anything in the world right now is to *piss you off.*"

The soldier lowered his weapon. If his look could kill, Dixon would be in pieces.

"Graves will hear about this."

"True," Dixon nodded. "He will."

It was a threat. A gambit. But was it a true one? The soldier clearly couldn't tell. Violence, the man could live with. But reprimand from the man with the scar, should Dixon turn out more important than this man realized? *That* would be unforgivable.

The soldier turned, walked, turned back, then finally disappeared.

"Let's head back to my office for a minute," Dixon told them when he was gone.

"Why?" Adrian asked.

"Because this situation is fucked."

I4

THE ROUGHNECKS

And it was. Fucked.

Dixon explained it all to Ray and Adrian in a rush, and given Dixon's usual rat-a-tat cadence, "rushed" became almost too fast to follow.

He explained by pulling up plans of the building complex they were in, pointing out the location of the Magnitude 35 rift, the warehouse through which they'd entered, and then a third building that seemed to have no doors other than a massive vault mechanism that Dixon said always stayed closed.

Officially, that big vault door — which Dixon was able to point out through his office windows, across the expanse — went into a munitions storage room. Officially, those munitions (being Zen munitions) were highly toxic unless properly contained.

That's what they'd be told, Dixon said to the Porters, if they asked anyone about the vault: that it was for storage. So of course later, when they *did* ask, Dixon's guess turned out right on the money.

"Zen rounds are temperamental," Patel said later. "It's that intentionality thing. Turns out they don't always shoot straight. We can maladjust a weapon's sights on purpose, then give that weapon to a soldier who's used to hitting her target. Within a reasonable window, the soldier's expectations end up guiding the rounds where they need to go, not just the gun itself. So yeah. When we deal with intelligent ammunition that can pierce bulletproof armor like butter, we like to store it behind a nice, thick wall just in case."

But before that, in Dixon's office, he told them that the real purpose of the vault room was something else.

"Graves's people said they're just now planning their first incursion. The truth is, they've already gone into that rift a dozen or more times. Weapons tech has vastly, *vastly* improved over anything you'd know on the brigades, and the armor they wear can, for fifteen or twenty minutes, completely withstand the heat. It allows them to go in for brief periods. The incursion they're planning now — the one you're meant to be part of — will be the first *extended* incursion, requiring the use of newer, extended gear. But it is absolutely not the first."

"So they've gone in for recon," said Ray.

"No. For fuel."

He brought up photos, clearly taken on the sly using his phone.

"This," Dixon said, "is in my opinion the real reason things have amped up lately."

Adrian took Dixon's phone. Onscreen was evidence of a cross-planar holocaust.

Having grown up in riftfare, the Porters were among the least likely people to feel sympathy for fiends. Ray himself had dispatched tens of thousands of them, and that was beyond okay because they were, officially speaking, evil. As most people believed, they'd literally crawled up from Hell.

The lore Adrian and Ray grew up with went even one step further, holding that fiends were demons trying to take over our world — and that if their aggressive intrusions weren't stopped, the world would end. The near-sundering had put an exclamation point on that idea, proving beyond doubt that the other side must be stopped by any means necessary.

All of that remained true. Fiends remained the enemy. The notion of "Hell" was a semantic one, up for debate among philosophers, but in practice it was true enough: another place, full of heat and sulfur, full of creepy-crawlies that seemed more than ready to scoop out your soul.

Still, even knowing that, Dixon's photos dropped the bottom from Adrian's stomach. It was like watching old whaling footage, or seals being clubbed.

Acres upon acres of fiends ferried from the rift and into the vault room through a dampening-field-covered set of rails, invisible to the larger room and entering through a door within the bigger door.

The photos showed fiend bodies in landfill-sized piles and laid in rows like meat. The bodies hadn't come from the usual rift-exiting soldier castes; Adrian could tell that much by how ill-formed they were. Eldon's theory of Primordial Form had turned out to be mostly correct in the past few months.

While boss castes tended to keep one form, the lower castes did not. They were indistinct until they encountered a human mind, then became what was most appropriate to encountering that mind: usually a final form that could claw and fight. *Until* that point, though, fiends were rounder at the edges, shaped only barely — sort of like blobs of goo that halfway stood upright.

Theory held that *most* fiends were probably like that, actually, if left undisturbed: a majority who never crossed a rift, the way most civilians never see front-line fighting even during war. The fiends in Dixon's photos were like that. It meant the fiends in the pictures hadn't come out fighting. Instead, Graves's unit had gone into the rifts, then systematically harvested them from whatever passed for homes.

"Cry over them or don't," Dixon said, but he was being facetious; even knowing what they knew now the man couldn't bring himself to feel bad for demons. "I'm not showing you this to get you morally outraged or some bullshit. I'm showing you because we know now that these things have minds, or at least the big ones do, or at least they have a few *clots* of mind that a bunch of these fucking Jell-O piles share. What would *you* think if these were humans?"

Dixon pointed at the piles of dead fiends in the photos. "What would *you* think if the fiends were the ones who opened a hole into our world that couldn't be closed, then set up shop on the other side? What would you think if every day — sometimes more than once a day — they came into our world, killed a bunch of civilians, then dragged their corpses back so they could render the world's most valuable substance from their blood?"

Ray nodded as he thought, jaw set. His face and body language finally looked like Ray again instead of the quiet follower he'd been since they'd entered this massive lab. This here, with the brutality and violence and go-smash-'em stuff — that's what Legion Ray was famous for. It was his comfort zone, where he finally felt qualified to have an opinion.

"I'd be ready to rip out some throats, to put it mildly," he said.

Adrian's head was still on deduction. On science as well as the real reason Dixon must be telling them this in the first place.

"This is where all the Zen Element is coming from." He'd been wondering; the numbers before now hadn't added up.

"They need this kind of scale given how much they've been using, don't they? The stockpiles aren't nearly big enough."

Dixon nodded. "The systemization you see here — this thing with the receiving hoppers and the little rail cars running back into the Zen refinery? That's all recent. Before now, things were like Patel told you. They killed the fiends that came out and rendered those. They obviously harvest the exhale, too, and it's substantial in a rift this size. But that's still not enough — especially since the fiends stopped coming, knowing how fortified the rift is. They don't even need manpower to protect it anymore. That line you see going into the rift? Part of it is a pipeline, like you heard. The other part is an AI-driven weapon that mows down any fiends that get close. To build what you've seen took all the Zen they had. It stripped the stockpiles to zero. So about a week ago, *this* started."

He tapped the phone, then took it back.

"Maybe you can tell me. What else happened about a week ago for the first time, Adrian?"

All the dots connected. Adrian understood. A week ago was when they started to see abnormal behavior from salt-and-pepper style rifts that weren't actually salt and pepper rifts. Those rumors they'd all heard about unusual incursions and disappearing fiend prisoners? They were all true, weren't they?

That was Dixon's concern: That there was only so far the other plane would allow itself to be pushed. As happened in any cold war, the risk was hitting a tipping point beyond which one side stopped taking shit. The fiends could have ended it all with the sundering, but at the last minute they'd pulled back, willing to try one last time to find another way. Humanity, however, hadn't been as accommodating.

When news came down that Hell had almost extruded into our world like an interdimensional hernia, people got scared and pundits demanded action and politicians eager to keep their jobs started rattling sabers and raising defense budgets. Even that had been fine. Even opening the huge rift had, in a way, been okay. But setting up a systematic rape-and-harvest from the people of their world? Dixon felt that was perhaps a bridge too far, and they wouldn't take it anymore.

And unlike Patel, Graves, and a lot of others, Dixon refused to underestimate the fiends. The military thought they had Hell on a leash, trained not to bite.

Dixon felt otherwise. All that had happened in the past week proved it.

"Find others you can trust," he told them.

But then what? Dixon couldn't say. He had privileged access through Spread and Containment, but he wasn't in charge and had no idea who was. Graves wasn't in charge. Even Patel wasn't truly in charge. Patel was taking orders from someone higher up, and probably didn't know much more than Dixon.

Things changed too quickly for any plans of any sort to be made outside of the official ones, but Dixon did tell Adrian and Ray that one thing was sure: the brass wasn't concerned at all about the past week's findings.

The rift was contained. The new rifts meant nothing. The disappearance of prisoners — all that Zen Element sucked back into the fiend plane through micro-rifts — meant nothing. Same for the tentative, trying-things-out nature of the popcorn rifts. Even the fact that Adrian's perfectly secure, perfectly intact Stitching rig had magically been drained of its Zen resin when he got too close to a new rift meant nothing.

To Dixon, the military's blind eye was staggering. Clearly the fiends were consolidating what power they still had. Clearly what they'd seen in the past week was prelude to a strike.

To the military, even a strike would mean nothing. Because

after all, what could the fiends do at this point? They couldn't try to sunder again; the planes' topology was mostly known now, at least around Fortune and the Gore Point, and detectors monitored anything that might possibly perforate. They couldn't come through the big rift thanks to all its armament, and rifts bigger than popcorn could be detected early enough to be handled by the brigades now that Legions carried better blunt-force tools and effective multi-weapons.

The military wasn't even concerned about what Dixon had mentioned earlier: the fact that micro-rifts could be weapons in themselves. What, so they could assassinate one or two people at a time, and cause a bit of political disorder? Who cared? Humans had what amounted to interplanar nukes now. That's what Graves's team would be taking into the rift for their first extended mission — the one Ray and Adrian were supposed to help lead, having had the most experience.

So, sure. The fiends could take their tiny little pot shots if they wanted. They'd be laughing out of their second half-headed mouths right up until the bomb obliterated their primary nest, taking out that queen everyone kept talking about.

Dixon wanted Ray and Adrian on a special team — something he could control, running just a bit ahead of the stampeding military machine. He didn't know what form that would take, though, or when. Until the time came that he knew more, "Find others you can trust" became all he could tell them. Whatever came next would be in days, not weeks.

"And until then?"

"Train," Dixon said, "just like they want you to."

So they trained. Day and night, they trained. Sleep moved to the middle of the day, confusing Adrian's faculties and making him foggy. That was the idea. The hardasses wanted everyone prepared for everything.

They were shown how to use all the new weapons. How to use all the new detection and recon hardware. On heat gear and breathing, Adrian and Ray became the experts.

It clearly bothered Graves, who already hated them. Whenever they talked about formations for marching through the Hellscape, Graves always planned for the brothers to be on the left-side — and less-defended — wing. He clearly didn't care if they died, and might even want that.

In between, they left the compound and went home. It was necessary, if non-ideal by security standards. Unfortunately for Patel, the Porters were still celebrities. The *Brigade* reality TV show had ended when rifts stopped appearing, but people still stopped both brothers on the street for autographs.

Ray had a publicity agent, who was constantly fielding potential sponsorships. If the Porters disappeared, people would ask questions. Paparazzi might start to look for them, eager to snap photos.

The last thing Patel wanted were investigative reporters on her doorstep, so although it was less than ideal, she had no choice but to let them live their lives between training sessions. They slept at home, not in the troop and scientist-civilian barracks. They didn't even have to sneak around to meet with other members of Brigade One, quietly combing through them to decide who among them were best to trust. There was a strong brotherhood among riftworkers. Finding people they could absolutely trust was beyond easy, leaving the bigger question of "Who is best to recruit?"

A hard question to answer, seeing as they didn't know what they were recruiting for.

On the third day, Graves gathered his unit and finally answered the question of how they all planned to survive the heat and breathe.

He held up a syringe, all the jarheads looking on.

"Listen up. This here's GEN's special sauce. They've got a long name for it that's half numbers and dashes, but personally I just call it 'Frog.' Frogs are amphibians. They can live just fine in air or underwater. That's gonna be us, ladies and gentlemen, only instead of water we're gonna learn to breathe inside the Devil's asshole. Frog will show us how."

There were more explanations, but the soldiers didn't need them. Almost didn't want them. It seemed to be a point of pride to simply accept their CO's orders blindly. The more elite the soldier, the more obedient they were. This group, without hesitating, would walk into a vat of acid if ordered.

Adrian was less presumptuous when he explained Frog to Lee, Shannon, Oliver, Dee, and Harrison in the supply room at the brigadehouse.

"Zen Element is a mutagen," Adrian told them. "Used indiscriminately, it's toxic like cancer. But once targeted, it can *cure* cancer."

He paused. Long enough that the others began to stare, curious why he didn't go on. He'd stopped because he'd realized how hypocritical some of this was. In all probability, his mother's own cancer had probably only been cured because of the genocide and exploitation Dixon had shown them. It was the only way to get enough Zen for all the experiments everyone wanted. There was no denying some of this was a zero-sum game: Using the other plane like a supply closet definitely made life on Earth better.

He made himself continue. "Element can reverse scars. It can heal wounds that shouldn't be able to heal. It works by taking normal human cells and turning them into something else. Something a little more like *them.*"

The room waited for the punchline. What Adrian had just said, they already knew. Ray and Adrian had told them absolutely everything that happened last year, plus everything about their recruitment by Dixon and Patel right down to the fiend holocaust. All seven people in the room (the trust-bound group that Ray for some reason called The Roughnecks) knew about Erika Dale, too. That she had planned to actually become a fiend herself, or at least a hybrid able to live both places. She'd offered her fate to the brothers.

"I'm told that Frog will thicken our skin and establish something just below the top layer that works a lot like the energy shields we saw in use at the warehouse. We might get suntans, but we won't burn or boil on the inside. It will adapt our lungs, making us able to breathe superheated air with very little oxygen. We won't need full heat suits, or oxygen tanks, which would explode over there anyway, or rebreathers. It's not permanent. When this is over, a complimentary injection of Zen can return us more or less to normal."

"More or less?" Oliver asked.

"Uncharted territory," Ray said. "It's taking a risk."

"None of you have to do this," Adrian reminded them. "This will be a lot more dangerous than fighting a predictable rift the way we used to. Legions, you guys have never crossed a rift. It's disorienting. It's also terrifying. I don't know yet how it'll slot together. I don't even know if you'll have to enter the plane at all. We don't know because Dixon doesn't know."

Then Adrian repeated his conversation with Dixon, where *find people you can trust* was the only mandate he could give. For all any of them knew, Adrian and Ray would enter with the military unit as planned and the other five would just sit outside, monitoring vitals and doing paperwork.

It was the worst way to plan anything. To compensate for all the unknowns, Ray and Adrian simply tried to cover all the bases. If they'd all enter, Dixon would find a way to get enough Frog for all of them or get them somehow on the official mission roster.

The rest was just knowledge, so the Porters taught it all. Weapons. Defenses. All current mission specs, scant as they were.

New intel gathered whenever they went to the warehouse cluster and, strictly outside of bounds, poked around to see what they could learn.

The names and all else they knew on the soldiers, on Graves.

Eldon's thoughts and research. That was something the Porters knew better than anyone, and their father had proven smarter than anyone figured — enough for his legacy to save the world once already.

And all the while, Dixon kept poking. That was part of the problem. Colonel Patel was half politician, and as such, did her best to play nice with Dixon. But Graves kept withholding, working against Dixon at every turn.

"I guess I think too much," Dixon explained.

Graves, Adrian decided, didn't enjoy thinking at all. He didn't ask questions and discouraged them from his people when they strayed outside of strict mission requirements and into the realm of *how* and *why*.

Thinking got in the way. Graves operated more like a rock flung from a medieval trebuchet. Once fired, no thinking was required. There was only one place it could go.

Train.

Sleep.

Train.

Brief the Roughnecks.

Train.

Sleep.

Train.

It only went on for four days, but by the end of it Adrian felt like a man caught in an endless loop. His dreams hadn't stopped. They intruded every night, or perhaps every day when his cycle was inverted, and in each one he saw Laurel at a great distance as if her mind was moving farther away from his. In each one, the enormous form of the captive dreadnought sat on a throne of skeletons in the corner like a huge red king, its head so high above it seemed to be in shadow.

It made subtle noises, like grunts in the emptiness. Adrian could barely see its head and enormous horns, but still he felt it looked into his eyes the entire times.

"Bad dreams?" Ray asked.

"It's okay. It's the only way I can tell sleep from awake anymore."

"I know the feeling." They were beyond exhausted. Legions were tough, but Graves's training was several levels beyond brutal. They both thought it was on purpose — a way to shake the Porters out, to break them physically or mentally before the mission began.

Train.

Sleep.

Train.

Sleep.

And all the while, it seemed to Adrian that the dreadnought's influence on him was growing stronger while Laurel's backed away. Fatigue was eroding him like a stone into sand.

"Why didn't they take it back?" Adrian asked. This time, sleep was in the middle of the night where it belonged. "The dreadnought, I mean."

Ray was barely conscious. He'd gone out of his way to insist Adrian wake him whenever there were dreams, or messages from the other realm. But he wasn't always awake when Adrian started speaking.

"Dunno, Ade. Write it down and tell me in the morning."

Adrian didn't bother. Ray wouldn't know, and it was pointless to confuse him beyond the bafflement both men already felt. But it did preoccupy him. Perhaps the dreadnought was too big for the fiends to take back through rifts like they'd done with the soldier demons in all the prisons. Or maybe it was another reason, and that bothered Adrian in a way he couldn't quite put his finger on.

One difference between soldier and boss castes was their size.

The other difference, though, was their minds. Soldiers had a collective consciousness. Soldiers were primordial before emerging, without a single fixed form. Bosses seemed to keep a single form to go with their singular minds. Unlike all the prisoners who'd been sucked back to consolidate Zen on the other side, the dreadnought was an individual. It might have real thoughts.

Did have them, if what Adrian felt in his dreams was to be trusted.

The next day, when Adrian was passing in front of Captain Kaur's empty office, the phone began to ring. It stopped the second he was past the door.

Adrian paused, and the phone began again. One ring, then stop. One ring, stop. Like a signal buoy in landline form.

Adrian looked both ways, then pulled a key from his keyring. Kaur had given him the key last year before the saboteur mess, so he could use it and its resources to figure things out. He'd never returned the key. Now was the perfect time to use it.

The phone was silent. It didn't ring again until Adrian's hand was hovering over it, wondering if he should pick it up and check the dial tone.

He snatched it mid-ring without saying hello. Dixon's staccato voice greeted him.

"Adrian. It's Dixon. Five minutes. Be outside with your crew."

"My crew?"

"Your Magnificent Seven." Dixon liked that name better than Roughnecks. "I know they're there."

"How did you know *I'd* be here? How did you know I was walking past? How did you know Captain Kaur—"

"Jesus, shut the fuck up. Look at the bookcase. Lower right corner of the second shelf."

Adrian did. A tiny rift was there, and inside the rift was another, this one with Dixon's eye visible through it.

"Don't make me explain. I don't have the fucking time."

But did he *need* to explain? They did all sorts of dangerous, unnatural things at the warehouse complex. Opening rifts for surveillance felt like the least offensive among them.

"Loading dock. Five minutes. Get in the van that comes. All of you. You don't need gear of any kind. Just yourselves. Oh. And whatever you do, don't kill the driver."

Adrian blinked, unsure he'd really heard that last one. Dixon kept rattling on, giving him no choice but to let it all wash past. He'd known it might happen this way, after all: a sudden summons without warning. He just had to make himself ready fast like he might need to.

He nodded, more for himself than because Dixon might see him through the spy rifts. "Okay, we'll be there. Why is this happening? What's going on?"

"I just got word that Team Graves is going into the rift tomorrow. Patel wants me to thank you for your expertise, but you're no longer invited to join them on the mission itself."

"Okay, then why—?"

"Because what they have in mind might just cause a new sundering, and for that reason your little monkey squad is going in today."

15

WE ARE MANY

Adrian rushed into the squad room, sighted his people by looking each one in the eye, then ticked his head sideways to indicate that they should follow him.

Only the Roughnecks were expecting anything like this; only the Roughnecks saw Adrian's look and came. He had to resist an impulse to just call out for everyone. They were all good recruits for the squad the Porters had assembled — every Stitcher and Legion in the room. There wasn't a man or woman in the brigade that Adrian didn't trust entirely, now that Matt and his oddness were gone.

And they could be trained, right? Really quick — like within two minutes — they could all be brought up to speed and ready to roll ... right?

Of course not. Seven are ready so seven will go. You're just afraid, now that the time has come.

It was true. When you were ordered to invade Hell, you wanted all the familiar faces around that you could possibly get.

"Loading dock," Adrian repeated.

"Now?"

"Now."

By Adrian's watch, they had two minutes remaining. He felt certain for some reason that they were entering a clockwork affair: not ass-on-fire urgent, but precise down to the second. Dixon was S&C but everything around him for the past half year had been military. If the clock said there were two minutes left, they'd better not be ready in three. Things, until they were on the other side, would likely run like a German train schedule.

But two minutes was two minutes and he'd been told to bring nothing, so they could afford to take their time. The loading dock was just across the station, so they'd use that time to walk over slowly. Seven of them running for the door would look suspicious, and if Adrian couldn't bring everyone, the last thing he wanted were questions.

They went up and over: taking the far set of stairs, crossing the upstairs bunk room, then coming down in the hallway near the captain's office. Kaur was actually in his office with his head down, so they had to sneak past one at a time.

They arrived at the loading dock as a van was pulling up: white with no windows in the rear. The cab's windows were so heavily tinted, they couldn't be seen through even when Adrian approached them. It was probably more of that new Zen tech GEN had developed. All sorts of things were possible, if you didn't mind harvesting your enemies and drinking their blood.

They moved to the sliding door on the passenger's side. When it opened, Ray was the first to see, or to draw his M9 and aim it inside.

A gray-skinned halfskull was behind the wheel, its severed brain flat above its rotting, chattering mouth.

"FIEND!"

Ray's shout made the others scramble, some grabbing sidearms as Ray had and others reaching for collapsible Rollards that whipped to full extension like expandable batons.

The fiend turned its head and hissed — a sound like rattlesnakes in a pit.

Ray kept darting glances at Adrian, eyes panicked at this most urgent of times. "Where's the people Dixon sent? Is there a rift?"

He jerked his gaze into the rear of the van, looking for an ingress point, or for more fiends to spill forth. *"Where's the driver, Adrian? What did it do to them?"*

The halfskull chattered again, now creeping forward with one of its decrepit hands on the headrest. The other hand held something Adrian couldn't see.

Ray cocked his pistol, then raised it to fire. Bullets counted as blunt force. At close range, plain old gunfire would kill anything lower than a boss.

Other weapons up, other weapons cocking.

"Sayonara," Ray told the halfskull.

Dixon's voice rang in Adrian's ear: *Oh. And whatever you do, don't kill the driver.*

"WAIT!"

"What?"

"Don't kill it."

"The fuck you say?" Ollie still had his Rollard up. He was squeezed into a too-small shirt that made him look even more massive than he already was, and had been wearing mirrored sunglasses indoors for some reason.

"I SAID DON'T KILL IT!"

The Roughnecks lowered their weapons halfway. Adrian was the quiet Porter — the pushover of the pair. He didn't shout or assume command of anything. The others' backing off came more from surprise than obedience.

The halfskull hadn't moved. It was still half-turned between the van's driver and passenger seats, its body crouched to accomodate the low ceiling, reeking of sulfur. Something like fog or mist was rising from its paper-like skin the way body heat makes bald heads steam on a frigid day.

Had they ever seen that kind of thing before? Adrian had no idea, even having reviewed more repellences on video than probably anyone in the brigades. There usually wasn't time to notice nuance. Things happened too fast, and killing halfskulls was Fortune's version of stomping roaches. They were the stock soldier, even in the old days when only one class per rift was permitted.

It came from somewhere hot enough to burst eggs inside their shells, Adrian thought. *Of course it's still steaming.*

He'd never seen a live one this fully before. It was horrific and fascinating. The thing they usually called a brain did, in fact, seem a lot like a brain that'd been dried out by fire and sun. It also didn't look finished in itself; it looked a lot more like a complete head containing a complete brain had been cross-sectioned diagonally by the swipe of an extremely sharp sword. Its jaw protruded, exposing blacked teeth in deep-gray gums. The thing had a tongue, too: another thing he'd never noticed, thick and pointed like a tree's taproot, not flat and supple like a human's.

They stared at each other: Adrian squinting forward, the thing breathing like a spray paint can with a BB in its throat. Beneath the sulfur smell was something earthier, like mulch.

"Jesus," said Ollie, meaning everything about this right now.

The halfskull extended its hand. Forcing himself not to wince, Adrian recognized the gesture of offering and extended his own. Beside him, Ray re-raised his weapon and firmed it in his grip. He'd heard Adrian just fine, but if his brother was wrong, Ray stood ready to blow the fiend back to Hell.

There was something foreign stuck to the side of the half-skull's head, below where a human's right ear would be. A small matte black circle, about the size and thickness of three US quarters glued together. No wires ran from it, self-adhered to the thing's skin.

It placed an identical object in Adrian's hand, its finger brushing Adrian's palm. The fiend's flesh wasn't as hot as Adrian assumed it'd be. He could feel heat deep down, but the creature seemed to have several loose layers of skin above it as insulation. The outer one was brittle and dusted partially away at Adrian's touch, reminding him of a wasp's nest.

Adrian looked up at the thing. It didn't have eyes, but a pair of structures at the rear of its cut-off brain — ventricles, maybe — gave the illusion of sight. The fiend seemed to nod at Adrian's silent question about the object, running the illusion home.

"Don't—" Dee Scott started to say from Adrian's other side, but he ignored her and pressed the thing to the skin below his right ear anyway. It was light, but felt cool and brushed like gunmetal.

"Adrian," Harrison said, "I don't know what the fuck's going on with this thing, but—"

Adrian held up a single finger to stop Harrison. Because now that he'd attached the device, he could hear the halfskull inside his head.

I am many. We are friends. Get inside van.

"It wants us to get inside," Adrian said.

Ollie laughed.

"I'm serious. I can hear it." He tapped his head, then

touched the device. "It's some sort of a GEN-made translator. Look. It's wearing one, too."

Aloud, the halfskull's voice was just hissing and the chattering of bones. The voice inside Adrian's head wasn't translating; it was doing what he'd done imperfectly back at the GEN hangar before it'd become a military base, when he'd mentally spoken with the first dreadnought humanity had ever seen.

Erika Dale had told him then that you had to project your feelings and intentions to speak telepathically with fiends. This seemed to simplify the process, turning what he'd found hard to pin down into concrete words.

Although, still … not really words. More like a voice in his head, clearly coming from somewhere else.

Tell them. All will wear.

And it gestured into the van's rear, pointing more or less toward a small cardboard box.

Hurry. I am many and we are friends. Dixon says come.

"Dixon sent it." He reached for the box, inside of which were more translators. "It wants all of you to wear these."

Dixon says hurry.

"On the way, though," Adrian said, pushing Ray's gun down with finality. "Pile in."

16

THE SPEED OF THOUGHT

It took some effort to get used to talking with the halfskull, but Adrian quickly realized that the effort was on his end and more or less beyond his conscious control. Using the translator (which was more accurately a *communicator*; it seemed simply to mediate the normal mental chatter they were all capable of) was less like learning a language and more like seeing past an optical illusion. He was reminded of old computer-generated "Magic Eye" images, where fractal patterns suddenly became 3-D images if you stared at them long enough with de-focused eyes. He didn't have to hear and then understand words being spoken one at a time. It was more like receiving a packet of mental energy, then reframing all of it from a human point of view. Or, perhaps more accurately, from an *Adrian-Porter-specific* point of view. There was too much familiarity to the voice, once he got used to it, for his own mind not to be involved.

After learning the trick, talking to the halfskull was like talking to anyone else.

They don't trust me, Adrian.

And Adrian sent back: *Give it time. I doubt your people trust us much, either.*

He could use colloquialisms because they weren't actual words. He could hear familiar cadence and personal modes of speaking because no real speaking was happening. Each conversant was his own broadcast tower, and each receiver shaped what they received into a form that made sense.

It was more like hearing himself talk than hearing anyone else.

The others sat in the back on long, side-mounted benches. They'd put on their communicators, but from what Adrian gathered, you couldn't be overheard unless you wanted to be. It was probably the same tech he'd seen at the facility, in those big over-ear noise-blockers. Wearing those, you couldn't really be accidentally overheard, either. It meant Ollie, Lee, Shannon, Dee, Harrison, and even Ray were not hearing the exact conversation Adrian was having with their driver — who had already explained that it drove the van at least in part with its mind as well, thanks to a box mounted under the dash.

Yet despite the others not hearing Adrian talking to the fiend, they were definitely hearing something. If thought was the medium, the halfskull might be talking to all of them while also speaking to Adrian. It might be sending them a group announcement of sorts, letting them get used to hearing inside their heads and responding in kind.

Adrian could hear them back there, trying to get the hang of it. Ollie kept speaking aloud first, hoping he could force his mental words out that way.

The van drove out of Brigade One's jurisdiction in the direction of the Army encampment, but detoured short of its gate, heading into an older, disused property several miles down the road: a custom residence district that had housed the original Army who'd used the base, back in time fifty years or more — when riftfare was new, Eldon Porter was alive, and even GEN was just a twinkle in some government scientist's eye.

The place was a legit neighborhood, not barracks — complete with curving roads bearing charming names, mailboxes, and sidewalks rising from a concrete curb. Yet it'd been military housing, run wholly to support the base that Colonel Patel now ran. A ghost town, liminal and existentially haunting.

On the drive, the fiend told Adrian all he needed to know. The mental bond only felt like a conversation some of the time. If needed, it could move at the speed of thought instead. Adrian found entire concepts dropping into his brain intact and all at once: the sort of thing that would normally take hours to explain suddenly *there* in his knowledge base as if he'd known it all along.

He understood their multiplicity now, for one. It was mostly as they'd believed: the soldier castes tended to be hive minds whereas the bosses were usually more individual, usually a whole mind in and of themselves. Those were still just tendencies; fiend intelligence was collective deep down but "doled out" at the surface. It meant that bosses like hellbringers and macerators could be part of a collective if there was need, and even halfskulls and slitherenes could think for themselves if there was any reason to.

The best way to describe their approach to individual bodies (versus a core with disposable cells on the outside) and individual minds (versus the hive) was "fluid."

Unlike rigid humans, fiends became what was most useful for the whole.

When it'd said "We are many," that was Adrian's unpracticed mind interpreting its attempt to convey the same balance. Now that he understood his own brain's role in parsing what the halfskull sent him, he would have explained it to the others differently, and would do exactly that if they were still confused or wary when they reached their destination.

Now, he'd say that the halfskull was mentally tied to several hundred other halfskulls on the other plane and *could* and usually *would* think collectively with them ... but because humans understood working with individuals, it was no big deal to imbue its single body with a consciousness that was more or less singular, too.

More or less? Adrian asked.

The group mind comes and goes, the halfskull answered.

Adrian kept looking over as they "talked," doing as he would if their words were aloud. He was committed on the anthropomorphization by now, meaning the thing's brain ventricles would, for Adrian, forever be its eyes.

But if it's easier, you can treat me as one.

What should we call you? With this, Adrian sent him one of those complete blocks of knowledge — in this case, the most baseline facet of human individuality: that of a name. Adrian needed one. It was too weird talking to someone who always said "us" and "we."

I've never had a name, the creature thought/said. *What name would you give me?*

Adrian looked hard at the halfskull. It was strange: He was talking to an actual demon — a thing that looked as terrifying as people felt demons should be. Yet hearing its voice inside his head (or perhaps "its thoughts" was better than "its voice") erased all of that. Right now, considering the thing's question, Adrian was looking right at it. The creature was naked, sexless, with flaking-away skin and an exposed brain. Its hands were three-fingered claws and its teeth seemed stuck with flecks of leftover meat. It stank of sulfur and radiated heat. And yet

Adrian didn't see a horrorshow. Some trick of mind had turned the fiend behind the wheel into an unusual-looking person for him now, nothing more.

Carl, Adrian said.

Carl? Why Carl?

Why not? You look like a Carl.

"Yeah," said Harrison from the rear. "Carl works."

They'd heard. Because it had been appropriate for them to hear. It struck Adrian that his little crew was now effortlessly doing what no human group was known to have done before by forming a hive mind.

In the last few minutes of the drive, Carl the Halfskull (who'd already taken on masculine pronouns in Adrian's mind) delivered everything the others needed to know directly into all of them. As with prior concepts, most of the information arrived in pre-existing chunks. Carl spoke of factions forming within the fiend plane, but somehow knew without being told how exactly those factions had come together.

By the time the van parked outside the empty neighborhood's abandoned rec center, everyone in the Roughnecks understood all they needed to know.

For one, there were the factions they'd heard about. On the fiend plane, there was as much discord and disagreement about the whole of riftfare as on the human side. Adrian wondered why he'd ever assumed otherwise. It was easier, when fighting an enemy, to think of them as entirely different.

And, of course, *evil.*

In war, every enemy soldier was a criminal, an abuser, a cruel miser, a rapist. Every enemy soldier lived only to burn your society and disembowel your family. It was too hard to fight real people with complex motives and drives — enemy soldiers, for instance, who might not like killing any more than you do.

So of course riftfare, which didn't involve enemy humans at all, was an even more extreme version of that all-or-nothing way of thinking.

But in any war, the enemy was in fact *never* unanimous. On every side, there was good and bad. That's what made wars so strange: in most cases governments waged them, not the people.

Carl had told them: *We are friends.* Translated now, the same sentiment would have come to Adrian singular: *I am a friend.* But it was still plural, wasn't it? He could sense that meaning in Carl as well. The fiend was one body, imbued with more individuality than was usually given to a halfskull when it rose from primordiality and took shape.

But there were many like him: Many on the other side who had not wanted the sundering. Many who, despite the impossible idea of diplomacy, would have preferred a pass at handling affairs without bloodshed.

It was complicated. *Oh*, so complicated.

Fiends were like humans in all the important ways on the matter of strife and warfare. What Graves's unit had done under Patel's command? The part where they stopped harvesting Zen Element and had moved instead to raking it from their base population?

That part made Carl's singular consciousness furious. There was an element of an-eye-for-an-eye, but at the same time Carl — and the larger, plane-resident intelligences that stood behind him and existed in their own rights — allowed that things weren't quite so simple. Perhaps two hundred people knew the warehouse facility even existed, and a smaller number than that knew the facility contained a massive, man-made rift. A subset of *that* group knew the rift had been opened on purpose and why: to keep the fiends on their knees so they couldn't attack by robbing them of all the energy they could suck from the rift. And finally, how many people within that smallest number had made the decisions that led to the rift being opened?

Given the amount of secrecy and control Adrian and Ray had seen on their visits, Adrian was willing to bet he could count the biggest human offenders on the fingers of both hands. Maybe even on the fingers of *Carl's* hands.

Dixon is a good man, Carl told them all. *Dixon is the best friend that those who think like me have.*

Last year, Adrian had thought of Spread and Containment Special Agent Dixon as one of the world's biggest cocks. He'd recruited Adrian, promised Adrian wouldn't have to turn rat on his friends, and then had inverted everything Adrian gave him to serve his own agenda ... an agenda that originally included nailing every Legion in Brigade One to the wall. Chances were, every other human inside the van still saw Dixon that way. But seen through Carl's brain ventricles, the man was something else entirely.

There were cruel, warmongering assholes on both sides. As with any war, each group's leadership had committed the most sins and the worst atrocities. Fiend leaders had sent soldiers into the human world to rip innocents to pieces. Now, human leaders were doing the exact same thing.

There were those among the fiends, contrary to Erika's admittedly warped testimony, who had wanted the sundering to destroy Earth and still wanted to destroy it now ... but there were also fiends who saw violence and destruction as ploys of last resort. The dreadnought Adrian had met on Sundering Day had been willing to propose a Devil's bargain: Laurel traded for ending the apocalypse.

Although, was is even correct to say "Devil's bargain"? Or was that just more propaganda, because the other side in any war were *always* devils?

Dixon had been put in an impossible position. As senior S&C agent in the sabotage-and-sundering matter, he'd been the logical man to head the investigative and GEN-centric part of the post-sundering response, in concert with the military. But whereas Carl said Dixon had wanted a complete debrief and re-analysis of all the new information first and foremost, he'd been overruled. Politicians had trumped him because their human constituencies were scared and out for blood.

When scorpions came into your bed at night, you wanted to eliminate rather than understand them. *That*, post sundering, had been the opinion the powers-that-be had listened to.

And so instead of the comprehensive investigation that would have made sense after riftfare's entire body of knowledge was turned upside-down, Dixon had been ordered to find a way to annihilate the fiend plane instead.

Can't guarantee that rifts will close up and stay closed forever? Well, then, better burn down their houses instead.

Those were Dixon's orders, but he'd known it was a mistake, Carl said.

Even now Dixon wanted to take a deep breath and pause, but Graves's mission tomorrow had forced him to violate those orders in secret. Sending a crew with a bomb would obliterate all chance of peace between the planes once and for all. Dixon, as the civilian at the top, had therefore been given a choice: Should he do as he was told? Or should he disobey, doing the wrong thing now because he felt it was right in the end?

Stop. Think. Communicate, Carl said. *That's all some of us want. There are Dixons on our end, too — bosses who will listen, if given a chance. If that fails, the result will be catastrophic. Right now, your side has all the strength, but we arm in different ways than you — ways your people cannot see or understand. If our queen is struck, she will strike back. It's a mistake to assume that even with group minds, we are all the same.*

The fiend plane was the size of the world, not just the size of the city it'd punched its holes into. Of course its people weren't homogenous even in their hive-think and hive-mediated opinions: even in groups, the fiend population was far, *far* too large for that. It would be like declaring all of Earth united in a single, sadistic, evildoing opinion.

The notion was absurd, and yet that's exactly what the human brass (which meant the US brass, since the Gore Point was in Utah) said was true of the fiends. They were *all* evil. For fuck's sake, they were demons!

But what is a "demon"? Carl asked, his thoughts familiar enough to Adrian now to sound rhetorical. *Yes, some of our number are large and red and have horns, and yes, those things match your legends of a place called Hell. But we do not know your holy books well enough to work deliberately against them. In truth, we do not care. The shapes we take come partially from your own expectations; even your scientists know that now. Before the rifts, we simply existed and knew nothing else. We are what we are, even though we look strange to you.*

Then Carl said something else, and every one of the Roughnecks heard it:

To us, you are the demons.

17
FULL CIRCLE

eapons.

Dixon explained there was only so much he could do to equip them. He offered some new weapons of the kinds Adrian and Ray had seen recently, but between the seven of them, they were only able to take two or three people's worth of the very best stuff.

It's okay, Dixon said, *because your goal isn't to fuck all of them up like Graves. Just stay ahead of him and only fuck up the fiends who come at you. In this situation, you can sort of assume the ones who come at you are their "bad guys."*

And to this Adrian asked, *Sort of?*

Dixon just shrugged, as if it was a Zen koan with no real answer.

Armor.

Very little armor was in the offing. What Dixon gave them was a little better than what the brigades were using but nowhere near as good as what Graves had. But that was sort of okay because:

Frog.

The mutagenic resin was in high supply, and handled some of what armor would normally handle. There was a chance someone would notice that their weapons and armor had gone missing, but the odds were slim of anyone noticing seven syringes' worth of Frog. It had been brewed in vats large enough to fiendify the entire city. When Ray observed as much, Dixon explained: Yes, that was *exactly* how much Frog had been made for the military to hold in reserve: enough for the city. They needed to be prepared should a critical-scale incursion occur — "critical scale" being about as shit-hits-the-fan as an asteroid headed for Earth.

If another sundering threatened, Emergency Plan Z (which the grunts called The Diaper Contingency, because that's when you started shitting in your pants) would treat everyone inside the effected area with Frog. Dosing citizens as a last-gasp contingency would at least (hopefully) mutate them enough that the heat and oxygen starvation of massive planar collapse wouldn't, by themselves, broil and suffocate everyone within the event's radius. It was a literal case of "If you can't beat 'em, join 'em."

Weapons. Armor. Frog.

What they got was what they got. It wasn't much.

"Officially, you assholes stole all of this stuff, which is one reason you didn't get every little thing you needed," Dixon said after they were equipped and assembled. "Officially there was a break-in. Officially I was alerted, called the base guards who for some reason didn't get the same alert, then ran to the encampment to wake their lazy asses up."

Ray looked around as if the guards might be coming now.

"I haven't done it yet," Dixon said, seeing Ray. "I'll be there in ..." He looked at his watch. "Forty-one minutes. The official record won't show that I'm here right now. According to the record, I never came here at all. In fact, right about now the record will show me giving your captain hell for interfering with an official, Federally-appropriated Spread and Containment operation. Our argument was pre-recorded on station surveillance and everything. I'm probably telling him *right now* that I don't care what the brigades used to be; right now they're just a bunch of fucking mall cops. No offense. Right about now I'm probably calling Captain Kaur 'Paul Blart.' No offense."

Ollie Davis grunted. He was still wearing his sunglasses indoors.

"I don't think I have to tell you that this didn't happen," Dixon continued. *"None* of it happened. Nobody called you on Darren Kaur's phone, Adrian. All record of our chat back at the station will be erased from the brigadehouse comms database when the time index on my little playacting video with Kaur gets changed to make it look like that video happened now, while we're actually here doing treason. The goal isn't only to save my ass, just so we're clear. If Patel has any idea at all that I sent you into the other plane, she won't just have me arrested or shot. It's worse than that. She'll remove me from the mission."

The Roughnecks looked at one another, trying to understand Dixon's priorities.

"If they remove me from the mission, protocol insists they *change* the mission. Obviously they won't tell me the new plan, and that's bad for you. Without my guidance, you'll end up flying blind. You'll also end up playing out a plan that absolutely won't work after all the parameters are changed. This situation requires that officially, you went rogue. You somehow learned what was going on, broke in, stole this equipment, and were able to enter a rift before anyone — including me — knew you were gone."

"How exactly would we do any of that?" Ray asked.

"The story we'll tell is that Kaur figured it out, pulled some strings, and weaseled you guys in here. When you see your captain again, you all owe him a hug. A big one. Even if everything goes perfect, he still might spend the next twenty years in jail. But he knows *exactly* what he's doing and what you're doing. I told him everything. He's falling on the sword to make this happen with full knowledge of why it's necessary. Which it is. I think we're all clear what that means for you."

"Don't fuck it up," said Shannon.

"Don't fuck it up. Kaur and I staged an argument. Said all the right things. What happened next, officially speaking, is that Kaur didn't like my answers. He found a way to get into the departmental assignments and found enough in yours—" Dixon pointed to all of them. "—to put together what you were up to. We'll say he figured out how I was tracking Adrian's dog tags, then saw the way the tracking disappeared when Adrian went onto the grounds of the old GEN warehouse, which just so happened to be the epicenter of the proposed sundering. Kaur's smart and he knows a lot of people in important places. Oh. And Denny Brennan. We're going to try keeping him clean, because it'd be good to have a source with access to GEN, but Brennan also knows everything. I needed his opinion, as a professional. He agrees with our assessment of the situation and is fully on board. The two of them are plenty believable as your co-conspirators even if everyone believes I'm not involved. They were the ones who made this happen."

Adrian wanted to ask what "this" referred to, since Dixon still hadn't really told them what they'd be doing other than "entering the other plane." But before he could speak, Harrison Kim asked a different question.

"What *is* Denny's 'assessment of the situation'?"

"That the strange things we've seen lately are signs of a larger problem. The fiends in that holding facility didn't just 'explode.' The Element inside them was sucked back into the other plane through those little rifts you saw all over the place, leaving a few pounds of dry organic matter behind. They proved they could pinpoint the Element inside your filler rods when you got close to the large rift, Adrian. They gave it back because they didn't want us alarmed, knowing everyone here would assume it was an equipment malfunction. It wasn't, though. They can reach into our side and pull Element back to theirs. They did it with your rig, they did it with the fiends in the prison, and they've done it with several key stockpiles."

Dixon nodded toward Carl the Halfskull, sitting off to one side, radiating heat and reeking of sulfur.

"The other plane's resistance movement has taken the same middleground as ours has. Their people tell us that all this consolidation of Zen is prelude to either an attack or a counterattack. They also tell us that if they've taken back as much Zen as we know they have — and especially if they can take more as they need it, which seems likely — our forces will easily be outmatched. Now. Patel's no dummy. She believes all of that and has equipped her teams with a weapon that might be strong enough to flatten their side. Only problem is that the resulting conflict might flatten ours, too. With extreme prejudice. I'd rather not take that chance."

Carl tapped the side of his half-a-head. Inside Adrian's mind, he heard the most colloquial thing he'd interpreted from Carl's so far: *Tick tock.*

Dixon's hand went to his own translator. He nodded; Carl seemed to have thought it for everyone to hear. "Right. Enough playing with ourselves. With luck, nobody will know you've taken any of this equipment until after word comes down that you're gone. That part's inevitable, but I'd like to delay it as long as possible."

He reset, then answered the question Adrian hadn't asked.

"Okay. Official story. Now that you've stolen what you need, you will go to what Brennan calls a 'quiescent weakness' — a place so thoroughly worn down by repeated past incursions that opening a small rift now will likely stay below the detection threshold. You'll enter the rift and the Stitchers among you will close it behind you. With luck, nobody will notice. Your mission is to reach their leadership and make contact. Graves's team will go tomorrow. They will be better equipped and have superior intel, so expect them to move faster. You have 24 hours' advantage and are likely to need all of them."

Tell them the other thing, Carl thought/said.

"I'm getting to it," Dixon told Carl. "Keep your head on."

Adrian scanned the Roughnecks. All were doing their best to keep cool while they talked about nightmares. The Legions, although big and strong and nominally brave, had spent their careers knowing that rifts were something to avoid. To many of them, secretly, Stitchers were braver for crossing the boundary.

"The other thing," Dixon continued, "is that the second Graves passes the threshold, their equipment will tell them you're already inside. That gives them two missions: the original, plus finding and killing all of you. On top of that, I will be helping them to do exactly that. S&C has all sorts of detection tricks up our sleeves of which the brigades have never been aware. They know I have all sorts of ways to get one up on a group of rouge traitors like you, so I can't hold back. I'll do what I can to help, but most of my job until this is over will be to end you. To stay believable, I'll need to open a few cans of whoop ass on you. They will send reserve units into the rift to take you out, as well as to safeguard their original mission *from* you. That's why your first 24 hours are crucial. They're the only time you'll have any real chance of success at all."

He again nodded to Carl. "Our friend here will be going with you. There are cells of others like him on the other side, plus a few among the boss caste sympathetic to our cause. You won't be totally alone, but their resistance members won't be able to officially avow you any more than I will. Carl knows the plan and will brief you on the way. Follow it and you'll have a chance. We — meaning, you know, all of Earth — will have a chance. Personally I think it's even money. I give the odds of success as 50/50."

Dixon went silent. Everyone looked at everyone else.

"Now ..." Dixon pointed toward the open warehouse door and the crew van still parked there.

"Where is the insertion point?"

"Full circle," Dixon answered. "You'll make your ingress at the heart of the Gore Point. It's so roughshod, there are more weak spots than fully-healed ones. Specifically, you'll be opening at what Brennan says is a fifty-year epicenter, right by Cecret Lake. Should be nice. Have you heard? It refilled. It's blue again now."

The familiarity of seeing a rift inside the Gore Point again seemed to comfort the others, but Ray and Adrian traded a glance. There was a reason the old black lake was legendary in riftfare circles, and it wasn't for its blackness. Dixon wasn't just sending them to *a* chronic rift location. He was sending them to *the* chronic rift location. Right beside Cecret Lake? That was the spot of the first big banger. The place a Classical-class hellbringer came out of Dorn-class rift.

It was where their father died. The start of the long con. The beginning of everything.

The group turned toward the van, but Adrian stopped when Dixon grabbed his arm and held him back.

"There's one last thing you need to do. Not everyone. This is just for you."

"What's that?" Adrian asked.

"Keep an open mind."

"I always do."

Dixon shook his head. "That's not what I mean. I mean, turn off your defenses. Carl's been watching your thoughts. He can only see what leaks out — the things you think that are too loud for you to control. He keeps telling me you're trying very hard to hold something back."

Adrian understood. Carl was hearing his guilt. Adrian didn't want to admit many things out loud, but recently the person to whom he'd wanted to admit the least was himself.

"Whatever you're repressing, knock it off. I don't give a shit if you were diddled as a kid or if you like to choke yourself when you beat off. The future of everything depends on you letting it all hang out. Remember, you can't *talk* to our fiend allies. You have to *think* at them, and that means you'll just cause a shitload of critical communication problems by bottling up. So don't shut *anything* down, do you hear me?"

Adrian looked at the departing others, now almost to the van.

"Why just me? Why aren't you giving this 'clear communication' lecture to everyone?"

"Because you're the compass."

"What's that mean?"

Dixon gave Adrian a half-annoyed, half-frustrated face. The look seemed to wonder why Adrian hadn't figured it out by now. Why Adrian was so stupid.

"Officially, you didn't get mission guidance from anyone who actually knows a damn thing," Dixon told him. "Remember? I didn't tell you anything you didn't already hear from Patel, so how exactly do you plan to explain how you knew where to go?"

"I'll say we stole it. Kaur stole it, the same way he did the rest."

Dixon was still shaking his head. Lower, still using his *you're-an-idiot* voice, he said, "You're missing the point. Yes, you have to explain how you did what you did. But even I can't tell you what you need to do *after* you're inside. How would I know? How would *anyone* know, without the sensor-and-mapping equipment that only Graves's team has? Even our allies on their plane are mostly just soldiers."

Adrian was starting to understand. He blinked, unable to believe this impossible, dice-rolling thing was really their mission. "You have no idea what we're supposed to do, do you? Carl can get us around, but he doesn't know where we have to go."

"Right."

Adrian heard Dixon say again, *Because you're the compass. The future of everything depends on you letting it all hang out.* Then he heard someone else: Patel, the voice of his enemy. *We need you to guide an exposition. We want you to lead us to them.*

She'd spoken of Adrian having access to a homing beacon.

And then it all made sense.

"Figure it out yet?" Dixon asked.

"You want me to follow my thoughts to Laurel."

"That's right."

"And the fact that Patel kicked me off the mission even though she needed me to lead them to Laurel ..."

"That's right, too. Either they found another target ... or *they* found a way to track her, too."

18

EYE OF THE ENEMY

Find the heat, then follow it home.

That's what Laurel's messages had told him. Adrian's own mind had collaborated on the form of her messages, twisting them with his own fears, prejudices, and paranoia. He saw her in pain; he saw her covered in blood; he saw her suffering. He understood now that he couldn't take those things as literal, because they'd come from guilt and a lifetime of fear of the other side.

Adrian had no idea how Laurel was doing, but that last most dominant communique, he could almost trust. But even the meaning of the final clue had changed, now that it wasn't about heat or energy or entropy or thermodynamics — all those scientist concepts Laurel tended to think in.

Now, it was about him and her. He didn't need to watch the back-sucking of rifts and chase the heat that entered them. He didn't need to follow anything but the magnetism he increasingly felt within his chest — an interdimensional magnet, calling him home.

Home. Is that what it is?

He'd thought the word without meaning to. It'd just popped into his head. Now Adrian wondered if thinking *home* was accidental. He'd spent six months now chasing oblivion. Believing Laurel dead or worse, his deepest desire had only been to pay for doing her wrong. If that meant dying himself, it would be a blessing.

So he had to wonder: Was that why calm had descended over him while at the same time, nerves were descending over the others? Was Adrian relaxed now because he was finally at the eye of his own demise?

Calling me home.

Into Hell. Into pain and suffering. Maybe he wasn't the compass they needed.

Maybe if Adrian was to lead them, it would be into the maw of forever with him.

Don't, said an internal voice.

Adrian looked up. The van was parked at the edge of Suicide Flats just inside the tree line separating the still-strange vegetation from the still-mostly-dead zone. Dee, Shannon, Ollie, Lee, Ray, and Harrison were mostly debarked. The door was open. Inside, Adrian and Carl were alone.

For a blink, Adrian stopped seeing him as the ally he'd already become mostly accustomed to and saw him again as a creature. *Fiends. We call them fiends.* He'd been meaning to find a new term to use now that he knew some were on their side but in that moment he couldn't remember why. Two feet away was a naked, gray-skinned thing with sharp, chattering teeth, no face, and an exposed brain. He was still calm. It was good, that this horrible thing might rip him apart.

I said don't.

Don't what? Adrian thought back.

Don't let it in.

Let what in?

The dreadnought. They are powerful influencers on our side. You might call them a brain caste. Our intelligence is fluid, and dreadnoughts influence where that intelligence goes. They do our thinking for us. Surely you know.

Adrian was going to say he didn't, but he did. Ray, too. They'd watched a dreadnought emerge from that black whirlpool on sundering day, then use its mind to send wave after wave of soldiers for the brothers to fight a few at a time, as a test. Their conversation was with the dreadnought. Same for their bargain. The others were just its limbs. Just dumb flesh to its commanding mind.

The one you have in custody is extremely dangerous, Carl said. *It changes minds. It gets inside you in the same way it gets inside us. If you aren't careful, it can make you do things.*

Adrian supposed he knew that, too. There'd been rumors about full guard units set to watch the dreadnought inside its magnetic prison, all of whom had reportedly killed each other or killed themselves. It was clear now that those rumors were true.

But hadn't the dreadnought's proximity, at the bunks at the brigadehouse, facilitated Adrian's dreams of Laurel? Should that make those dreams suspect? Wasn't it possible they should *not* be following Adrian's heart to Laurel at the other plane's center? That maybe this was the dreadnought's intention all along?

Keep it out. Have discipline.

But Dixon told me to keep my mind open.

You must do both. Let us in. Keep the dreadnought out. Get those backward and it will just be the dreadnought leading this mission, through you.

How do I keep some things out and let other things in?

You DO, Carl told him. *You do it by doing it.*

Carl left the van, their conversation apparently over. He

didn't walk like the humans. He was half bent-over most of the time. The one time Adrian had seen him run, his gait was like a diseased horse.

The rift was not difficult to open. Ray had been given that particular set of instructions and they worked a treat. The resulting rift was small — just two or three feet tall, up to Adrian's lower thigh. It exhaled as rifts were supposed to, and its aurora was exactly the colors they all expected. When it was done, Ray stepped back and seemed to see what his brother saw: a new eye to Hell in exactly the place their father had died.

"Now?" Lee asked.

"Sure," said Ollie, who wasn't qualified to give that answer.

Lee, who post-sundering had taken EMT training as a way to make ends meet, had been given custodianship of the Frog syringes and instructions on how to use them. He pulled a small case from his pack, opened it, and laid the needles on a sterile cloth atop a rock. The injection process didn't look difficult, and when he injected Adrian, it didn't feel bad, either. He'd expected pain, to feel his skin thickening and his face and body changing. Like what had happened to Erika Dale.

But this was GEN-official, not assembled as a mad scientist's experiment like Erika's had been. They seemed to have gotten out most of the bugs and (so far, anyway) side effects. Adrian's movements felt a little stiffer thirty seconds after his inoculation and his breath felt cooler, like inhaling air from a freezer. His body felt cold, too. It made him don his Stitching coat for warmth, rather than shielding from warmth.

Lee, after injecting himself, looked wary. "I dunno, guys and gals. I thought I might get ballsy like Superman. Any of you feel like walking into a furnace right now?" He was looking at the pet-sized rift. "It won't protect my hair, will it? Is my hair and eyebrows gonna burn off?"

"Hell, I'll go first," said Ollie, rubbing his bald head. "Not a problem here."

He got on hands and knees, paused, then crawled forward. Halfway through, his tentative steps gave way to quicker, more confident ones. Then he was on the other side and looking back out at the rest of them, eyebrows still intact.

"Come on in, kids, the water's fine."

Still, Adrian hesitated. It didn't matter that Ollie was in, or that Frog worked, or that this was the mission. He'd crossed rifts a thousand times in the past, but always with the knowledge that he'd walk right back out. Even his and Ray's crossing, before the sundering, had been easier than this. That had been a crisis: *do or die*. This was voluntary. Even after Laurel — after all he'd endured since she'd gone — his instincts rebelled.

He looked to Ray. "Last time we did this, it was a trap."

"Sure it was," Ray replied. He set a hand on his shoulder and gave a devil-may-care grin. "But in the end, why we do *anything*, Ade?"

It was absurd enough to make Adrian smile: a callback to their twenties, when both had been more reckless. "For good times and good stories," he replied, and found himself able to move.

It was hard to believe, but when Adrian got down on all fours like Ollie, he found that the hot breath of the rift no longer felt especially hot. It, plus Ollie's presence on the other side, gave him the courage to crawl forward. It was no big deal. His unprotected hands pressed into the coal-hot rocks, but it only felt warm.

He stood, then took off and re-stowed his asbestos coat.

One by one, the Roughnecks followed and Carl assumed the rear. It was a thoroughly unusual experience. They were able to breathe the atmosphere and didn't burst into flame — not even their hair.

The Stitchers in the crew turned to the small rift. Then, with a small and justifiable reluctance to cut off their own world, they closed it.

"No fiends," said Harrison, looking across the red stonescape when it was done.

"'Visitors.'" Adrian looked toward Carl, reminding them who in the group was risking it all by turning traitor in the eyes of his fellows. "Let's go with the word 'visitors' for now."

"Fine," said Harrison. "No *visitors.*"

A way has been made for us, Carl thought at them, *by a splinter faction just like yours. We won't stay invisible forever. We need to keep moving.*

"Where?"

Adrian didn't see who had spoken, but all eyes were on him now. Plus Carl's ventricles. He hadn't counted on that. You'd think that in Hell, the demon in your group would at least have the decency to take point.

"I ... I don't know."

Surprisingly, Ray came closer, putting a palm flat on Adrian's chest. "Come on, Baby Brother. You know."

Adrian tuned inward. He tried to find Laurel inside, but unearthed only his neuroses about her. He saw himself stabbing her in the back. Throwing her into a bottomless pit. He saw himself shoving Laurel into a fire to burn alive.

He shoved it aside and closed his eyes. Then, behind his lids, he saw a path between two tall, horn-shaped rocks. Laurel stood between them, covered in blood again, beckoning him forward with one slow, curling finger, mouth closed and eyes peeking through all the red like stark white moons eclipsed in the center.

He opened his eyes. Turned in a circle. And saw the rock formation far in the distance.

Inside his head, as they started out, he heard a bloodcurdling scream. Only he'd heard it; nobody else even looked up. The scream was in Laurel's voice. He blinked and saw her impaled with a great, broad spear. He saw her split in half, entrails like party streamers.

Keep it out, Carl told him.

Adrian wasn't sure what that meant, because inside it all blurred together.

What was Laurel, what was his own internal guidance, what was the plan, and what instead was the influence of the dreadnought? He could actually *see* its hold on him if he squinted, if he allowed himself to believe that thought could be seen. It made a straight, faint blue line that yawned into the distance, toward some tiny rift nobody had noticed. On the other side, the dreadnought's mind waited patiently.

It's watching us. It's trying to touch us.

Nobody heard Adrian's thought. Not even Carl.

Adrian kept walking, choosing to believe it didn't matter. But what if it did? What if he wasn't taking his group of Roughnecks toward Laurel at all ... but instead into the eye of an unknown enemy?

19
MILLIONS UPON MILLIONS

The march was endless. After a few initial bursts of chatter, all conversation within the group died.

Now that nobody was speaking, anyone who *did* speak stood out in a way that felt, to all, acutely uncomfortable. Maintaining their pall of silence somehow felt safer, though they'd still seen no fiends.

No *visitors*.

The Hellscape was flat and open, dominated by imposing red-rock formations that never got any closer no matter how long they walked toward them. Noise, in this empty and alien world, felt like ringing a dinner bell. Even the wordless parts of their communication stopped, maybe because if Carl could hear them asking questions mentally, others might hear them as well.

And so very quickly it became a dirge. A death march ... until they could bear the quiet no longer.

"Jesus Christ," Dee said, finally breaking the silence. "How do we even know we're going in the right direction?"

"Shh," said Shannon.

"*Shh* yourself, Shannon." Then she muttered, *"Uppity bitch."*

"What did you call me?"

"Easy." But Ray looked at Adrian anyway, legitimizing Dee's question. Soon everyone was looking at Adrian.

"Wait. Do you have a map, Adrian?" Harrison asked. "Why hasn't anyone shown *me* the map?"

"There's no map, Harrison," Ray replied.

"Well. That's super. So I guess we're just kind of following *Carl?"*

Harrison said Carl's adopted name with clear effort, just barely forcing himself not to say something else — something worse.

Adrian couldn't hear the thoughts of the other humans, but he didn't need to in order to understand Harrison's almost-gaffe. On the Earth side of the rift, everyone had seemed to improbably accept Carl as just another member of the team because the mental bond had a way of ... well ... *bonding* them. It went beyond skin-deep, and once wordless talk was normalized by everyone's individual language filter, "beyond skin deep" more or less made them the same.

But things had changed after crossing. The six other humans now looked drawn and full of blame. If he was being honest, Adrian felt mostly the same way. They were trapped in this horrible place, and whose fault was that? Why, it was probably this fucking *demon's* fault. This fucking *creature.*

Didn't they used to kill monsters like "Carl" all the time? Didn't it used to be their reason for living — the very thing for which they'd been put on the planet, to help save humanity from the ravages of evil?

He clamped the angry thought stream shut. It felt poisoned, like a grudge without cause.

"We're following Adrian," Ray told Harrison. "Now shut the fuck up."

"Ray ..." That last *shut the fuck up* had struck Adrian as a bit too hard edged, even though it was justified. After all, Harrison was being an asshole.

"The hell you say to me?" Harrison said.

Ray stepped forward. They were both Legions — both egos given arms and legs.

"I told you to shut the fuck up. We're going where Adrian says."

"Okay, *Adrian,*" Harrison said, turning his head but not his body, which remained chest-to-chest with Ray. "Where exactly *are* we going? Other than fuck-all?"

"Toward those rocks." Adrian pointed toward the horns, which after a half-hour or more of marching still weren't any closer.

"Why?"

"Because."

"Oh. Really." Ollie now, his voice dripping with sarcasm. *"Because."*

"You signed up for this mission."

"Let it go, Ray," Adrian told him.

"I got this. I'm fine."

"You're not *fine*, Ray. You're trying to win." And that, right now, was really pissing Adrian off.

Ray's need to show off and be the bigger man had diminished significantly since the *Brigade* TV show, the sponsorships, and the leagues of adoring fans had gone away, but something about this mission was reviving all of his worst qualities. Adrian would know; he'd dealt with his older brother's dickhead showiness — his inborn need to prove he was better than everyone else — since birth.

Ray was insecure. If he wasn't waving his dick in everyone's face, he wasn't living.

"So now *you* have a problem, too, little brother?"

"Not a new one. Just the same old Ray Porter bullshit."

"I'm on your side." Ray turned his macho, inflated chest from Harrison to Adrian instead.

Adrian almost laughed at his brother's predictability. A peacock, always displaying his feathers. Would it kill him to let someone be the Alpha for five minutes? Would it destroy his pride so completely to let someone else lead, the way Dixon had told them Adrian pretty much had to if their mission was to succeed?

"Let it go, Ray."

"Let what go? There's nothing to let go."

Adrian rolled his eyes, turning away.

"I'm *used* to letting things go. Otherwise, how would you ever get anything?"

"Oh, fuck off, Ray."

"I guess it's a good thing I let *Laurel* go. What if I'd held onto her? We'd be so screwed, Adrian."

Adrian simmered, turning from his brother.

"If I hadn't let you have her, how would we be able to use your baby pecker like a divining rod?"

Adrian snapped. In one smooth motion, he spun, leapt, and tackled Ray to the ground.

He genuinely hadn't seen it coming; Adrian was the cooler head, always turning that other cheek. Right now, however, he didn't feel like being the bigger man. He'd never wanted to hurt his brother more.

Adrian got in one good punch — right across the cheek, making his hand smart — before Ray found his wits. He slammed his fist into Adrian's stomach, voiding his lungs.

Adrian wheezed, unable to inhale, and in that time Ray rolled them to reverse their positions.

He hovered above Adrian's face, between him and the stormy red sky.

A line of drool fell from his furious lips, ice cold when it hit Adrian's chin.

Ray's face was delirious with out-of-control anger. He pinned Adrian with his knees, then moved both hands to wrap his brother's neck.

"*Ray,*" Adrian said, but it came out like a squeak.

Ray squeezed, pressing thumbs into Adrian's windpipe.

Adrian saw swimming darkness. His brother was going to kill him.

Then Adrian saw slow movement. Something smooth and black pressed against the side of Ray's head. It touched his skin and sizzled like a steak in a skillet.

"Easy," said a voice.

Ray's dark eyes cleared. He blinked. Over and over again. When his hands left Adrian's throat, it was like he'd snapped out of a trance. They went up at his side in surrender, his expression horrified.

As Ray moved away — slowly, minding the M9 Shannon was still pressing against his temple — he looked beyond compliant. Like a man who regretted everything, and wanted to put himself in handcuffs so nobody else would have to.

But Shannon's focus hadn't broken. She moved with Ray as he shifted position, every muscle tense and ready to paint Hell's rocks with his brain.

Then Adrian noticed something else: Carl the Halfskull was beside Shannon, pressing a clawed hand flat against her shoulder.

It was a bond, Adrian realized. They could already speak without words, but this was something more. This was Carl pushing his mind right into Shannon's. He wasn't controlling her. This was more like speaking very seriously and sternly, so she'd be sure to understand.

Fortifying her, perhaps, against the influence of this place.

"Easy, Ray," she said.

Ray was upright now, hands raised in surrender.

"You good?" Shannon asked.

"Jesus, Ade. Jesus, I'm sorry."

"I said, You good, Ray?"

He was still blinking. "I don't know what came over me."

"This place came over you," Shannon said. "Over all of us. *You good now,* Ray?"

"I ... I think I'm good."

Carl moved his hand away from Shannon. As he did, Shannon lowered and re-holstered her sidearm. Some of the certainty she'd seemed to have seconds ago collapsed, leaving her looking about as unsure of things as Adrian felt.

Adrian got to his feet, rubbing his neck.

"Adrian, I ..."

"It's okay."

"I could have killed you." Ray swallowed, wide-eyed. "I *wanted* to kill you."

"It's okay," Adrian said again.

It was a little hard to talk, and hard to act as if everything was fine after nearly being strangled to death. But what Shannon said felt true, so he did all he could to believe his own words.

Something about the vibe of the other plane was worming beneath all of their skins, making them irritable and angry. How could it not? Even rainy days can change a person's mood, and they were in a literal other world.

It's not just being here, Carl's voice said. Adrian could tell Carl was projecting into all of them because every one of the

Roughnecks turned to face him, as horrorstruck by what'd just happened as children would be. *It's the dreadnought.*

Adrian rubbed his sore throat, recognizing the truth. He'd hoped the dreadnought's influence miles back was a hangover of some sort: psychic poison that'd leaked through from Earth's side. Now it seemed that influence was walking with them instead of being left behind.

The ninth member of their party: a shadow thing, playing tricks.

"The dreadnought," Dee repeated aloud. It came off like something she'd needed to voice just to get it out, so it wouldn't consume her.

"I ... I hear it, too." Harrison so far had trouble even hearing Carl. He was a literal sort, barely believing in rifts and creatures even though he'd faced both every day of his adult life. "It's inside my head."

They all stopped, all listening to the wind.

There *was* wind on the red plane, too; Carl's mind told Adrian that just as on the Earth plane, the hottest of the hot air rose and sometimes cooler (but still scalding) air rushed in to replace it. When the wind didn't blow, there was very little. The place seemed to hold a kind of standing echo: a subtle hum that simply existed, reflecting no source beyond the aether itself.

But Adrian could hear what Harrison heard, too.

"Carl," Adrian said aloud.

Carl answered in his out-loud voice: a guttural chatter, coming more from throat than tongue. Inside his head, Adrian heard the English version: *That's not the dreadnought.*

Then something new happened. Up until now, the half-skull's communication had arrived in Adrian's cortex as words in his native tongue. It wasn't coming from Carl that way; the bond and the chip stuck to the side of his head were working to translate on Adrian's end.

But now Carl was agitated; Adrian could feel it in the bond along with the message. He wasn't used to being singular. None of them were, in the lower castes. Carl's singularity was working against him as fear came. He, like any soldier, was new to terror as well.

Fear sent the message differently to Adrian. The information came too fast for words to convey, so instead he found himself assaulted by images and feelings. The sounds Harrison reported hearing in his head were explained like flash cards.

Adrian absorbed only the primitive core of them at first: not descriptions, but instead a sense of overwhelm, of danger, of alarm ... of something coming that under normal circumstances shouldn't be here.

Images of conquering, of destruction, of mayhem. He saw darkness as if he'd been covered with bodies, hiding what passed for the sun in this place. His nerves jangled. It was senseless, instinctual panic without antecedent, as if something horrid had invaded his brain's oldest parts, playing rhythms on his amygdala.

The feeling did not pass, but the worst of the adrenaline did.

The group slowly raised its heads, which had bowed in panicked contrition to nothing at all.

"There," Lee said, nodding sixty degrees sideways from their line of travel, where a ridge of tall red rocks blocked their view. "It's coming from over there."

They looked. The direction Lee indicated had brightened, as if someone had turned on a rainbow lamp somewhere beyond the ridge.

Carefully they moved upward, staying low. Although danger was present in this direction, Adrian's senses had returned enough to tell him the threat was more generalized: perilous, but not for them specifically.

Dee saw first, and gasped.

Soon enough Adrian and the others were behind her, looking across Hell's sprawling valley.

An enormous flaming eye glowed in the distance. It was the rift, he knew: the rift Patel's team had opened inside the ad-hoc Army base. The rift through which the little train cars went, to kill and render the bodies of their citizens. The rift through which, tomorrow, Graves's team would come.

Knowing its actual size, Adrian judged the rift to be at least two Earth-miles away.

Between the Roughnecks and the rift was an endless, millions-strong mass of soldier demons, just waiting for the exodus.

They know, Ray's thought said from inside their collective bubble. *Somehow, they know Graves is coming for the queen.*

It could have been a good thing. If the fiends stopped Graves at the gate, Adrian and Ray's team wouldn't have to worry about what Dixon had said — about how the war machine, including Dixon and his intel, would have no choice but to chase the Roughnecks as they chased their target.

It *could* have been a good thing, but Adrian knew it wasn't. He kept thinking of what Carl told them: that the queen, if she was threatened, would strike back.

This was good for their team.

But an abomination for humanity as a whole.

The fiends — the visitors — had been consolidating Zen Element. Weaponizing it. Adrian knew that now; thanks to the translator beneath his ear he could practically smell it in the air. Some of what came was from Carl: visions of defenses nothing at all like humans would make. These beings were *made* of Zen. They were natives, born of it. So of course they wouldn't refine it, making incendiary rounds to be fired from clunky metal tubes. They wouldn't make bombs and missiles like the Army.

The visitors' new weapons would be subtle. Like a touch that brought instant death. Like a slow-bleed poison. Like biological espionage: a sentient disease that could infect, hide, spread, and strike at will.

When Patel sent her troops through the rift tomorrow, the visitors would send theirs. It was as Dixon said from the start — the very reason he'd risked everything to send the Roughnecks in the first place.

Any battle that came now would not go smoothly. What came next would be worse than the sundering.

"We have to reach the queen before Graves enters the rift," Adrian said. "Somehow, we have to get her to stand down."

Nobody answered. It was too preposterous. Too impossible to believe. But what could they do other than attempt to complete their mission? The rift they'd came through was closed, and the only other known rift was the one they saw now: a carpet of visitor soldiers on one side, the American military industrial complex on the other side.

The queen, Adrian thought at Carl. *You have to get us to her.*

Immediately, as soon as Adrian had the thought, the demon version of a murmur rippled through the ranks of creatures ahead. Their perfect rows undulated. Heads turned, as if looking for someone who'd dared to throw a rock their way.

They all ducked low, trying to hide.

Even though Carl did not have eyes, he seemed to stare hard at Adrian with the flat slots of his half-brain ventricles. A chastising sort of stare, telling Adrian that he should understand how this worked by now. They were a psychic people, based on collective thought. Thinking about attacks and the queen was as rough a choice as yelling a slur in a room filled with the people that slur most offended.

Laurel, Adrian thought-said instead. *I meant, we have to find LAUREL.*

Laurel, who had called to him from across the planes. Laurel, who was far smarter than Adrian had ever been. Laurel who, if they were extremely lucky, might already be working on this problem — might already have some idea of what to do.

Was it a pointless hope? Perhaps. But either way she was still alive; Adrian felt sure of it. He knew because he could still hear her mind beneath all the chatter. Her message had changed, though, now that his perspective on it (and hence his internal translation) knew more.

She no longer spoke of *heat*.

She spoke of something more precious.

Find your heart, her mind seemed to tell him now, *and follow it home*.

Maybe Laurel could help the mission and maybe she couldn't. Either way, Adrian knew now, she was her own end in this. And that was okay. He could easily follow her — follow his heart — no matter what else happened between two doomed worlds.

They peeked over the ridge again. Disturbances rippling through the lines of visitor soldiers had stopped, the ranks once again settled. They were all looking forward again, toward the massive and glowing rift.

Yes. This is why Dixon sent us. This is how he knew we could be invisible to them in a way Patel's people can't. Somehow the visitors know Patel is planning conquest, so they're ready to face it. But us? We aren't after ...

He stopped himself, unwilling to even *think* militant

thoughts. Unwilling to risk thinking about the queen even in the privacy of his own mind.

We aren't after anything else, he finished, *other than finding Laurel and bringing her home.*

The others seemed to hear Adrian. Carl certainly did. Maybe bringing Laurel home wasn't the literal mission, but that literal mission — communication, contact, maybe a bit of understanding — would come along the way as long as she remained their focus.

Chasing Laurel was the advantage Dixon had seemed to know all along that his little squad would have. They had to keep tuning in to Laurel, not crusades and violence. Keep *Laurel* front and center in Adrian's thoughts, and the collective visitor mind wouldn't care.

Fortunately, focusing single-mindedly on Laurel was easy.

Ever since the day he'd doomed her, Adrian had never been able to stop.

20

CRYSTAL

Lieutenant John David Graves marched back and forth in front of the tents. He'd been in some hellholes in the past, but this was ridiculous.

He didn't understand the science of their current encampment, or remotely care to. All he knew was that goddamn scabs used to come at them every single fucking time they crossed the boundary, and his forward line usually had to expel a few whirligigs and a lot of boomer rounds to show them their place. By the end, the scabs had gotten as docile as puppies, pretty much accepting that the squads were going to come in, kill them, and cart them away to be squeezed like oranges.

Resistance, as the expression went, had become futile. But here and now, the scabs didn't even look their direction. Couldn't see them, maybe. Again, Graves didn't care. They had a foothold in Hell now, and according to the geeks, as long as they stayed inside the perimeter, Hell's residents wouldn't know or care.

The geeks called the big black cases in a rough circle around the tents "responders." What they "responded" to was yet another thing about which Graves didn't give half a shit. He only knew that they looked like big tall sets of Marshall stacks, as if their group planned to throw a concert. He knew they supposedly masked thought from the scabs, and without responders' protection, the fucking diaper wipings that called this place home would somehow hear their intentions.

It was seven ways FUBAR, having your thoughts dangling in the breeze like a forgotten dick. As little as Graves hated fighting behind too much technology (it felt dishonest, less pure somehow), he was reluctantly thankful the geeks were able to shield them.

The guys and gals in the unit called the responder-surrounded camp they'd made here "the bubble of glee." Maybe that was how it worked. Maybe while everyone inside the camp was itching to thrust a big fuck-fist into the scab nest and turn their queen to paste, all the scabs saw from the outside — thanks to the thought-disguising responders — was a big ol' bubble of glee.

Intolerable unicorn and rainbows shit. He couldn't wait for Phase Two to begin.

He marched the perimeter, looking repeatedly at his watch. From this far off, they couldn't even see the warehouse rift. Supposedly it was awesome, seen from a distance on this side. Looked like a giant hairy pussy hanging in the sky, only instead of pussy hair, it was waves of light. Like the pussy of existence itself. You had to fuck it with a nuclear bomb.

His communicator buzzed. Patel.

"Yes, ma'am."

"They're inside," said Patel.

"Yes, ma'am, my comms chief has already made that determination. Our sensors seem to be working just fine. We clocked the first cut at fourteen twenty-one. Closed fourteen twenty-six. Body count plus eight. But we also got eyes on them and saw they sent their pet halfskull along too. 'Course we can't track that one. It's *supposed* to be here."

"Eyes?" Patel asked.

"Ma'am, we sent a whirligig. Stilled its blades and sent it as a drone."

"Your orders were to stay inside the perimeter."

"Yes, ma'am, but this seemed acceptable risk and necessary to pursue at the time. We couldn't risk breaking radio silence due to a short in one of the responders. Comms could not verify that the b—" He stopped himself. He'd almost said "bubble of glee." "—the obfuscation field was intact at the time. I made a judgment call. It felt vital to properly recon, given the mission's requirement for stealth. Ma'am."

"It's stealth I'm concerned about, Lieutenant," Patel said.

"Yes, ma'am. But our bird was not seen and we have not been seen. Not by the targets and not by the scabs."

"So it's working. The field."

"Yes, ma'am; we're five-by-five. Out here in the red plains the scabs don't seem to wander much. I assume they're sticking closer to their domiciles. We sent a second bird out in the direction the civvies gave us, and although we were unable to see any signs of settlement, we did see tracks in the dust."

"You sent a drone out past your field?" Patel sounded aghast.

"Yes ma'am we did," Graves replied. "As expected its range was extremely limited. Even heat-shielded the EM was immediately toast. The bird crapped out, but not before we got some good readings. I'd say the assessment is spot on. For all parties. Tracks suggest major movement from a central source toward the prime rift. Mr. and Mr. Porter are on a line to intercept that line. We're behind both, staying out of sight and out of mind."

"Goddammit, Graves. If you're ditching drones over there, you're hardly out of sight."

"It's not a problem, ma'am," said Graves, a little impatient now. This bitch was safe in an office back where oxygen existed and you couldn't set a piece of paper on fire by holding it out in the open. Patel hadn't injected her with Satan's diarrhea, turning herself half-fuckwad like his people had. She wasn't on the ground, and in his mind that only gave her so much right to an opinion, commanding officer or not. "The grounding here is sandlike. It moves with breezes and forms dunes. Chances are more than excellent that our downed whirligig is already buried and out of sight, but if you want, we can break cover to—"

She cut him off, annoyed. "No. But from now on, I want complete adherence to protocol. I mean one hundred percent. Is that clear?"

"Crystal, ma'am."

"You've seen the rift?"

"Before bubbling up we sent a two-person team. Yes, ma'am."

"And?"

"Like you said. Every munchkin in Oz is there, just staring at the door and waiting for some asshole to waltz right through it. You want to see something really special, go down to warehouse prime and ride one of our little rail cars over — guarantee you it won't go clockwork this time. There might be ten million scabs ready on the other side — mostly soldiers, but we saw a few bosses. If you'd like, I can list—"

"Not necessary," Patel said.

"Well then. SitRep says all's well here south of the border. Enemy is behaving as anticipated."

Patel went quiet, probably digesting the news. It had happened exactly as the geeks predicted, but no one outside the geeks really believed it until they saw it with their own eyes.

It was unnerving, to know the scabs really could read a human being's intention. Almost made Graves shiver with the feel of a close call. The original mission was for them to Frog up and march right through the giant rift instead of quietly finding themselves a back door. Just in time, some genius decided the fiends, who communicated semi-telepathically, probably knew what they were planning. No specifics, but the general purpose.

March in. Take a bomb. Kill the queen. Annihilate the rest.

That was supposed to rip the guts from this place and these fucking cockroaches, and Graves was pretty sure it would have. Problem was, they'd never have gotten a chance. The scabs could sense their murderous intent and lined up at the front door good as you please.

That's why Plan B happened. Graves himself was willing to take credit for that one.

It started with Adrian, the more dickless of the Porters. You didn't have to be psychic to read his lovelorn bullshit like a highway billboard. He walked around all hangdog, with his head down and his bitch titties swinging. His idiot brother explained without question the first time anyone asked.

Oh, poor Adrian lost his woman to the scabs. They snatched her like a barbarian's bride. Boo fucking hoo.

Somehow Adrian felt guilty about it, too, although Graves had no idea why he'd hung *her* bullshit on *his* balls. In the end it didn't matter. All that mattered was that through every bit of training and briefing and drilling of the bomb-and-kill mission, Adrian would only ever think about his woman.

But then the geeks started running that shit up the flagpole about how the scabs might read their minds and know they were coming. So Graves said, *What if they didn't know we were coming?* He repeated it then, emphasizing the important part: *What if they didn't know WE were coming?*

The caveat mattered. There'd been so much buildup already that the scabs would never believe they'd given up, should they try anything obvious like entering inside a bubble of glee, hiding themselves until they could creep close enough to the queen and her scab city to attack.

The sudden silence from the human side, in itself, would put them on the lookout.

So they needed a decoy: someone to invade their plane as planned, but on a mission the fiends wouldn't care about — and a disposable decoy, just in case they did. That's when Graves had told Patel about Adrian Porter's bullshit and how he wouldn't stop whining.

Send the sad sack, he said. *Then instead of following the queen, we follow him.*

The parts, taken separately, made perfect sense. Whereas the fiend army would detect the plane-conquering intentions of Graves's unit, they wouldn't detect any conquering from a unit headed by the Porters — not if it was an unofficial one. Maybe they'd let that unit be. If they did — if they allowed Porter's small group to try to find his woman on a mission of peace — then Graves's team, duly camouflaged by repeaters, could enter behind them.

Of course, it would only work if Adrian knew he wasn't being followed. He'd never let himself be used as some sort of human tracer round. Fortunately, the warehouse detection team spotted someone taking unauthorized photos of the rendering room. It was Dixon. Patel wanted to step on him, ruining his life and career for trying to turn the Porters into spies against them. Graves convinced her not to.

Let Dixon think he's getting away with it. We both know what he'll do, if he thinks his hand is forced.

And of course Dixon had. He went right to the Porters, who went right to the team they'd been training in "secret," but not actually secret at all. They opened a small rift inside the old Gore Point, intending to reach Laurel Gantry and likely the queen before anyone else.

Since then, Dixon had been preparing to act surprised, ready to jump straight up with faked surprise and indignation when Patel told him that the Porters had gone missing, likely into the rift. Dixon would play both sides, pretending to hunt down his own team while actually helping them.

He'd seen too many movies. You didn't build what they had inside the warehouses without the ability to know everything.

"Where is Adrian Porter's team?" Patel asked.

"Two clicks in the direction we're calling west. Assuming clicks are still clicks." Direction and distance didn't make a cunt hair's sense over here; they'd had to make shit up just to have a way to discuss any of it. "They found the prime rift and had a look at the waiting party. I have a scout wearing a portable repeater out keeping an eye, radioing back whenever he comes close enough for us to get a signal. Scout says they're preparing to move out."

"Toward the city?"

"In the direction of the fiend tracks, ma'am, yes. We're assuming that's the direction of the city."

"Tracks headed out, not in."

"Yes, ma'am, also as anticipated. There's obviously no way to know how many of them stayed behind to protect Her Highness, but we do know that a fuck ton of scabs did *not* stay behind, prepared instead to meet us when we walk right in."

That would be fun. Graves almost wanted to ditch the mission just so he could stand back and watch millions of scabs wait and wait and wait. They expected commandos to burst right in; that's what whatever their intel came from seemed to tell them was imminent. That could have been Graves and his unit: a handful of humans with some ass-kicking weapons. Chances were that if they'd missed this switcharoo and gone in as planned, the scabs would have surrounded them, preventing them from bugging out. Their weapons were serious shit; they might be able to kill three, four, maybe five hundred thousand before running out of ammo and getting overwhelmed. Either way, they'd end the day dead and then the queen would unleash whatever-the-fuck. Their failure would have replaced Custer's as the most epic.

Now they had this quiet little tactic: some guerilla action like crawling belly-down in rice patties, able to sneak up from the rear and shoot their leader in the back.

The bomb would level them before they thought twice. Graves would like to see that. Supposedly the bomb wasn't really concussive. It didn't superheat air and send out a deadly shockwave like a true explosive. This was something else. Something the geeks said would work only on the scabs. Supposedly they could stand right in the epicenter if they wanted, watching it go off safely while all those goddamn roaches bit the dust.

"Stay close to them, Lieutenant," Patel said. "We don't know where Gantry is or if she's even where everyone hopes. She might not even be alive. If Porter's group finds the wrong thing and you're not ready, they might decide on a new mission on the spot and all those fiends might return."

"Yes, ma'am. We're anticipating the same, ma'am."

"Don't let Porter know you're following them. Let him keep thinking you won't enter the rift until tomorrow. Stay close, and watch for signs."

"And what if we kill the queen and bomb their shit, but then it turns out Dixon and his pet monkey are right?"

"Right about what?"

"That the scabs have a failsafe. The halfskull they've got

seems to have individualized. I guess it told Dixon that if the queen goes, everything goes."

"Let us worry about that, Graves. Follow your orders. Exactly. No deviations. You are to pursue at a distance, remain unseen, and strike only when they get you close enough that coming out from under your obfuscation field no longer matters. At that point it won't matter if they know what you plan to do because you'll already be doing it."

"And if there are still too many inside the city to be dealt with? If we're overwhelmed?"

"It won't matter. All that matters is that you fire the incendiary and take down the boss when you do. And Lieutenant?"

"Yes, ma'am?"

"I don't have to remind you it's the mission, not your lives, that matters most here. Do I make myself clear?"

"Crystal," Graves said again.

21

BLUE

Adrian got used to her feel, the longer he walked. Her quiet psychic trail was no longer a distraction, now it was the mission's point. After a while, a nonspecific sense of Laurel became everything for Adrian: distant, yet all there was.

The sense of her was a little like smelling the last specter of her scented soap, but not quite. A little like finding her fingerprints on the glass coffee table or one of her bookmarks in his books, but not quite.

Closest was the aura of her empty home office. It'd always been Laurel's private space — so private and completely hers that Adrian almost never entered it ... not when she was around and certainly not now. In the time she'd been gone he'd only opened the door once, on accident, after sleepwalking there and waking with his fingers dipped into her Zen garden.

The thing was the size of a tabletop: black sand forming a Yang and white sand forming a Yin, each with a small circle of the opposite color in the fat parts of the commas. He'd stayed a while after waking, returning his hand to his side but remaining anyway, soaking up the nighttime quiet and feeling Laurel's palpable presence in this place she no longer occupied.

The lights had been off. He could see only shadows. And yet he'd seemed to feel her, very clearly, standing right beside him. It wasn't sight, or hearing, or touch, or scent that told him Laurel was somehow still present. It was all of those things and none of them. It was a generalized gestalt that insisted some of Laurel had stayed behind after her body had gone: a tiny bit of her soul, perhaps.

What Adrian felt now, walking through heat strong enough to bend sight lines with haze, was like that. Eventually he stopped trying to pin it down and instead followed the deepest part of his gut. When he felt comfort, as if an invisible hand held his, he knew he was guiding the Roughnecks correctly. When agitation rose and that hand went absent, he would tweak his direction until he found it again.

Soon enough he began to have walking daydreams. After seeing the assembled visitor army, nobody spoke — either humbled by the size of the force humanity was facing or afraid on some instinctual level of being overheard. There was still a phantom wind, its cries loud as it rounded rock formations, but beyond it Adrian mostly heard only their footsteps.

The group's rhythm was a steady metronome that soon enough seemed to have no start and no end. They were the marching dead, carrying forward only because there was nowhere else to go.

And so, with the steady *thrum-thrum-thrum* of bootsteps and all this nothingness to see, the small but omnipresent sense of Laurel grew until it took over all of Adrian's under-stimulated senses. His memories of her took on the shape and substance of present-moment dreams.

Her beside him as they walked the streets of Fortune

during good times, not the sulfurous misery of this horrible place.

You keep promising me we'll leave, Adrian. You keep telling me you'll talk to Kaur and ask for a transfer, so we can move somewhere away from all this Hell.

Even in his fantasies, Adrian let her down.

First it was duty to Ray that kept you here. Then the Captain asked for your help with the saboteur investigation. Even then it was supposed to be weeks. Then Dixon and Brennan. Then you thought the saboteur was your brother so of course you had to stay again. I kept taking you back no matter how many times you failed to keep your promise, Adrian. Why? Because I loved you. Did you ever truly love me back?

He kept reminding himself that the daydream was only a falsified memory, and that this version of Laurel wasn't real.

Even after everything, I stuck with you. Remember when the sundering started, and I ran to help you? Remember when you told me that you and Ray were planning to chase Matt Baker through the rift, but instead of hiding, I volunteered to stay behind and help in any way I could? I might have been slaughtered the minute you left me, Adrian. I was in fiend country, alone, with no way to protect myself. Ray gave me his Rollard. What did you ever give me but broken promises?

"Stop it," Adrian said aloud.

Ray looked his way, seen from the corner of Adrian's eye. When Adrian didn't turn his head, Ray seemed to let it go.

And now look what happened to me, Dream Laurel said, her hand still in his, warm while her words went cold like some disingenuous game. *You left me alone, but even that wasn't enough. The second you got the chance, you betrayed me. To save your own skin, you let them drag me to Hell.*

"I said—!"

"Shh!"

They all stopped. Harrison was holding a splayed hand in the air, his single syllable somehow conveying urgency and stillness in unison.

Dee and Shannon raised eyebrows at him. Harrison shook his head, hand still up, ear still cocked for a sound nobody else had heard. Adrian saw Lee's mouth move: *Where?*

Harrison listened again, then pointed in a way that seemed only lightly certain.

His finger firmed, indicating a long, shallow hill they'd been walking beside for the better part of an hour now. It looked like one side of a halfhearted drainage ravine, if this place ever saw water.

"H—" Ollie began, but even his quiet tone struck Harrison as far too loud.

The finger Harrison had been using to point shot back to press against his lips. He shook his head slowly, then pointed again. At first there was nothing to see, but then a miniature pebble scree jostled from near the feature's top, dribbling down like rain.

Someone was up there.

Harrison began to gesticulate, taking command, using finger gestures they hadn't rehearsed in advance to, presumably, indicate a plan of attack. Whoever was up there needed to be dealt with just so.

Then another set of fingers entered the field. Four of them, wasp-nest gray and ending in claws.

Carl shook his head, then pointed into the distance. His agitation was clear, likely exacerbated by the fact that half-skulls were almost always part of a collective mind, seldom cut off as individuals. Carl wasn't used to being on the outside, having to make decisions without a hundred others in the mix. Watching him now, it wasn't clear if he wanted them to stay or go.

Then he pointed into the distance more urgently, and the answer became clear to everyone:

Go. Run. It wasn't coming from their own little collective, spoken internally using Carl's psychic voice. The words came as concepts, from body language alone.

Too late, Adrian realized why. Harrison didn't want Ollie overheard, but it seemed now that Carl, speaking mentally, didn't want to be overheard either.

But that meant—

Halfskulls. Rising over the shallow hill. Hundreds of them. Thousands.

Carl had told them that the collectives they formed were intentional and volitional, that nothing could be overheard unless the thinker wanted it. Even that certainty had gone by the wayside, now that so many Carl clones were nearby. Maybe he'd heard them. Maybe their collective mind was reaching out to his, trying to persuade him back home.

But the halfskulls, Adrian realized as Dee raised her hands at them in some futile attempt at peace and others tucked to run, were not exactly the same as Carl. They were as tall, and as broad, and as cut-in-half up top to expose their working wet brains, but their skin was closer to blue than gray. Their presence seemed to cut the red dim they'd been walking through, creating what could only be described — and not at all ironically — as a purple haze. Were they creating that light? Or was it a trick of the eye?

Dee dropped her hands. It was clear that these were not friends. They were as the first dreadnought had conveyed on sundering day: more like skin cells than organisms. Whatever larger mind they had was the real intelligence here. Actual halfskulls were as disposable to that brain as bullets were to a gun.

Ray acted first. Instead of reaching for the weapon Dixon

had given him, his hand went to his standby. He raked the latched-back Rollard from its catches and went to work.

A blink. Then no hesitation at all.

Ray became a dervish. Seconds later — and yet it seemed to take an eternity — the others in the group took up arms. The remaining Legions in the group (Ollie, Harrison, and Dee) grabbed Rollards once Ray unleashed and began doing business with his. The Stitchers, who hadn't spent years used to the heavy ballet of Rollard work like the Legions had, equipped with projectile weapons instead. Adrian, whose sudden transition from tortured daydream to wretched reality had left him foggy, was the last to raise his gun.

But instinct, not training, guided him. Everything they'd learned with Graves was a mishmash. Everything Dixon told them when this began had flown out the window. Adrian had been listening, but nobody expected their first real encounter to be an ambush.

Halfskulls were supposed to be mindless. Even the collective mind, when directing soldier castes, was supposed to be largely mindless. Even from his father, Denny Brennan, and the psychotic ramblings of Erika Dale, Adrian had never heard of fiends plotting and strategizing ... which, if they had indeed followed the Roughnecks and bided their time, this seemed to be.

Was it another way the second plane had hustled mankind — able to make elaborate plans all along but never showing it? Or was this instead something new: a variable they'd never faced ... because until rifts started inhaling and Zen started consolidating, it hadn't *existed*?

Adrian forgot all the weapon's settings. There was no time to figure them out — not in the half-second he had left before three blue-glowing halfskulls took him down. So Adrian pointed the muzzle and pulled the trigger, believing but far from sure that once equipped there was no safety. He had no idea what he'd be firing — only that triggers, when pulled, had a way of making bad things stop coming.

The weapon hung low and heavy, operated from the hip rather than aimed at the eye. Using it felt like playing an electric guitar onstage. It kicked, surprising Adrian. What shot from the barrel was like fancy buckshot. It exploded outward with a belch of either smoke or steam, the thing's fat stock punching backward into Adrian's upper pelvis. The rounds then arced outward in a curve: a trajectory that seemed to follow the bell shape of a classic musket — a shape the multi-weapon didn't actually have.

With one shot, Adrian turned not only the three coming at him to paste, but cut those in a wide swath around them nearly in half. Its angle of fire was impossibly wide: not straight out like a pistol, but covering something like 120 degrees of field in front of him.

"Save the rest, Adrian!" Dee barked, and then Adrian remembered. What he'd just fired was meant to be a close-quarters finisher: an impressive, reaper-cutting blast that could only be fired thrice before the energy required to work it was gone.

The blue halfskulls had surrounded them. Carl was nowhere to be seen; Adrian hoped too late that he hadn't accidentally taken him out with the blast. The weapon was called Energesis. It fired what looked like buckshot, but was actually charged pellets made of grit gathered into balls by internal magnetism. A human could take an Energesis round in the chest and barely feel it, but the chemistry cut right through fiend flesh.

He'd gotten lucky. Assuming he hadn't hit Carl, none of his party was actually in danger.

Not in danger from Adrian's panic fire, anyway. There was plenty from the ongoing attack.

Everything was a blur. Adrian saw very little than the huddle that had formed around him and Lee Barnes, who was handling offense much better than Adrian even though he too was a Stitcher. He strained to see the others but could only make out Ray — and only knew because of their familiar, fraternal bond. Without trying, now that Ray's adrenaline had kicked in, Adrian could hear Ray's voice inside his head, counting his kills.

Twenty-one. Twenty-two. Twenty-four.

Then: *Shit.*

Something was wrong. Ray's words were more jumbled emotions than genuine words, conveying only controlled panic. He had made a life out of close calls and pushing limits. Even inches from being overtaken, Ray could be cucumber cool.

But it wasn't just Ray that Adrian sensed now; he could see pockets from above as he moved with the battle: places devoid of halfskulls and high on bodies, meaning places his fellow Roughnecks were busy fighting. They were no longer doing the courtesy of attacking in few-body waves. Unlike the time Ray and Adrian had been tested by their warehouse full of enemies, these soldiers were playing for keeps.

They'd mounded up on something large; one heavy Rollard rake and Ollie Davis appeared from beneath it, still in charge by the skin of his teeth. But there were also smaller scrums, and those could mean Dee, who was short, or Harrison, who fought from a crouch. They could also be places where one of the Roughnecks had fallen, and the halfskulls were finishing them off. Adrian tried not to think about it.

He fought on one hand, changing weapons and finding his groove with the new attachments, working to understand the scene on the other. His foes had backed him mostly up one of the rises by now, giving him an aerial view. He spotted Dee, Shannon, Lee, and Ray in an instant. Two more battle points meant at least two of the other three were still out there scrapping. He finally saw Carl, too. He'd scaled one of the tallest rocks — easy for halfskulls; they climbed like black bears.

What was Carl doing: the lone gray among all these blues? Carl had no face, so he couldn't be read visually. He projected no talk, so Adrian couldn't hear him. His mouth was his only expressive feature by human standards, and it had always looked monstrous. So was this conviction Adrian was seeing: Carl angry, preparing to leap in and fight? Or was it fear? Was Carl capable of fear?

Or was cowardice more true?

Halfskulls came. They didn't move the way they used to out of rifts; these arrived not as a single carpet attack but instead from all directions. He needed a wall to his back but couldn't find one. Right now a rampart would protect him more than limit him. He didn't need to back up. He needed at least one clear direction, now battling in three hundred and sixty degrees and barely keeping them at bay.

Zen, said Laurel's voice, now rational instead of accusing. *There's too much Zen Element inside them. Don't fight the bodies. Fight the Zen.*

His thumb toggled the weapon's function. A new nozzle rotated forward and snapped to full extension. They'd always known that certain weapons empowered particular classes of fiends instead of harming them; that's what made mixed-class riftfare so difficult. That's why so much emphasis had been placed on developing newer and better blunt-force weapons. Smashing and dicing was the only thing that worked on every class.

But with Laurel's hint, Adrian was starting to understand

why they weren't making as much headway with the halfskulls as they should be.

They had much, *much* more Zen Element in their bodies than was normal. And instead of dying after they were shot or bludgeoned or cut in half, many of the halfskulls were getting right back up — sometimes in pieces — and maintaining the fight.

His mind went deep, marrying what he'd seen and what he felt Laurel's ghost was trying to tell him to the body of knowledge he already had.

Halfskulls are Dorn class. Knowing what we know now about the collective mind, they should be controlled by a boss, which for Dorn class probably means a macerator. You fight Dorns with Rattlers. Resonance — and of course plain old Rollards — were what it took to defeat a Dorn.

But here and now, that was only partially true. There was no macerator nearby. They were too big to hide behind any of the obstacles within sight. Rollards weren't doing the job, and neither were the other, newer brute-force projectile weapons. Even bisected, these halfskulls still charged like the severed parts of zombies. Rattlers seemed dubious; he'd spotted Ray trying to use one moments ago without effect.

Don't fight the bodies. Fight the Zen.

She was telling him to ignore their classes, but to instead see the truth before him.

"P-Paulsons," Adrian said to Lee, who'd stayed close. "Use your Paulson attachment!"

"What?"

Lee didn't budge. He certainly didn't flick the selector to rotate-in his Paulson muzzle. By the old rules, just about the worst thing you could do when fighting Dorn class would be to fire Paulson rifles. They shot Zen rounds. Fire Zen at Dorn soldiers and they'd just lap it up to become even stronger.

But right now, Adrian's instincts told him the rules had changed.

These halfskulls were *already* full of Zen Element, their blood soaked with it well beyond normal.

Zen rounds were used against Gallance class rifts because Gallance soldiers were also overfilled with Zen. Shooting more Zen their way was like overfilling water balloons. When you fought Gallance, you fought the Zen, not the bodies. Classes meant nothing in themselves.

Classes were useful only because they told you something about the makeup of the fiend's body — vulnerabilities in that body that could be exploited. It used to be true that the bodies of Dorns, like halfskulls, were low on Zen element. But these fuckers were so full of the stuff they kept glowing blue. Half-skulls or not, their changed physiology made them more like Gallance than Dorn.

That meant Paulson rifles, firing Zen rounds. It made sense, but Adrian could only take it on faith.

He pulled the trigger and hoped. The front end of the thing exploded, launching a starburst of rounds that instead of rocketing at their targets, drifted toward them instead.

At first there was nothing. But then one by one, the creatures in Adrian's firing cone began to shake and glow even bluer. They stopped fighting, seeming to swell and distend. Mouths opened. Demonic cries filled the sky. Then something would rupture — usually the exposed brain — and a heavy azure rush would spill out.

Bodies collapsed, staying down for good this time.

Lee was watching, fighting one-handed, his mouth open in a gape.

Then his eyes focused and he shouted, "USE YOUR PAULSONS!"

The tide began to turn. Once equipped and firing, holes

started to open in the battlefield. Their new multi-weapons could self-reload Zen-based attachments if there was Zen in the air, and right now there was plenty.

Adrian spied Ray; as soon as he cleared himself a circle, he spray-fired at the ground around him, shooting the corpses of the fiends he'd killed earlier with his Rollard — kills that kept crawling forward and refused to die. The Paulson stopped them for good the same as it stopped the intact ones.

The halfskulls turned once they saw Paulsons being fired, intending to regroup. That wasn't supposed to happen. Even under the direction of a boss, no soldier caste ever turned back, just like no soldier caste was supposed to fight from all sides, storming their enemies like individuals.

"Don't let them get away!" someone yelled — Ray, Adrian thought. "They'll tell others we're here!"

The idea was weird, but felt true by now.

The halfskulls ran like sprinters, as best they could on their bony, brittle joints. The Legions and Stitchers were immediately at a disadvantage, too bogged down with equipment and armor to catch them and no way to cut them off at the rear.

Worse, there seemed to be a low-slung cave ahead — one whose floor appeared to arc down into a subterranean cavern. There could be anything down there, and already this battle had nearly ended them.

It looked like all was lost until a single figure interposed itself between the cave and the three hundred or so remaining blue halfskulls. The figure was gray, and against the wall of onslaught seemed very small.

It was Carl, standing with clawed feet wide, teeth chattering, as much of a scowl as was possible on his false face. His arms were up, hands hooked forward as if he planned to fight every one of the escapees hand to hand. But instead of advancing or retreating or engaging them, he merely seemed to tense. To Adrian, who blessedly had nothing left to fight, Carl looked like an amateur wizard trying to cast a spell.

One by one, the halfskulls stopped. They slowed casually, as if not sure why they were slowing at all. Then, slowly, every single one of them adopted the exact same posture as Carl: legs wide, arms wide, claws out and scowling.

"They'll rip him to pieces," Lee said.

But no. They hadn't stopped to fight Carl. They weren't in attack pose at all.

They were mirroring him.

Carl lowered his arms. The others lowered theirs. He brought his feet together. The others brought their feet together. Then Carl turned around, and the others followed suit.

They were facing the Roughnecks now, standing mute and dumbly. The wings of the wide fleeing formation tucked in as Carl walked in semicircles, soon becoming a tight scrum.

Do it, Carl thought at the humans when it was done.

Adrian understood first. He re-raised his Paulson and marched forward.

The others did the same. Shots fired, and soon the red plains around them were bleeding blue.

BUT NOT ALL OF the others did the same. It was only after the halfskulls had been dispatched that anyone thought to make a head count.

The attack scrum was Lee, Adrian, Dee, Ray, and Harrison, whose arm had been claw-raked so severely it looked like it might fall off. Ollie and Shannon were missing.

They found Ollie easily, due to his size. He'd been cut open by the halfskulls, overtaken by sheer numbers. A few half-living fiend corpses were still crawling over him, trying to feed.

Without words, Lee sprayed the scene with another blast of Zen rounds and all movement stopped. The Zen wouldn't hurt Ollie's body. When applied to human flesh, the element either mutated or healed. Ollie was too dead for either to happen now.

Finding Shannon took longer. They'd backed her into a corner, then beat more than cut her to death. Another Paulson blast cleared the second scene, and then with grim emotion Ray took charge, dragging both Ollie and Shannon onto two of the space blankets he'd had in his emergency pack.

Ironic that he had any, packed out of old habit from their conventional riftfare days. The last thing anyone would need, on this plane, would be to stay warm.

Once the bodies were on the blankets, Ray removed single-shot pneumatic injectors from the kit Dixon had given them. Each contained a compound with a long scientific name that everyone simply called *Undo*. It reversed the effects of Frog, meant for use only when the mission was over. It *was* over for Ollie and Shannon, though. Now it was time to retire with honor.

The injection took effect immediately. The internal protections given to the bodies by Frog evaporated, and once unprotected, both of them began to steam in the heat. First the water boiled away, and when that was done, the ambient temperature was enough to set them matchlessly aflame.

The air, according to a high-temp thermometer hanging from Dee's pack, was well over sixteen hundred degrees Fahrenheit. Within fifteen minutes, all that remained of Ollie and Shannon was ash.

Wordlessly, Ray shook the ash from their clothes and set them aside. He bundled up the space blankets and tied them with cords, then stowed both. Ollie had been massive, weighing in at over three hundred pounds of muscle. Desiccated, they'd later weigh his remains at eight. Together, the remains of their compatriots only added eleven pounds. The rounds they'd panic-fired at the battle's opening salvo had weighed more than that, leaving their party lighter, still, on exit than on entry.

The clothes caught fire and began to burn soon after. From the fire, Ray kicked out Ollie's sunglasses.

He set them on one of Hell's many rocks, upright and facing the direction they had yet to travel, so that even as he rested, Ollie could still look out for them.

22

THE HOURS AND DAYS

The march became a funeral procession. Literally, given the ashes on Ray Porter's back.

The emotional oppression of the place — that crushing, pessimistic, eager-to-fight feeling that'd come over everyone shortly after they crossed over — hadn't diminished at all. They'd forgotten it, gotten used to it, and gone on despite it, but that changed nothing. Adrian had no idea if the dreadnought was somehow still causing the down-dragging emotion or if it was the place itself making them morose and dull-eyed, but that didn't really matter. It didn't even matter that the subtle, corrosive malaise existed in the first place, seeing as they were professionals in a dangerous field and had dealt with worse.

What mattered was that they were coming to accept the feeling as normal. It was one thing to be crushed and another entirely to have no clue that you were even *being* crushed — to feel that "crushed" was normal.

There were two bodies, turned to dust, inside Ray's pack. There would probably be more before this was over — maybe so many there'd be nobody left to bring their remains home. If it was even possible to *get* home.

Only now was Adrian trying to remember if Dixon had ever mentioned a return trip. Maybe this was a suicide mission. Maybe they were supposed to already know that and already have accepted it. Maybe the best outcome would be to do what they had to do … and if they died in the doing, it would have to be enough.

But what exactly *did* they have to do?

Adrian no longer knew with much certainty. They talked about it over dinner that night: an event whose time came when nobody's legs would go any further and the clock seemed to suggest enough time had passed. The sky didn't darken here, suggesting evening. Nor did it lighten. The vista was always the same monotonous red-gray, like a cloudy place on an LSD trip.

"We're supposed to find Laurel's trail, then make contact with their queen. Or if the queen isn't amenable, maybe make contact with the visitors' resistance instead." Dee explained it as if Adrian had simply forgotten.

"I know what Dixon said," Adrian replied. "I *remember* just fine. I'm just not sure it feels right anymore."

Unbidden, he heard his father's voice in his head.

Sometimes you have to do the wrong thing, because real life is filled with grays, and sometimes there's a lot more to things than anyone else sees.

This wasn't exactly what Eldon had meant, but it just so happened to fit like a glove.

"They aren't *making* new weapons. They're *becoming* weapons. This is how they'll fight us — by becoming things we can't beat. We got lucky this time. I figured out the *they're-over-filled-with-Zen-Element* thing quickly enough that we could dial in on its weakness, but …"

Adrian paused. Actually *Laurel* had figured out the Zen Element thing (their need to use Paulson rounds, which had felt like suicide at the time), but he didn't want to tell the others. For one, it sounded crazy that she'd be talking to him from a distance. And for two, Laurel was just one more thing he wasn't sure of anymore — one more always-shifting variable he'd had to take on faith in a place where faith was hard to come by.

Who was to say that Laurel's voice wasn't just one more lure? They could be using her, seeing as they were capable of strategy now. She might not be the pot of gold at the end of the rainbow, but instead cheese on the trigger of the mousetrap.

"But at least there was something we could do about it this time," Adrian continued. "When they're pumped that full of Zen, brute force doesn't stop them. You chop them up into pieces and the pieces keep coming. So, we can't use Rollards or Punisher rounds on anything that glows blue, but at least we figured out Paulsons would take them down. But what happens when they come at us with a *different kind* of modification? A different kind of brand-new fiend — one that's not Zen-based? This time we were able to use Gallance class weapons, what if next time they don't have the weakness of a class we know how to fight, or we can't figure it out in time? The visitor armies are *learning*. Isn't that what Carl said, when he told us *he* wouldn't be able to do again what he did today?"

Nobody answered his rhetorical question. Truth was, they'd leapt with both feet into something far out of their league. Humans adapted by building new things. Fiends adapted by *becoming* new things — by sharing minds and knowledge without needing to stop and discuss. They would be ready for Carl's hive-mind trick if he tried to pull it again.

This time they'd made an ambush, and that might only be the beginning. Next time, Adrian's group might not find a weakness before they were all dead. Next time, Carl might try to woo the enemy and simply be ripped apart because they'd made their minds immune.

There was no getting around the terrifying fact that the Roughnecks were a mere six people without home-turf advantage ... and there was no way to forfeit, surrender, or call a time-out. They were staring down the barrel of superior offense and defense, yet had no choice but to play the game to the end.

The question fell away, unanswered.

They slept.

They woke.

They marched.

There were skirmishes along the way — uneven fights against sparsely-populated clusters of guardians who Carl said served the queen and who, blessedly, were not overwhelming in adaptation or number. Not all of them glowed blue; not all had been pumped full of Zen. Carl could tell friends from foes using his mostly-singular mind-bond, though so far he'd identified only enemies. If there were resistance members here (Carl had promised them Bosses like Dixon, more willing to talk than kill), they were few and far between.

Most of what Adrian had started to think of as visitors were still fiends, coming at the Roughnecks intent on destruction. So far, they'd been possible for Adrian, Ray, and the others to handle. But would that last forever?

Meanwhile, Adrian's feelings of Laurel only grew stronger. Sometimes he swore he could almost see her beside him. Sometimes she was a companion. Sometimes she was guilt and rage personified. The randomness of it made Adrian wonder if maybe he, not she, was the wildcard.

Maybe her signal was always the same, but his own mood vacillated, turning her raw psychic message into comfort or malice depending on the hour. Did that make his compass unreliable?

They were all beaten down. Morose. Discouraged. Sad. The two deaths had deepened all those ill feelings. Ollie and Shannon's fates sometimes felt inevitable for the rest of them as well. There were moments all of them seemed to waver, wondering if getting that inevitable thing out of the way now might be the better call.

They watched their rear. The huge rift, leading into the human-side warehouse complex controlled by Patel's army, had long ago stopped being visible even as a glow on the horizon. Adrian wondered at the physics. Was there an atmosphere here, beyond all the sulfur? Without an atmosphere, you could see forever. Was the fiend plane spherical, like Earth? Or was this a dimension where flat-Earth was possible? If their world was round, how big was it? How far had they needed to walk, before the horizon's curvature swallowed it?

Despite their inability to see the rift, they kept watching for signs of Graves's entry onto the fiend plane. Dixon had taken stabs at allowing them to communicate with him once the mission was underway, but nobody had any real hopes that it was possible.

Turned out it wasn't; they were now entirely cut off. The Army might be able to communicate cross-plane (Graves speaking to Patel the entire time he was here, for instance), but the Roughnecks sure couldn't. And so there was no way to know if Graves had entered. Dixon had told them only that it would happen "tomorrow," and now tomorrow was today.

Adrian's group would need to hurry. Graves would rush to the city and detonate his bomb, and their mandate was to arrive first and prevent that detonation.

Where *was* the visitor city? Adrian still had no clue; the

assumption upon which their entire mission was based seemed now to be a flimsy one.

The city was where Laurel was, and Adrian could find Laurel. But was that just a guess? Had anyone done advance research and recon to be sure, or had they simply rolled dice and hoped? Even if they could find the city, what about the bomb? Was it even a real bomb, or some other destructor the Army merely *called* a bomb?

Yet another thing about which they had no idea. The bomb, too, was yet one more facet of this that Dixon had known little about, and hence told the Roughnecks next to nothing.

I don't know, Dixon had said. *I just know setting it off will be bad.*

Bad because it will kill off their population? Or bad because it might sunder the planes?

Adrian, as he walked, no longer cared about the first one. So far he'd met exactly one fiend he would save, with other "on-their-side" visitors being merely hypothetical. His memories of the rendering room — all those supposedly innocent beings stolen from their hellbound homes and squeezed for Zen like oranges for juice — were now both distant and academic. Right now he cared about Laurel, he cared about his group, and in a vague *if-I-must* sort of way he supposed he cared about the fates of the worlds ... though in this place, he could take worldly salvation or leave it. Everything else could go to Hell. Again: literally.

Bad because it'll piss her off, Dixon had answered. Meaning the queen.

That's what Carl said, too — probably the reason Dixon believed it in the first place. Patel was underestimating her enemy. So was Graves. So was everyone everywhere. The public party line since sundering day was that there'd been a very near miss, but have no fear because government was here!

The blustering of politicians had led everyone to think that Fortune's little rift problem was solved. The demon-things people used to be so afraid of were nothing more than very stubborn roaches. But just like climate change, which had also seemed bad at first, politicians had talked about it a lot and that meant things were okay now. Fiends were no big deal after all the hot air, budget expenditures, and irrelevant law-making were over. It's not like a bunch of roaches would wage a counter-attack or anything. It's not like if we hit them hard, they'd strike right back.

Nobody was afraid of what the queen might do to humanity if humanity attacked the queen. Only the Rough-necks, who'd been here and knew just how terrified everyone should be — not of the visitors as things stood right now, but of the visitors if Graves tried to shove a grenade up what passed for their assholes.

That's what Adrian meant, about how being here changed everything. He didn't want to disobey Dixon's orders, or anyone else's. It was more that he was starting to wonder if those directives were obsolete — had maybe *been* since the day they were made. Only the Roughnecks had seen the blue half-skulls, so full of Zen that no amount of slicing and dicing could kill them. Only they had seen a group of soldier demons launch an ambush — something they were supposedly too dumb and roachlike to do.

Nobody else had been here. Nobody had felt the hard hand on the soul they all felt constantly now, creating an irresistible urge to dispair and give up.

Why get up? Why even bother?

That's what every one of Adrian's fellows said with their eyes whenever it was time to get back on the road after taking five.

Harrison's injury had been very bad. Now, fourteen hours

after being treated with a Zen Element ointment from the First Aid kit, it merely looked painful. Adrian had treated burns with Zen ointment last year and healed quickly without a scar, but the ointment Harrison used seemed at least twice as effective.

There was no question that Zen was powerful stuff. Valuable stuff. *Heaven-sent* stuff, really, though everyone on Earth called its origin point "Hell." Even Ray and Adrian's mother had received Zen treatment for her cancer. Now, doctors said she was in full remission. Did that make them hypocrites?

They were here to argue for peace.

Dear Queen: We are sorry for the raping of your people and your land. It was wrong, and we want peace. Zen Element is yours, not ours. We're some of the good ones. But if you wouldn't mind bleeding into this cup for us, that'd be great. Everyone on our plane wants to exploit what you have, and that's wrong, but our mother is the exception. We don't believe in exploitation except for this one case that's convenient to us.

Humanity was the worst.

That's what Adrian kept thinking, until he looked up and saw the storm-strewn red sky and felt the hand on his heart all over again, knowing it was influencing his thoughts and making him dour. This place got into your head. Made you want to give up. Either that, or the dreadnought was still reaching into his brain, with some stubborn tie to Adrian's fears and insecurities that transcended time and space.

Why me? Why can't I shake it?

Maybe because his tie to Laurel made him vulnerable — or perhaps visible — to the dreadnought's mind.

Or because there was no Laurel and never had been, and what Adrian thought was her reaching out to him was actually something else.

No. No. I can tell the difference. He told himself this over and over, over and over.

As they kept walking, following the most tenuous of feelings, Adrian focused in every empty moment on the feel of Laurel Gantry. He relived and sharpened old memories. He made his mind speak for her, so they could have conversations, and ignored the dissonance.

But deep down — or maybe right on the surface — he wondered if he might be lying to himself, creating something from nothing at all.

The more I deliberately recreate her presence, the more possible it becomes that I'm imagining her real signal out in the world. Maybe there is no signal, because Laurel is dead. Maybe I'm hypnotizing myself. Maybe I'm not even here. Maybe Ray never woke me up back in the bathroom that day. I was delusional then, so maybe I'm still delusional now. I could still be on the cool tile floor, dreaming every bit of this. Ollie and Shannon are alive, but I might be in a straightjacket in the real world, all of them around me shaking their heads as I ramble about my walk through Hell to find Laurel, knowing without question that the absence of her has finally made me snap. I'm not here. Or even me anymore.

The only consolation Adrian had, in fighting the hypnosis and unending monotony of this place, was that the others in the group seemed to feel the same way.

"We're being followed," said Lee Barnes.

Ray, beside him: "We're not being followed, Lee."

"We are. I keep seeing movement behind us. Someone's right behind us. Hot on our tail."

It wasn't true. Either that or whoever was chasing them was very good at hiding. Lee had been saying it for half a day now, and twice Dee had broken away, circled around while the other five marched on, and tried to spot their tail. There was none.

"Then maybe it's fiends. *Visitors,*" he corrected, though by now the euphemism was either a joke or said for Carl's benefit.

The idea of allies on this plane felt like a possibility that had withered into a lie.

Adrian knew, through some leakiness of their bond, that most in his group were like the population now, more than willing to think of this plane's residents as roaches.

"It's nobody," Dee said. "Not humans, not f … Not visitors."

"Maybe they can turn invisible. Maybe they can look like rocks."

Ray scoffed at this so abundantly that it was immediately clear to everyone that Lee should not be taken seriously. But Adrian's mental bond to his brother, thanks to the translator and Frog and Carl's mediating influence, was secondary only to his bond to Laurel, if it was her he was hearing. And he knew the truth: Ray had considered Lee's theory, about visitors being able to camouflage themselves. He kept looking back, wondering if rocks were their enemies.

Jesus. What if there were windmills here? Look at Ray. Look at his eyes. He'd run at them with Rollard drawn, attacking windmills just like Don Quixote.

Adrian laughed to himself a little, then stopped. He kept forming thoughts like spoken sentences. But to whom was he speaking? Who had that joke been meant for, if nobody could hear it?

Laurel. It's for you, Laurel. Answering her directly, because he needed to believe that she heard him.

But then her connection seemed to sever entirely, snapped like overstretched taffy. Stretching, stretching, then popping clean away if tugged. The suddenness of it made Adrian stop in his tracks.

The others stopped around him.

"What?" Ray asked.

Adrian didn't answer right away. When Laurel disappeared, she'd been replaced inside his mind with a picture clearer than television. It had lasted only a blink, and as he stared across the alien landscape Adrian began to think he might have imagined it.

But that couldn't be. Laurel was all that kept him going. If he'd lost his lead on her entirely, he might as well just kneel down right here and die, because what else was there — anywhere, anywhen?

The picture showed her in a protected room, surrounded by glass. Beyond her windows was a city made of flame. She'd looked a little different, probably because they'd changed her the way Frog had changed them. They'd taken her so she could teach them to refine Zen Element and make it stronger ... and that meant they needed her alive.

Alive for *then*, at least. But maybe not for *now*.

Adrian imagined her inside that room choking, slowly unbecoming the thing they'd made her. Slowly becoming human again — a body that, like Ollie and Shannon's once made human again, could do little else in this place but burn.

A city made of flame.

Dear God, he could see it on the horizon.

The queen was there, along with their mission's end. And Laurel, whose clock he felt sure had just begun ticking, was there.

He looked again. How far could it be?

Hours, not days.

23
ALL THE ZEN

Harrison Kim came to Ray an hour and a half later.

"Ray, you need to see this."

He took the small, handheld instrument Harrison gave him, but for a while Ray didn't so much as look down at it. Five minutes earlier, they'd come around a corner it'd taken them a half-hour to round, and now that they were past it they could see Hell's city so much better than before.

It didn't resemble a human metropolis at all, but there was no denying what it was. Even farther back, Ray had spent the rest points using the group's heat-shielded binoculars to study the place, trying to understand its impossible architecture. He understood now, seeing it closer through those same binoculars: Their buildings were made of rock and bone. When fiends died, it seemed their bodies were repurposed here. It even made sense: GEN had said for decades how incredibly strong fiend bones were. And why not? They were hardened like steel in a forge, apparently tough enough for construction. Why invent steel? They *were* steel.

Ray considered the device, but what he saw made no immediate sense to him.

"What am I looking at?"

"Energetics," Harrison told him. "Something about the sky over those structures is letting me bounce a signal down onto them. Look, Ray. Look how much Zen Element they have ahead."

Ray saw it now. Harrison was right; the energetics around the city were immense. That wasn't entirely unexpected: More visitors in one place was sure to mean more Zen. But this was more than that. It looked like they'd drained every human stockpile from the other side to have this much in one place. Or (and this felt possible, maybe even likely) this could be Laurel's doing, if she succeeded in teaching them how to refine it.

"These readings can't be right."

"No, man," Harrison said, tapping the pad. "I compensated for any bounce refraction. I'm telling you; they're stacked. This right here is either a giant wall made of the shit or ..."

"Or?" Ray waited. Whatever Harrison said next was the real answer. There was no point in making an actual wall of Zen Element.

"Or it's something like half a million fiends."

"There's no way."

"You sure? How many people are there in New York City?"

"Yeah, but you're talking about soldiers. There might be a few million *citizens* in New York, but ... what? Maybe you could wrangle a few *thousand* soldiers."

Harrison just watched Ray's eyes. Ray understood; with fiends and their collective minds, citizens were usually interchangeable with soldiers.

"We're walking right into this, man. Adrian's walking us right into it."

"He knows what he's doing," Ray said.

"He knows where he's going. That's different. You know what I keep thinking about? Nobody ever assigned a mission commander. Nobody's in charge. What's going to happen when we disagree?"

"We're a unit. We make decisions as a unit."

Harrison didn't answer. He just looked at Ray with concern — they both knew that was bullshit. They'd been deferring to Adrian because he was the compass. But navigators deferred to generals in the real world.

"I already showed this to Adrian," Harrison said. "He didn't care."

"Then he must have a plan."

Harrison stabbed the screen with his finger, frustrated now. "This is his plan, Ray! To march us right into it! He's not thinking straight. He's lost his fucking mind."

"Watch it," Ray said.

"We aren't equipped for this. Not even close. How big was that ambush? A few hundred, all halfskulls with the same fighting pattern, all falling with the same rounds? You more than anyone know that primordial form shit is true. *Look*, man."

Again Harrison slammed his insistent finger into the screen. "You can read this same as I can. There's two percent here that are differentiated. *Two percent!* And look what they are! Bosses. Look." He scrolled on the aerial map view, touching identified markers and bringing up their IDs. "Boss. Boss. Boss. *Super*boss. Jesus Christ, Ray. You think this outfit can handle even one boss? We got three Legions and two Stitchers. *Three people* who've faced a boss before, and that was under the old rules. But hey. Let's be optimistic. Let's pretend we can defeat the bosses. We got multi-weapons now, so maybe we can. *Maybe*. But—"

"I get it."

"—ninety-eight percent of the Zen here is undifferentiated. Ninety-eight percent! That's almost all of it!"

"I know how math works, Harrison."

"Then you know that ninety-eight percent primordial Element plus five people and a halfskull equals fucked right up the ass! We can't take down that many even if they *have* taken a class form we understand and know how to fight. But they haven't taken form! We walk in there, they'll know we can't handle variety. A bunch will become Classicals, a bunch will become Dorn, some might even Voltron-up and combine to some goddamn superboss we haven't ever seen. That's nothing but naked options ahead of us, brother. They can turn into whatever kind of demon suits them. We'll be overrun in seconds. Forget minutes. *Seconds*. Are you hearing me, Ray? We're walking into a blender and your brother won't listen!"

"Okay. I'll talk to him."

But it was like Harrison said. Adrian wouldn't hear him.

"She wouldn't have called us if we couldn't get through," Adrian told Ray.

"Who? Laurel?"

"Of course Laurel."

"It's half a million of them at the gate. Laurel must be assuming you don't need to be told you should go around them."

"'Go around'?"

Ray nodded. This was Harrison's idea, planned in detail. He explained, showing Adrian a path through the newly-mapped land ahead, thanks to Harrison's sky bounce. The city was nestled inside a cup-shaped feature in the land, surrounded on three sides by rises like mountains, leaving only the front flat and open — something the fiends might have ground down themselves for access. The flat, open spot was the only area that was guarded. The mountains, on the other hand, seemed to be free and clear.

Adrian listened, but never slowed. They'd analyzed while continuing to march. "No. We aren't going through the mountains."

"'No'?"

"It'll add days to the journey."

"So?"

"She doesn't have that long."

"Who?" Then he realized. *"Laurel?"*

"She's in trouble, Ray. I think she's dying."

"How could you know that?"

"I know."

Now Ray could see what Harrison had seen in Adrian — the thing that'd made him say that his brother was losing it. He was wild-eyed, gazing ahead, mouth slack as if in the grip of some weird palsy. He wouldn't even look at Ray. He could only see his goal, right through all the carnage in between.

"You know what they told us," Ray said. "This bond thing you have isn't literal. *Can't* be literal, because half of it is you and half of it is her. She's sending, but it's your mind that's interpreting. You could be interpreting wrong."

"I'm not wrong."

"When she was talking to you earlier. When we were back at home. She didn't tell you exactly what to do, did she? No. She spoke to you in image and metaphor. 'Follow the heat.' Why didn't she say something more specific and helpful? You know why. It's because everything she said was filtered through you."

"I *know* her, Ray."

"We can't march right through that many soldiers."

"She'll make a path for us. Somehow. She knows them. Maybe even knows the queen."

"'Knows the ...' Shit, Ade, do you even hear yourself?"

"She's calling me, Ray. She needs my help. She wouldn't call if I couldn't reach her."

Ray grabbed Adrian to stop his single-minded walking. Adrian pulled Ray's hands away, shoved him hard, then kept on walking.

"Will you just think for a minute? How the fuck do you plan to get through that many of them?"

"Resistance," Adrian said. "Allies in the crowd. You heard Carl; they're not all the same."

"So they're just going to let us walk into their city?"

"We can explain! There's a psychopath somewhere behind us, and he has a bomb! We can explain that we're friends, and they'll let us in!"

"Adrian. My brother. Just think. If this is a problem for us, it'll be a problem for Graves. He'll have to go around same as we will. This doesn't jeopardize the mission to make contact with the queen."

"It jeopardizes Laurel."

"This is about the goddamn human race, not saving your girlfriend! You can't risk the greater good just because you think she's in trouble!"

"I don't *think!* I *know!* I know Laurel's going to die if I don't reach her!"

"How the fuck could you possibly know that for sure?"

"Because I can't hear her anymore! I can't feel her! She's gone!" Adrian looked like he might fury-cry, but then pulled it together. "I won't abandon her, Ray. I won't."

Ray stepped in front of Adrian fully, again putting both hands on both of his brother's shoulders. "Listen to me, dammit. If you lost the bond, you know nothing. You're fucking blind. I won't let you get us all killed and ruin our chances of stopping Patel and Graves just because you feel guilty."

Adrian paused for a moment. Then he slapped both of Ray's hands away and socked him in the face. Ray staggered, then fell to the red dust below.

"The only possible bond to the queen goes through Laurel. If she's gone, that bond goes through me. You can't talk to the queen without me, Ray. Without my consent, this mission dies right here."

"Absurd."

"Maybe absurd. Maybe true. Maybe I'm making it up, and anyone can talk to the queen." He flicked his eyes to the others, who were seeing all of this but hearing few of their words. "But this has gone on my gut from the start. Even Dixon said that."

Adrian gave a smile with no joy.

"Let me ask you this, Ray. When it comes right down to it, who do you think the others will believe?"

24

A POTENTIAL SOLUTION

The communicator crackled.

Graves wanted to smash it and go on instinct. Fucking demon technology. Sometimes it worked, sometimes it was total balls. It took much longer than normal to get a signal, but then Patel was on the line amid a billion fireflies of static.

"Come in, Graves. I'm barely reading you."

"I said we're nestled right up under their city's balls." Last time he'd said "close to the city," but all this difficulty communicating — and all the cat-and-mouse spy shit, instead of good old-fashioned action — was making him testy. Graves didn't care right now if Patel thought he was out of line or vulgar. She could deal with his language or she could walk through the giant flaming vagina herself and try to do better.

She was smart enough not to nitpick. "I have your scout report. The people here downloaded visuals from the drone you sent back and agree with your assessment."

"How nice of them, back on their comfy couches."

"The terrain on three sides is highly problematic. Carry the frequency bomb that high and you'll likely get sparking from the electrical systems above. It might damage the equipment. That means you'll need to find a way to enter through the low-elevation apron at the front. Somehow, you'll need to clear a path."

"Exactly like I said."

"Excuse me, Lieutenant?"

"Exactly like I said … *ma'am*."

Patel didn't like that, but again: He dared her to come down here and do this herself. Her ass wasn't broiling right now. She wasn't being asked to hold her dick in her hands, babysitting Dixon's fucking traitor squad without being seen instead of charging in with guns drawn like real men would.

"We have a potential solution," Patel said.

"As do I, ma'am."

"Explain."

"I have already solved the problem of a frontal assault. And at the same time, I have solved the problem of Dixon's little shit suckers."

"Your orders specify that no harm comes to the Porters' team, Lieutenant Graves."

He grinned at that, happy their call was audio-only. Harm had already come to the so-called Roughnecks. His people had watched it live through a stabilized spotting scope. Two of their number had been eaten to death. Two down, five and their little pet to go.

And who really cared about the rest? The Porters' purpose had been to guide Graves's team to the city without Graves's team's ill intent raising flags for all the scabs out there. That purpose had been fulfilled. With the city on the horizon, they could now creep up in their violence-masking bubble of glee and take down Queen Roach. All that was left was to get through the front door … but Porter could do them one last favor before dying, which was what Graves had in mind.

There was a huge burst of static. The call died, then Patel called back on a different frequency.

"Goddamn scabs are putting up some kind of psychic wall, I guess," Graves said of the static.

"It's not them. The interference is coming from our end."

Graves's eyebrows raised. "Oh?"

"It's a prisoner here. The one they call the dreadnought. It's ... up to something."

Graves snickered. "Nothing the couch-asses up there can't handle, I'm sure. *Ma'am.*"

"I still need you to explain your plan, Lieutenant."

"My comms man was scrubbing the frequencies earlier, and we found something really interesting on one of them. It's not an EM broadcast like radio or anything you'd expect."

"Then what is it?" Graves asked.

"Funny enough, my guy's a med tech in civilian life and you know what he said it looked like to him? An EEG. You know, one of those brain scan things where it makes little lines going up and down and—"

"I know what an EEG is."

"He thinks it was the bond between Adrian Porter and his girlfriend. Whatever he's been homing in on, listening to her bitch all the way from Hell's prison, it made real waves. A real frequency we can detect."

"It *was* the bond?" Patel repeated.

"Yes, ma'am. Past tense."

"Why past tense?"

"Because we jammed it, ma'am. Cut it off pretty as can be."

"*What?* Why?"

Graves explained. What they needed most, if they had to make a frontal assault, was a distraction. Porter was obsessed;

they'd seen and heard that much from whirligig surveillance. The theory went that if Porter stopped hearing from Laurel Gantry, he'd freak the fuck out, then become idiotic enough to charge into the lion's den. And that was bearing out just fine.

It was nice, in a way. Porter had led them to the front door, and now he and the others would die opening it. No loose ends.

"*No,* Lieutenant; do you hear me? Un-jam that frequency immediately. These orders are coming straight from the top: Adrian Porter is to be—"

Graves had started rolling his eyes the second Patel started protesting. Now he circled his finger at the comms man, who was already adjusting the settings to fuck up the reception — not interference, plain old sabotage this time.

Patel was still ranting. Graves ranted back, knowing she'd hear only chops and static.

"Graves? Graves, you're breaking up!"

"Sorry, ma'am. It's the dreadnought fucking with us."

Then he drew a finger across his neck, and comms cut the call entirely.

25

ONE AND THE SAME

Adrian grabbed his head. The others looked on, most worried for their immediate futures. Ray looked on for another reason: He was quite sure Adrian was losing his mind. They'd had their big public fight and things had gone exactly as Adrian said they would: Scared of the soldiers ahead or not, the Roughnecks would follow Adrian, not Ray. Even Harrison had been swayed reluctantly to Adrian's side, and Harrison was the one who'd brought the intel; Harrison should know better.

But Adrian said the only way to reach the queen was through him, and that meant trusting the resistance to somehow get them into the city. Trusting Laurel, who was either dead or giving her suggestions in absentia.

Ray stepped toward Adrian, but Carl stopped him.

It's the dreadnought, Carl said. *He is in your brother's head.*

The dreadnought on our plane? The one being held captive?

There is only one of his kind. And he is only as captive as he wishes to be.

You're saying he wants to be there, in our prison?

Prison for you, but staging ground for him, Carl said.

Staging ground for what?

For his return to the city.

Ray shook his head, not understanding.

You call him dreadnought, Carl replied, *but we call him king.*

It made sense. They'd met the great demon before. Ray himself had looked it in the eye. Its presence that day had changed all the rules. It had the power to command every army. To stop the sundering with a thought. To make their grand deal, and abduct Laurel through means they'd never discovered.

The combined brigades of Fortune had managed to capture the dreadnought and imprison it shortly after, but Ray and Adrian had spent a lot of time wondering how it had been possible. No known tech at the time could have felled the dreadnought, and Ray doubted their new and improved tech could do it now.

He thought of what Carl said: *He is only as captive as he wishes to be.*

It was just another con. The king had let himself be taken, and was now right where he wanted to be.

What's it doing to Adrian? Ray asked.

Asking for help.

What do you mean?

The queen gained enough support to turn our world against him. Now he wants a way back home. She has blocked him out. Removed him from the consciousness of the others. She controls it. Above all minds, our royals have the ultimate say.

And it thinks Adrian can help it?

Carl nodded — a strange gesture for someone with barely a head, but the halfskull had learned from the humans. *Adrian can.*

How?

No matter how many times we fracture, our world still has only a single mind at the highest level. Now there's a human among us.

Laurel?

Laurel.

Ray wanted to hear more, but Harrison was tugging at his jacket, demanding attention. This was new information, requiring discussion. He had a picture of Laurel as a grain of sand inside an oyster, on its way to becoming a pearl. She was a tiny fracture in a pane of glass — one tiny weakness in an otherwise perfect crystalline structure just waiting for a nudge.

Ray turned, ready to shout Harrison down. He stopped when he saw they'd been surrounded.

Behind them were six hellbringers, massive and unbeatable by such a small band as theirs even if they were taken one at a time.

The closest one came to kneeling, still towering high above them all. It spoke to Ray in the same way he'd heard their voices before, this one far less calibrated than Carl's mind. Its thoughts came out without smoothness, half images and half ill-formed words.

Lay down your weapons, it seemed to say.

The roughnecks looked from one to the other, each considering disobedience. Each then looking to the other five hellbringers, deciding it was smarter to comply. So this was how it ended? Ray's concerns about the millions of soldiers ahead were pointless after all. They hadn't even made the city. They'd been found within a stone's throw of it.

Then the lead hellbringer looked at Carl, and Carl, without eyes, looked back.

You found them. You brought them to us, the hellbringer said to Carl.

Ray looked from one to the other, wondering if he'd been

betrayed. He didn't know if he should relax now, or if his dying act should be to rip out Carl's throat.

Adrian came forward, looking between the halfskull and the six massive bosses. Then he asked the question every one of them was wondering.

Are you resistance? Or are you servants of the queen?

Both, the hellbringer said. *The queen leads the resistance. They are one and the same.*

26

EXACTLY WHAT HE HAD TO DO

Adrian thought he understood, though the situation was both political and complicated. Hell or not, the king and queen's story was time honored.

One had been in charge. The other wanted to be in charge. The rest was details.

Adrian and the others were transported in interlinked shackles that felt metallic but did not burn, and as they walked surrounded by hellbringers, Carl did his best to explain. The inhuman plane was not immune to human issues, such as power grabs and struggles. For as long as Carl knew, the royals had ruled as a pair, but Adrian's mind saw the arrangement as more like first and second than true equals.

There were no elections, no changes of rule, no opportunities for the less-powerful of the two to take command. Instead, the king would always be in charge. What he said went, no matter whether anyone — including the queen — liked it.

And as it turned out, even the shifting minds of the fiends were capable of feeling rage and strife. Of not liking the king's way of doing things at all.

The dreadnought they'd met on sundering day (the same dreadnought now held in Fortune, perhaps for his own reasons according to Carl) had been a tyrant. The shifting hive mind had done nothing to diminish the feeling of tyranny; even shared minds felt loss and strife and pain.

There was work to be done in Hell — structures to build, bodies to be shepherded before birth and re-integrated after death, and a sort of mental bookkeeping their shared consciousness required that Adrian's single mind couldn't understand at all — and the king worked his people to death to get it done well and fast and to his precise liking.

Of course there could have been room for leniency. Of course the work could have been done to lesser degrees that would have been fine and would have resulted in less strife, less pain. But that had been true in the time of human pharaohs, and yet they'd worked slaves to death for the pyra-mids — permanent testaments to their greatness.

This was the way of the dreadnought, and the rest of the shared mind had hated it.

The queen, Carl explained, had slowly gathered support behind the scenes. The higher up Hell's caste system, the more minds were separate. On sundering day, their king had told Adrian and Ray that the soldier demons the brigades slaugh-tered were so relentless because they were not truly individu-als. Instead, they were like skin cells on the hand of one large organism, unimportant in and of themselves.

That wasn't actually true, though. Although Carl was unique in having a single consciousness, the others still couldn't be dismissed as mere cannon fodder. The arrange-ment felt to Adrian like hypnosis. Soldiers did what their leaders demanded because their minds gave them no choice ... but still, beneath it all, even halfskulls could be reluctant and unsatisfied.

And so the queen had played on this, enlisting the help of the "mental bookkeepers" Carl had mentioned. She'd been able to shift the group mind in her favor, promising change in a skewed way the whole could almost understand. For nearly a year before the sundering, she made her plans, quietly consolidating power.

The sundering itself was the trigger for her plan. On the day Adrian met the dreadnought, the dreadnought had relented on the sundering: taking Laurel, allowing the planes to heal without ripping them apart. By that point, though, "the sundering of worlds" had been been sold to the other plane's population as the way things could finally change for the better.

Ever since Eldon Porter made contact through the first rift, Hell had been decaying from lost Zen. Lost Zen made the king's rule insufferable. Sundering was supposed to equalize the planes and relieve all that suffering … so when the king decided not to proceed, very few in Hell were happy.

Now they would have to keep suffering, counting on the human scientist to show them how to make their limited Zen powerful enough to reverse the decay. If relief was still coming through Laurel's work, it would now take years to manifest … years spent in Hell's version of Hell. It wasn't the news any of the fiends wanted.

So the queen struck, stealing the throne with the help of her many, many supporters. Her platform was simple: *We should have sundered. The king is weak. We must oust the king, and put the queen in charge.*

At the time, her uprising — which happened a-little-too-coincidentally-timed with the dreadnought king's being "captured" by the humans — felt like the victory of a resistance. Now, though, the picture Carl painted of queenly rule wasn't as rosy: *Meet the new boss, same as the old boss.*

The queen, who had once promised freedom from the tyranny of the king, quickly became a much bigger tyrant. She'd wanted power for a very long time. Now she had it and refused to ever let it go.

One of the hellbringers gave a mighty grunt and swiped at Carl, breaking his mental link to Adrian. Adrian saw the swipe happen inside his mind as well: the hellbringer's consciousness attacking Carl's for daring to tell Adrian too much. Beyond sensing it as a black sword through their shared mindscape, however, Adrian couldn't read or hear the hellbringer's thoughts at all. Its message was meant for Carl alone.

His reaction told Adrian everything: Carl's caste had supported the queen when she'd been "resistance against the king," and so had these particular hellbringers. Things had changed, though. *Were humans the enemy?* The answer seemed to be *yes* by default. Even the Roughnecks, who'd come to communicate and warn about the military, would be guilty until they proved themselves innocent.

Hey, Adrian tried to say to the hellbringer, though it was harder to speak mentally to anyone who didn't want to listen. *We're on your side. Give us a break, will you?*

The hellbringer either didn't hear or refused to acknowledge him. It kept marching forward, tugging at the chains that bound them all together.

"Lookie here," Graves said with a chuckle.

He handed his binoculars to Nick Biehn, laying prone beside him. The ground under their bellies, as they looked out across the Martian-like landscape, was hot enough to brand cattle. None of them felt it. Graves was really digging this Frog shit. Made them impervious like tanks.

As Biehn raised the binoculars, Graves gave the punchline:

"Dead assholes walking. That's even better than them charging in with Porter's balls in a twist."

Biehn spied, focused, and considered. He was a droll type — not nearly as fun as Graves.

"We wanted chaos. This is too orderly."

"Exactly," Graves said. "It's *better* than chaos. I hoped that dickhole would run in waving grenades, threatening the scabs and the their big fat queen unless they set his girlfriend free. That would have been a case of *Kill 'em all and let God sort 'em out.* Literally *God.* You believe in God, Sergeant?"

Biehn knew better than to answer that one.

"Now look at 'em," Graves went on. "Nice and tidy. Right now they're saying, 'We caught the folks we knew were coming. Somehow they got around our gauntlet, those sneaky little fucks, but we caught 'em anyway. Look at them, dammit."

"I'm looking, sir."

Graves chuckled again. "They think they're us. The army the human plane sent?" He pointed at the group in the distance, which looked like ants around a dropped French fry without the binoculars. "That's it, as far as the scabs are concerned."

"Sir," Biehn said, lowering his specs, "their guard line will still be intact. There will be no scramble. With them in custody, we still have to penetrate their forward defenses in order to deliver our ordinance."

Graves looked behind him. The rest of the unit was laying low behind the rise, their temporary encampment covered in a reddish mesh that served as camouflage. He could see the bomb beneath one of the canopies. It was an innocuous-looking thing, for all the power GEN said it had. It looked like a silver basketball inside a skeletal support structure. They had the makings of a catapult should they decide to lob it into the belly of the beast, but intel said it would be most effective if placed specifically, by hand.

Graves didn't want to live forever. It was more important that the job be done right than that any of his people go home when this was over. Biehn knew it. Everyone knew it. They'd follow orders, but Graves's death wish — or at least death-willingness — made them all uneasy.

"We will need to lob it in after all, sir," said Biehn.

Graves looked his man in the eye for a long time. Far too long. He needed Biehn to know he wasn't fooling anyone. The rest of the unit wanted to use the catapult — to lob the bomb into the belly of the beast. This was their excuse ... but that's all it was.

To Graves, who knew lobbing was an inferior way to do this most important job, their grasping of this excuse was pure cowardice ... and right now Graves needed Biehn to know he knew it.

"Nothing changes. Frontal assault. We punch a hole and push forward until we're close enough to shove it it up what passes for her snatch. You hear me, Sergeant?"

Biehn considered his CO's eyes. Then he nodded like a good little boy. "Yes, sir. But the distraction you hoped Porter would be still hasn't—"

Graves interrupted him with a knowing smile. "Give him time. Things might look grim for that crew up there in shackles ... but I for one still believe in the idiocy of love."

ADRIAN WASN'T sure why they stopped.

Maybe it was to scout ahead. He'd gotten the impression from Carl that not everyone in this plane was on the same page. There might be enemies around. Ironically, there was now a resistance to the resistance. Many visitors with individual or semi-individual minds had once supported the queen over the king, but now many of those same minds had turned to supporting something else over the queen.

What that "something else" was, Adrian couldn't tell. It was all still mental whispering. Beyond what Carl sent him deliberately, Adrian's human brain was still inadept at overhearing.

"What? What's going on, Ade?" Ray asked.

Adrian looked over his brother's shoulder.

Dee, Harrison, and Lee were standing behind him, watching them expectantly. This seemed to be everyone's question, not just Ray's. Carl was no help anymore. The hellbringers apparently doubted his loyalty after all that time telling Adrian the queen's history. Now they wouldn't let him out of their sight.

From what Adrian gathered, the group holding them in shackles now was the original resistance — those who'd helped the queen overthrow the king.

Carl was part of that group, which was why he'd led the Roughnecks to the hellbringers in the first place. But did that make Carl a friend or a foe? Adrian was torn. On one hand, Carl hadn't told any of them they were on track to rendezvous with anyone. But on the other hand, it was clear that Carl hadn't wanted his human compatriots in chains. He'd expected them to be greeted warmly by the hellbringers, not treated like prisoners.

In answer to Ray's question, Adrian explained what he'd gotten from Carl about the new resistance to the old resistance. Now that the queen and her supporters were in charge, the supposed benevolence of their platform had changed. Now others were rising against the queen, but this time she was taking precautions. The queen knew how she'd seized power, and didn't want anyone to seize power from her in the same way.

They were many-times fortified now. Highly suspicious. It made Adrian wonder who were the good guys and who were the bad guys. Or perhaps more accurately, it made him understand completely that there *were* no good guys. There *were* no bad guys. As the old song went, there's only you and me and we just disagree.

It left Adrian unsure how to answer Ray's follow-up questions. They were all variations on the same query: *Whose side are we on? Who, in this brewing civil war, do we want to win?*

The queen, who'd toppled the tyrant king?

Or those who wished to topple the queen ... so *they* could become the next tyrant in town?

"Do we still try to talk to her?" Ray asked, as if Adrian would have any idea. He jangled his chains, which had been nailed into a rock by one of the hellbringers as simply as clipping keys to a keychain. "Did Dixon say *anything* about a scenario like this?"

The answer, of course, was no, and Ray damn well knew it. Dixon had been making a guess. He'd assumed that anything the Roughnecks did to counter Patel and Graves's Plan of Destruction would be a step in the right direction. He only knew that if Patel got her way, the queen would have *her* way in response.

The Roughnecks confirmed that Dixon's fears were grounded. They'd already met one group of blue demons, so full of Zen Element they'd been nearly unbeatable and indestructible. If Graves accomplished what he'd come here to do, the queen's forces would loose Zen-stuffed demons through the big rift and any other rifts that remained. They'd eventually force the sundering the queen had wanted all along.

In the meantime, Fortune would become an occupied land — a literal Hell on Earth.

"Dixon took a shot," Adrian said. "He wasn't entirely right, and he wasn't entirely wrong."

It didn't answer Ray's question, or have to. There *was* no answer. Truth was, they were cut off. Truth was, they had no way to get orders — not from Dixon, not from anyone. There was no going back: The rift of their passage was sealed, the big rift was guarded from both sides, and nobody on the crew had any idea how to open new rifts.

They could only improvise. Simply guess, same as Dixon, and do the best they could with whatever information they had.

"Then what do we—?"

"I don't know, Ray."

"Can we—?"

"I said *I don't know,* Ray."

He wasn't entirely telling the truth. There were two bits of information Adrian hadn't bothered to tell him. Brother or not, even Ray might not understand.

Laurel had once told him about the dead zones that appeared around rifts — areas she'd called "zones of inhibition." She'd said Zen Element was bio-consumptive. It devoured living things from the human plane. Their shackles were strong because they were made of Element, their bodies protected from it only because Frog had made them part fiend.

Adrian also knew that his urgency had been building to a fever pitch ever since her beacon died. The sudden severing of her mental voice meant that she was in trouble; he felt sure of it. Her time might be running out. His time for drastic action was rapidly approaching.

He'd managed to work two small items out of his sleeve pocket during their last hour of death-march. The first was his supplementary Frog injector, provided by HQ should his mutation begin to fail. The second was the emergency tube of Adrenalix they'd all carried since the riftfare days: so-called Soul Balm, which could stop and restart a human heart to fix fiend wounds. They'd been warned not to use Adrenalix while on the fiend plane, since that start-stop might undo Frog's work, turning them mostly human again.

"We're going to march with them to the city," Adrian told Ray, "and then we're going to play it by ear."

Ray waited, but Adrian just stared in a way that was so unlike his usual self. This Adrian was harder. Colder. This was the Adrian Porter who, for once, meant to step up and do the foolish, foolhardy thing that only Ray would usually do.

Ray saw the look in his brother's eyes. Then, looking somewhat troubled, he walked back to the others, watching Adrian all the way.

Adrian watched him back, unblinking.

The rules had changed. Laurel needed him. Things might still work out the way Dixon wanted, but they also might not. He would hope for the best, but plan for the worst. Failure might once have been an option for Adrian. Now it wasn't an option at all.

Ray wanted to know what Adrian planned once they entered the city and were brought before the queen.

Adrian palmed the two small cylinders. *What would he do?* The answer was simple:

Exactly what he had to do.

27

THE CITY OF FIRE

An unknowable amount of time later, the Roughnecks arrived at the city while Graves and his soldiers watched from a distance, waiting for what Graves assured everyone would become their chance.

The lead hellbringer stopped the chained procession at the gates of the city of fire. The fire itself turned out to be more like a mirage than literal, though that made the spectacle no less impressive. The buildings weren't actually aflame, but only because everything in and around the city was essentially already burning. The licking yellow tongues they'd seen from the distance — proper flames, familiar to those on Earth — were mostly undulations in the rock that made up the structures. The rock seemed to have within it shifting crystals that rotated to catch scattered light rather than those same crystals being frozen in a matrix. The effect was a luminescent sort of wave effect, like burning. But atop it, the ground and walls and even sometimes the sky seemed to smolder and smoke, heat waves rising ardently enough that from the back of the procession, those at the front looked hazy — something like a mirage, or a fever dream.

Adrian found he could hear them. He could hear the demons in this place.

At first he didn't know why. Nobody else seemed to hear; only Adrian shot his head side to side, hair whipping, as voices appeared from all corners. But as he became used to the chaotic mumbling of what sounded like hundreds of thousands of souls (it was like party chatter: audible as a whole, but not a single voice distinct), Adrian began to understand.

It was the dreadnought again: reaching into Adrian's mind from distances that it turned out didn't matter, maybe because Laurel had opened a crack or maybe because Adrian, in his agitation, had grabbed that crack with both hands and ripped it wider.

Anything to hear better.

Anything to understand more.

She might be anywhere in this place. Anywhere at all. The geography of the fiend plane was incomprehensible to the mind of almost any human (Erika Dale's crumpled-ball theory was only now starting to be accepted), but the murmur of alien voices somehow imbued Adrian with disconnected bits of understanding, allowing him to see the truth.

Their plane was everywhere and nowhere at once. It spanned the Earth, yet folded back to this single city. Laurel had theories along those lines, playing off of Erika's first hints on the matter, and she'd told Adrian about it in mathematical terms he'd only grasped a little. Laurel's term for the whole thing was "reduction." She said that yes, their world was enormous ... but it could still be "reduced down" to a single populated place in the way fractions could be reduced to their lowest common denominators.

Right now, he didn't need to understand anything more

than the fact that there was only one place Laurel could be if she was still alive, and it was here. Even if he didn't understand the math — even if the topology theories were wrong — she could still *only be here* — with the queen, at the center of everything.

Laurel would be here because the Zen Element was here. She'd been abducted so she could teach them how to refine it and make it stronger. She'd do as they asked, because they'd give her no choice. Adrian knew these things. She'd been inside his head for days, and inside his heart for so much longer.

But *where* was she? Even if the Roughnecks had stormed this place with weapons — and if those weapons were sufficiently effective, which their current weapons weren't — they'd need to know where to look if Laurel was the endgame. And for Adrian, Laurel *was* the endgame. Dixon's plan would be accomplished along the way, if there was time for world-saving.

You're being absurd. You're going crazy. The world matters more, Adrian.

He ignored the voice inside. His teeth wouldn't stop gritting. He didn't care about surviving anymore, if survival was even possible. He'd made a Devil's bargain before. He could simply make another one.

Let Laurel go. Take me instead, the way you planned from the beginning.

If only you'd let us, said a newer, deeper voice with which Adrian was intimately familiar by now. *If only we'd sundered the planes, and you and your brother had come to our side to fight with us.*

The dreadnought. The voice of their deposed king, held in an Earthly prison.

Your father bridged the worlds, it went on, stronger in this place as if the city was its own antenna. *Eldon Porter left an imprint on us, as he made his first contact, just as we imprinted on him. He was part of us and we were part of him. You are his legacy. You and Ray. Things could have been different, had you listened.*

But Adrian had been in the moment, terrified, sure the world was about to end in a rain of fire.

He was human. He'd scuttled away from oblivion like any human or roach. He remembered with shame how quick he'd been to offer them Denny Brennan, because Denny knew how to refine Zen and help save their world.

Adrian had been full of justifications in the minute or so it'd taken for their deal to be made: Denny would want to help; Denny was smart; Denny's sacrifice would save the worlds. In that moment, Adrian had told himself that he and Ray would be able to save nothing, but Denny could save them all. And so he'd thrown Denny on the pyre and said, *Take him.* The fact that they'd misunderstood and taken Laurel instead was his just desserts: karmic comeuppance, paid to Laurel instead of the bargain's maker.

I wanted to help you, said the dreadnought's voice.

You wanted to destroy the worlds.

I should have, should I not? Instead I had pity. Instead, I thought like a human. What if I had been strong, Adrian? You'd all be dead. Things would be so much better.

Adrian thought briefly into it, then used what remained of his will to shut it out. A literal devil on his shoulder, tempting him into easy answers. *What-if, what-if?*

What-ifs didn't matter. Who cared what might have happened that day? Adrian had taken the easy way out — easy for Adrian — and that was all there was to it.

Adrian, you can still—

The voice cut off. Adrian could still *what?*

Suddenly, he felt desperate to know. The thought had a finality to it. A way to end everything. The message wasn't naked words; like all projections sent to him by Carl or the dreadnought or the whispering millions of fiends he heard around him now that he'd entered the city, the dreadnought's promise came with images and concepts that didn't comply to just one of five senses.

Somehow, those severed words made Adrian understand something promising but ultimately unhelpful: *You have power you don't realize. You can end this. You can find her, and it can all be over with two clicks of those ruby slippers.*

Adrian looked down, half expecting to see his booted feet wearing Dorothy's red slippers. But the notion was merely conceptual. He had power to end it. But how? And why, when he thought too long on that path, did he feel equal parts relief and doom?

Pass, said one of the guards at the gate, waving their group through.

Their walk became a visual gauntlet once they entered the brimstone city. Most here were part of the hive mind, meaning they knew what had happened without needing to be told. There were parts of their awareness in the hellbringers. Parts of them within the queen. Parts of them, Adrian suspected, even within himself.

Laurel's psychic connection had opened a crack inside him and he'd lain himself in it to keep it open. In Laurel, when he'd still been able to hear her, had been the echo of the fiends around her. The connection had been facilitated by the dreadnought, who for some reason always had a special interest in Adrian.

Carl's words, conveyed on a bounced thought Carl once told Ray: *He is only as captive as he wishes to be.*

Meaning the dreadnought. But why would it ever want to be a captive? All its presence on the human plane had done was to stick its fist into Adrian's dreams. Dreams of Eldon and Laurel.

The rock buildings had holes, like windows. The tallest were five stories high, arranged like mud adobes smashed into clusters like human apartments. Adrian looked up at those holes — those up-to-five-stories of watching fiend faces — and saw that among the red-dancing flame illusion, the fiends were half like Carl: brown or deep red, and the other half blue, like the altered fiends who'd ambushed them.

Queen's soldiers, full of Zen Element. Nearly impossible to kill.

The walk took long, arduous minutes. Adrian kept his eyes up and around, watching the abundance of blue-skinned fiends. Dixon had been right, he now knew for sure. Carl had been right. They'd said that if humans struck their city, the fiends would strike back. They'd said that the fiends were arming, stealing Zen Element from the other side and using it not to create clumsy metal weapons the way humans did, but instead to imbibe it and become the weapons.

He could hear in their mental chatter that the blue ones were not just stronger. Not just tougher. They could also hypnotize opponents. Fry them with Hell's equivalent of electricity. Suck the life and moisture from them, collapsing them into dust.

Dixon was right. If Hell attacked, there would be Hell to pay.

Wait here, said two of the dreadnoughts.

There was no choice but to wait. The remaining hell-bringers would not let their chained party leave while two went inside.

They returned and gestured the party inside the most ornate and largest building in the cluster, bedecked with what looked like jewels and beveled glass, though in this heat the actual substances would need to be much harder. It had to be the castle. The fortress.

The dreadnought was still inside him, clinging to his fears for Laurel. It fed on them. Chewed them up. It made him stronger. More willing to fight, should fighting come.

Beside Adrian, Dee exhaled with relief. They'd been brought into what could only be some sort of a throne room, told to wait where supplicants held court.

"Good," she said, nodding in a way that told Adrian she was whistling in the dark, a lot more terrified than she was letting on. "We'll get to make our case."

"What makes you say that?" Lee asked.

It was like Dee didn't hear him. Her breath was fast, just shy of hyperventilating. She didn't exactly answer his question, but instead continued her own chain of logic.

"We'll just tell her," she said to herself. "We'll tell her they're sending a bomb. Look how blue they are. They can stop it. That's right; they can stop it and then they'll let us go."

"Honey, we're not *going* anywhere," said Harrison.

"We'll tell her," Dee repeated, "and they'll get Graves, and they'll let us go."

"Goddammit, Dee. Can't you see that—!"

Harrison fell silent as the walls and floor began to shake.

The queen was here, filling the chamber with her size.

28

QUEEN

Ray couldn't read his brother at all.

Adrian had gone cold. It was like nothing he'd ever seen.

Ray had known Adrian for Adrian's entire life, and up until now he'd known him in a few convenient guises: dutiful son, reliable if sometimes contentious brother, adoring and yet boneheaded boyfriend, intellectual, killjoy, and Boy Scout on the job. Every one of those faces of Adrian had optimism and responsibility behind it — enough that Ray, who was pessimistic and wild, usually found him annoying.

Adrian was always the one wanting to call home to Mom when they were out carousing as kids, who wouldn't break rules that nobody ever obeyed, who didn't drink until he was 21, and who Ray honestly thought might betray his brethren to Dixon last year because although righteous in their reasons, Brigade One's Legions had technically been breaking the law. He was an angel. A good kid. You couldn't tempt him with chicanery or a cigarette.

But now there was very little blood in his face. Adrian's

mouth was down at the corners: hard and unsympathetic. He looked like one of those kids with the humanity abused out of him.

It was hard for Ray to see, because even though Ray tried to always be in charge, Adrian had truthfully been the leader here. He knew the most, believed the most, and had a connection to Laurel even across the boundary that Ray knew his soured soul never could have had. Adrian was sensitive and wise, the beacon who'd bring them through this, and save everyone.

Now he was upright and stiff, his expression daring them all to burn the world. And him with it. He frankly didn't give a fuck anymore.

"Adrian," Ray tried to say while the walls shook, while the behemoth approached.

But Adrian, without looking away from the queen's antechamber, would only shake his head slowly.

The queen was as large as the dreadnought. It must be true that fiends molded their shapes to human perceptions, because to Ray the queen was exactly what he would have expected a ruling demon denoted as somehow female (as if that made sense, for them) to be.

She was the color of burned bricks, like the dreadnought. She wore smaller horns than the king's, turned down instead of up. Something swayed at the back of her large head — flaps like skin that approximated hair. Pendulous leathery breasts swung like deflated punching bags: six of them, with two sets on her abdomen like udders on a cow. Her clawed hands had slimmer, more articulated fingers than her counterpart. Sharpened teeth in dual rows, stacked like shark teeth.

Ray Porter. Adrian Porter, she thought-said, using a deep mental voice slightly higher in pitch than the others'. *It would seem you cannot stay away.*

"It *knows* you?" Lee asked Ray, but Ray shushed him.

You have come, then, the queen said, *with the price of peace.*

"What's it talking about, Ray? Adrian?"

The queen ignored Dee. It looked right at Adrian, front and center.

But Adrian said nothing.

He thought nothing. Ray, listening to his brother's mind as best he could, didn't know how that was possible. Their thoughts were all amplified here in this place, as if the walls of the queen's keep were, in themselves, receivers or repeaters. Ray could even catch snippets of Lee, Harrison, and Dee thinking if he tried. They were holding onto bravery but were scared. It was exactly how Ray felt.

But from Adrian? There was only that cold, hard stare.

The queen turned her gaze to Ray.

Speak.

Ray had seen Adrian talk without words to the dreadnought, but that day little had worked between his ears. He was an upfront, out-loud kind of guy. Subtlety didn't come easy.

So he answered aloud. "We came because we were sent by someone who *wants* peace."

With its price.

"With its intention," Ray countered. This conversation carried assumptions on one side only. Ray knew there was something missing here — a kind of advance-paved path of which he hadn't been made aware.

"Carl," Adrian finally said, deadpan. "It's talking about Carl. Carl brought us here. As the 'price of peace.'"

Ray spun, feeling betrayed, but Carl was nowhere to be seen.

"Hang on ..." said Harrison.

"*We* are the price of peace," Adrian told Ray. "You and me."

Ray was still looking for Carl. "That motherfucker. That little piece of shit. He—"

"It's okay, Ray," Adrian said, still in that dead tone of voice, still staring directly at the queen's horrible red face rather than turning toward his brother. "I've known for a while."

"What have you known?"

"That it's another trade. They wanted *us* last time." He nodded toward the queen. "*She* wanted us last time. The bargain the dreadnought made, to stop the sundering and take Laurel instead of one of us?" Now he shook his head a little. "It was the last straw. Isn't that right?"

The last question was directed at the queen.

The great beast moved its head slightly, grunting with something like acknowledgement, steam billowing from its great nostrils.

"It was all another con, Ray. Laurel taught them what they needed, but they still wanted the sons of Eldon Porter. They understood him. Now they want to understand us."

"Why us?"

"Ask her." Adrian clearly already knew the answer.

Sons of the breach, the queen said, *to re-open the breach.*

"Dad was with the team that opened the first rift. It took me a while to understand. Erika Dale figured out how to open rifts, and she opened a lot of them. But they were just holes, do you see? Just like ripping holes in a screen door. Erika wanted to perforate the world. To drop the center into Hell and bring about her armageddon. But that came from malice. It was sloppy. Dad's intentions?" Adrian shook his head. "They were pure."

Parity, the queen said. *The door swings both ways.*

"They're all connected, Ray," Adrian said like a schoolteacher. "Every one of the fiends is tied to the others. Sometimes it's a hive mind. Sometimes it's a whisper. We're singular, but they're always parts of a whole. They can share between each other. *Become* each other. It's like Dad showed me: You're never just talking to one of them. You address one, but there's always another of them waiting somewhere behind you — as a failsafe, or as defense to stab you in the back."

"This doesn't make any goddamn sense. If you thought any of this was—"

"It's helped me to see, Ray. I didn't know. I listen. I listen to all they've been telling me. It's not me who's put this together."

"So why the fuck are we here?"

"To show them how to open rifts the way Dad opened the first one. Not randomly. Not to fulfill a strategy. No. His desire reached across the boundary and touched something here. It happened because he was curious. They don't understand curiosity. They don't understand what it is to wonder as an individual. They have the energy they need now. What they are *curious* about now, is how far they can go."

"They don't need us for that. A lot of people are curious."

"You don't understand, Ray. To them, heritage is our bond. Their influence made me dream of him. Made me re-live moments with him. They want to understand Eldon Porter, and our memories are the only conduits to him that still exist."

Ray let that settle. The way Erika told things, the fiends wanted them as fighters. But Erika herself hadn't understood. Adrian had comprehended the mind of the dreadnought much better than Ray that day, but Ray knew even he had understood more than Erika. Matt Baker was a zealot and a tool. Erika was ambitious and nihilistic, also a tool. But once Erika and Matt were gone, what was the first thing the dreadnought wanted?

Ray.

And Adrian.

The sons of Eldon, who they'd admired, who they'd lost before they could truly understand. Who they could never resurrect, so his sons were the next best thing.

Now you have come, said the queen.

"Not for this." Ray shook his head and looked at Adrian. "You knew? You knew what we were marching into and you didn't speak up?"

"There was no other way." Adrian sounded fatalistic. Not defeated — grimly accepting instead.

"Fuck you, Adrian," Ray snarled. "Fuck Carl."

"Carl was only doing what he thought was best. Sometimes you have to do what's wrong because you know what's right. That's what Dixon did. What we did, when we made the bargain."

Ray was backing away, into the baffled forms of Dee, Harrison, and Lee.

"No." He kept shaking his head.

"It was the only way," Adrian said, "to right the wrong."

"What *wrong?*"

"Laurel."

"Goddamn you! *You* made the deal. *You* sent her, if anyone sent her."

"Look around, Ray." The almost-casual tone of Adrian's voice made him want to cut his brother open and see what was inside. He hadn't just given up; he'd given up in advance, then walked all of them into the no-win situation he could have easily avoided. "Look how full of Zen they are. We only saw a little of what they can do."

He tapped his head. "I've seen the rest of it in here. The dreadnought has shown it to me. We're no match for them. This was the only way. The only thing we could do to keep the world from ending was to deliver them exactly what they wanted all along."

The price of peace, the queen agreed.

Adrian looked hard at the queen, and then Ray heard his brother speak directly to her, using her own thought language: *We have come. Let the others go.*

No, the queen said. *Any who leave will show others the way. Now there is peace. The big rift is guarded. Your gunmen will take no more of us. Once your path is erased, none will have intention enough to follow. We will know. Your path must be scrubbed from existence, so it cannot be used again. You will stay. You are like us now.*

Ray felt more than heard his brother sigh. This was the second time Adrian was betraying people he cared about, and he was human enough to hate it. But the bond inside was more than words, and that meant that Ray, in addition to hearing Adrian's words, could also feel the thoughts behind what his brother had decided. Looking at those feelings, Ray saw the truth: *Graves's team would never have found this city.* Only the purity of Adrian's compass that had let them get this far. If he hadn't come for Laurel, they'd have never arrived.

Instead, there would have been more ambushes — one after another until they were dead. The fiends were stronger now than ever, and there was exactly one way to peace.

Nobody else could come. Nobody could leave, lest they draw a path for men like Graves to follow.

We will obey, Adrian said.

"No we goddamn well *won't* fucking—!"

Adrian held out a hand to silence Ray. Then he mentally repeated, *We will obey. All of us are alone in the world. We know there is no use in trying to flee. We know you control the doors. We know you hold the keys. We know that you allowed us to approach, and that leaving is something you will not allow.*

The queen made a gesture that approximated a nod.

But there's one condition. We came willingly. Another did not.

Laurel.

"Laurel," Adrian repeated aloud. "Is she still alive?"

Hesitation. Then: *She is.*

"But she's hurt. She's suffering. Isn't she?"

The queen didn't answer, but maybe it was because she didn't understand the concept of suffering. This was still Hell, after all.

Adrian had told Ray how her signal just ended. All of Laurel just … *gone.* That was the root of his obsession. Why he'd come. Why, now, he'd happily condemn them all to stay.

"It's clear you know how to refine Zen Element now," Adrian went on. "I see proof of it all around me. They know it on the other side, too — they *must* know by now, from what they've seen. That means Laurel's work is done. If we're to stay, you have to let her go."

Any who leave will show others the way, the queen repeated.

"Not if you look into me the way you looked into my father when he opened his first rift. He was curious. I am part of him, and Laurel's a scientist; she's also curious. We can open a small rift — one nobody else will ever find. I've seen it." Again Adrian tapped his head. "I know it can be done."

There was a long pause. The demons in the room shifted.

So did the humans, and when they did Ray tried to guess how the other three felt about spending eternity here. They'd known it was possible they wouldn't return, right? This wasn't really that big of a surprise. Adrian wasn't really *condemning* them by simply making a choice, was he? Because what if Adrian said no; what if they *did* try to run home? Did anyone seriously think they had a chance of making it?

This way saved the planes. This way held the peace. And it was true that Laurel never asked to come, and that it was Adrian's love — and guilt — for her that had brought them here safely. That much, even the queen must see.

No, the queen said. *It risks too much.*

For a second, Adrian looked distraught. Then, without warning, he clamped his hands over his ears and gave a cry. His face twisted; it looked to Ray like he was hearing unbearable noise inside his head. He curled from the abdomen as if he'd been punched. The emotion-stream radiating from Adrian to Ray had turned black, feeling even to Ray like panic.

"Adrian? What is it? What's wrong?"

Adrian's knees buckled. He looked crippled, unable to stand.

"Ade?"

Ray took his brother by the shoulders. Adrian's face had grown tortured, as if what he was hearing was more than he could bear. What was this? What strange evil had so suddenly befallen his brother?

Finally Adrian's hands lowered from his ears, but his teeth remained clenched. His hands fell to his sides: a tense posture of giving up inside this given-up scenario. He began to fidget, still grimacing at something unseen and unheard by the rest of them. A strange, determined-yet-angry expression crossed what had previously been resigned — and then agonized — features.

"Release her," Adrian managed to say, dropping his gaze to the floor. "Let her go, and I'll do whatever you want."

You are not in a position to demand, the queen said. *You cannot flee. You cannot decline. If you do not cooperate, you die.*

Instead of answering the queen, Adrian's eyes raised just enough to look at his brother.

"I'm sorry, Ray. I just ... I can't." He was fighting to talk, as if to make himself heard over whatever was in his head. "I did this to her. I'm all she has. I'm sorry. I don't have a choice."

"What do you mean?"

Adrian's hands continued to fidget. Ray could see something in one of his palms, maybe both of them. He winced hard like he was in pain, then gritted his teeth as if trying to bear it. There was a sound, like sizzling. A smell, like burning.

Ray felt intense pain rock through himself on the carrier wave of his brother's hijacked emotion.

"*Adrian?* What's going on?" Because a new emotion was coming from Adrian: *anger*. And with it, native to Ray, came a responding emotion: *fear*.

Something bad was about to happen. Ray had never been more sure of anything.

Adrian's shackles hit the ground as if they'd never been fastened. Then Adrian moved very fast, desperation screaming from one brother to the other: a sense of Adrian's urgency invading Ray's mind, screaming because he had no options left.

With unbound hands and a device snatched from Harrison Kim's belt, Adrian ran toward the queen.

That's when all Hell broke loose.

29

GAMBIT

Around the time Adrian and Ray Porter were meeting the queen, a specialist named Jane Choy was running back to her boss with unfortunate news.

"Sir!"

Graves turned his head. He was drinking coffee. They'd gotten more comfortable out here in Satan's sphincter than he wanted to be. Around the time they'd seen a party of dreadnoughts approaching the Porter Boys' crew, they'd also begun catching intermittent sight of a flaming city in the distance. Without the Porters' roses-and-teddy-bears intentions swimming around to act as camouflage, Graves couldn't get too close to that city, which was clearly the Porters' destination — and, correspondingly, the destination of the rather large Zen Fusion bomb Graves's unit carried. If they got too close, the scabs inside and around the city would smell the unit's malicious intentions on the wind like some great and righteous fart. What they *could* do, until the Porters arrived, was to get *somewhat* close, hide, and lay low while they waited.

The pisser was, waiting took too long. It'd looked for a

while like the Roughnecks might be slaughtered by those hell-bringers, but instead the big red motherfuckers had put them in shackles and marched them off like some infernal chain gang. They'd proceeded to walk toward the city, taking their sweet-ass time. Graves and his people had watched using optics and a whirligig or two, trying to understand what was going on. Audio was hard to come by with the hellbringers around, so mostly they'd witnessed the scene from afar and guessed.

The halfhead thing that had been guiding them looked friendly (friendly enough for a scab) with the hellbringers, so maybe what they'd seen was some sort of a betrayal. Or was it? Hard to say. The humans didn't seem like they were being treated as friends *or* enemies. Instead, they were somewhere in between — maybe seen by the scabs as allies and chained as a precaution, or foes to be heard out before dying.

Things got frustrating after that. While Graves drank his fourth or fifth cup of canteen coffee, the whole procession moved inside a building.

Before now, Graves had been planning to improvise. Some-how. Earlier, Patel had been able to give him orders, but Graves had cut that tether when he'd jammed Adrian Porter's link to his girlfriend. Because he wasn't in a hurry to be yelled at, Graves had no plans to re-open communication with Patel until after he'd completed the mission. Right now, that meant he was on his own. He got to make his own rules, and do this his way. But that became a problem when the Porters and their captors moved out of sight, into a place Graves couldn't follow.

It might still be fine. The Roughnecks had acted like good little dogs, leading Graves and his bomb to where both needed to be — where they couldn't have gone if Adrian's lovelorn bullshit hadn't paved the way for everyone.

Now all he had to do was kill the queen and obliterate the

city. Then all would be well. But would Graves still be able to hand-deliver the bomb, or would he have to lob it in catapult-style and hope it was good enough? He sincerely hoped not. After all that had happened, he wanted this to end in hands-on fashion. He for one wanted a chance to say *Take me to your leader,* then shove his ordinance up that leader's ass.

"What?" Graves said to the specialist.

"Energetics says the city is protected by some sort of a ..."

"Yes?"

"I hesitate to use the term 'force field,' sir. But—"

"—but it's a *motherfucking force field,*" Graves finished. "Like some Spock from *Star Wars* shit."

"*Trek,* sir."

"What?"

"Nothing, sir." She scrambled, seeming to realize that correcting her superior on matters of pop culture was perhaps not the best idea. "It's creating some sort of repellant shell over the city, generated by magnifying certain magnetic character-istics of ore in the rocks. So yes, sir. It's a field of force, and I'd guess it'll work just like in the movies."

She waited nervously. Graves had a reputation for killing the messenger.

"So if something were to be launched into the city ..."

"I suspect it'd bounce right off, sir."

Again she waited. Again Graves seemed to consider murdering her.

"That'll be all, Specialist."

Choy nodded, then scuttled away gratefully. Graves stayed put: metal cup in one hand, the other hand rising thoughtfully to his chin. He looked into the distance, spying the flaming buildings ahead.

So that was that. They were down to one course of action, if lobbing the bomb into the city was no longer a choice.

They'd have to cart the thing in, then detonate it on site. That was fine. Ideal, really. Lobbing came with a huge margin of error.

They'd have trouble for-sure getting the queen, and who knew if the blast would take out anything important or instead obliterate a lot of non-vital bullshit. Graves had just been thinking how he wanted to take the bomb in and blow it up himself anyway. Anything less felt like a pussy's escape.

But how? The scabs had managed to build some sort of repulsion technology despite basically being animals, but it was magnetism, not magic. You could still come and go through the city's front door if you had enough people and arms to do so, seeing as the gates were guarded by scabs and not an invisible force.

What *about* those guards? Graves's speciality was punching into tight places, but this was a whole new bag. Frontal assault might backfire. It might make things worse.

What they needed was to enter unseen, but expecting the gates to suddenly be unguarded (or for a backdoor to open) felt like a pipe dream. The best chance remained for someone to create a distraction. That had been the plan before now: They just needed to drive Adrian Porter into doing something dumb.

If that happened — if there was enough chaos inside the city — Graves could cut his way through it, and find a way inside.

He walked over to comms. "Are you still jamming Laurel Gantry?"

"Yes, sir," said the officer.

"Stop jamming her, and replace the feed with screams."

No, the queen told Adrian. *It risks too much.*

Adrian considered blustering. He considered begging. But

what could he do? The queen of Hell wasn't known for mercy, or human in the way Adrian's heart was. He considered making demands — dare the queen to call his bluff — but saw little point. They were inside the fiend city, surrounded by bosses and their biggest leader. Beyond the hellbringers were tens of thousands — maybe millions — of lesser soldiers. Her tone, even inside Adrian's head, offered no compromise.

She would not let Laurel go ... and there was exactly nothing Adrian could do about it.

His body half-collapsed. He thought it might all melt into nothing (all this effort and pain and hope, and for what in the end beyond nothing?), but something else happened.

Laurel's thought stream returned as suddenly as it had died ... only now, it was all bloodcurdling screams.

Adrian had never heard Laurel shriek in terror before. Not really, not in a way that was serious. She'd been surprised by jump-scares in movies, and had certainly yelled at him when he'd deserved it. But this was something else.

So this is what she sounds like when she's in pain, he thought. *This is what it sounds like when her soul is being ripped apart.*

It was impossible to take. Adrian slammed both hands over his ears to shut it out, but it was deep inside: impossible to silence.

He cried out. Everything clenched, curling him like a blow to the stomach. He almost fell, staggering to keep upright.

"Adrian?" Ray asked from beside him. "What is it? What's wrong? *Ade?*"

Adrian tried to answer — tried to even look up — but Laurel's pain had become his agony. It was only sound — only untold decibels of misery — but in it was everything Adrian had ever feared. It was one thing to be in peril yourself and another entirely to hear someone you love going through the exact same thing.

Not just someone you love, said a cruel voice — maybe his own, or maybe the mocking tone of the dreadnought coming from outside. *Someone you sent to this place. Someone who sounds like she's being tortured ... because of you.*

Adrian felt Ray take him by the shoulders. He couldn't look up; his sympathetic pain was too great to move more than inches.

You know what you have to do, the voice told him.

"Release her," Adrian croaked — his last effort at futile diplomacy. "Let her go, and I'll do whatever you want."

You are not in a position to demand. You cannot flee. You cannot decline. If you do not cooperate, you die, the queen replied.

Yeah. Well. Adrian didn't give a shit if he died. He had become anger. He had become rage.

Pictures — his own, concocted by his mind — joined the chorus of screams. He could almost imagine Laurel contorting, trying to survive whatever someone was doing to her. It didn't cripple him this time. He felt only fury instead.

They would pay. He would make them pay.

The screams continued, still barely recognizable as Laurel. But the worst of Adrian's panic dissolved, and determination replaced it.

You know the plan, that same internal voice said.

Grimly, he looked up at his brother. "I'm sorry, Ray. I just ... I can't. I did this to her. I'm all she has. I'm sorry. I don't have a choice."

Ray looked equal parts confused and fearful. "What do you mean?"

But Adrian was already doing what must be done. He'd dropped the Adrenalix he'd moved to the inside of his sleeve, as preparation should this be necessary, into his palm.

He used his thumb to push the button, injecting himself.

The pain was immediate and excruciating. Too late, he

remembered how Adrenalix worked: it stopped the heart, then quickly rebooted it.

A thousand knives stabbed him in the chest, tight bands of pressure gripping his ribcage and left arm. The injector fell away, and Adrian began pumping his free hand, either for circulation or just to push through.

He waited to fall. Waited to collapse. But the restart seemed to ride behind his partially-fiend biology, keeping him on his feet.

The pain in his heart diminished, but more torment was coming. This was the part he'd known. The part he'd steeled himself to face.

The changes that Frog had made to his skin and lungs reversed themselves slowly. Seconds after the heart-attack symptoms stopped, he began to feel warm. Then hot. Then very hot. Then so hot, it was like he was laying atop a frying pan.

His skin thinned to human thickness, then began to blister. He couldn't breathe. The air was nuclear in temperature, drier than any desert and devoid of oxygen. The smell of sulfur was so intense, he almost vomited.

Ray was still beside him, seeing Adrian's agony but not understanding its source. Why would he? Why would anyone intentionally turn themselves human again in the midst of all this Hell?

Ray was saying something beside him. Feeling something beside him. The skin and muscles at his wrists were the worst; they alone were in direct contact with the white-hot metal shackles.

Adrian gritted and bore, gritted and bore. It was taking seconds that felt like weeks to do what he needed.

Soon he'd fall to the ground. Soon, he'd suffocate, broil, and die.

Had he overestimated how long this would take? Or how it would happen?

His skin sizzled against the shackles, popping like a steak in the pan. The smell was as intolerable as the sound. His hands felt like they were melting as they hung at his sides. He couldn't inhale. He was lightheaded.

One way or another, this would all end soon.

He saw more than felt the shackles slip from his melted stumps. There was no feeling left to be had; he'd burned most of his nerves away. When his cuffs hit the stone floor, the sound of their dropping was muffled. They'd landed in what used to be the meat under his thumb, the breadth that was once flesh on his hands.

He was barely able to work the other injector. The one with the emergency top-off dose of Frog. He could only swing and stab, no longer feeling his grip. If he missed, or if it didn't deliver the injection …

But he struck his leg. The dose coursed into him. Almost immediately the pain began to diminish.

He could breathe. The Frog in the top-off doser was meant for panic situations; Dixon's people told them it was specially formulated to work fast.

And so as Adrian looked down, he saw black, burned flesh begin once more to take on color. Veins and capillaries were forming from nowhere, his muscles re-forming, his skin toughening again to withstand the heat.

But there was no time to heal fully. Everyone had seen his cuffs drop away; soon the guards would come to grab him.

So Adrian lunged for Harrison Kim, snatching one of the Zen grenades hanging there. Ordinarily, they'd be a strong punch to any sizable fiend, little more. Adrian was willing to bet that would change, if you got close enough and didn't care what happened next.

Adrian rushed the dais with the grenade, shoving it against what he had to assume counted as the great queen's guts. "Let her go."

The queen's voice had become indistinct, confused. Adrian took it as a good sign.

"LET LAUREL GO! RIGHT THE FUCK NOW OR I SET THIS OFF!"

More confusion. Even, maybe, fear from the queen. The guards came forward, but Adrian's eyes warned them back. There were two ways to set off a Zen grenade. One was with the pin, on a short delay. The other was to push a button whose safety catch Adrian had already disengaged. The makers of the grenades knew who would use them. Suicide, if it meant taking out your enemy, was always an option.

"Adrian?" Ray said, still unclear what had just happened. "Adrian, what are you doing?"

"Getting what I want."

"Adrian? Set that off and you'll die." Ray swallowed, looking at the guards. "We'll all die."

"I don't care if I die." Adrian wouldn't let himself hear the rest of what Ray had said.

He didn't want Ray or the others dead when angry guards took them, but he was improvising. Priority One was making Laurel's screaming to stop.

The world had paused. Adrian had shoved the grenade right into the queen's abdomen, but he seemed to have gotten lucky that it wasn't a toothless threat.

Nobody moved.

Until Ray came forward with both hands up — comical, almost, because he was still in chains. "Easy, Ade. What now? What exactly happens next?"

"They let her go."

"Then what?"

"I don't know."

"You don't know?"

"I don't know, Ray."

Ray nodded as if to say fair enough. Nothing got better but nothing got worse.

Now using a normal voice, but deadly earnest and grim, Adrian looked up to tell the queen, "If you think I won't do it, you aren't very fucking psychic at all. *Get her. Get Laurel,* or you end right here."

The queen stayed obediently still, unspeaking. She'd sent some sort of mental message to a pair of hellbringers; Adrian had heard its tone but not its contents. They were already gone, presumably to fetch Laurel. That meant he needed to figure this out, and soon. How would she get home?

And why had he just been thinking of his father?

Why had he just been thinking about rifts, and the role of intention in opening them?

A point in space began to grow white, like a tiny floating LED, on the other side of the queen's dais, dripping downward like wet paint. Soon it was a line, open in the middle, like an eye.

A rift parted by Adrian's single-minded, Porter-minded focus. Tiny, and only semitransparent. Nobody could fit through it. But what else did it take? Element for sure. Thulemite could be used to control rift openings; Erika Dale's interdimensional sabotage had taught him that.

But he wouldn't need it; he didn't care about control. Would the grenade open it the rest of the way? What might happen if, once Laurel was present, he told Harrison to lob another Zen Element grenade into the rift's iris? Did it just take two things, coming from a Porter: desire, and a big bang of Zen?

Yes. That would do it. But as before, the internal voice didn't sound entirely like his own.

Because it was the dreadnought, still speaking into him.

There was a shuffle. Adrian looked over and saw Laurel standing unbound between the two hellbringers. He almost couldn't breathe again, looking at her. His relief was so complete, he almost dropped the grenade, losing his advantage on the spot.

"Adrian?" she said.

He wanted to run to her. He wanted her to run to him.

But he couldn't do that — not until she got home, which might mean maybe not ever. The thought that he was likely facing his own end did not hurt as much as the fact that it meant he might never touch Laurel again.

"Harrison," Adrian said, keeping his grenade pressed tight to the queen's front while eyeing the grenades still clipped to the other man's belt. "Harrison, I need you to ..."

Harrison paused, then short of shrugged for Adrian to go on. But Adrian had forgotten about the grenades. He'd forgotten about the plan.

He was looking right at Laurel, who didn't even seem hurt. She didn't look like a woman tortured. And for sure, she wasn't being tortured right now.

So why did he still hear screaming inside his head?

"What, Adrian?" said Harrison.

"I ... I ..."

There were no words. No comprehension.

Fortunately, that all stopped mattering when the walls fell in.

30
ACT OF WAR

While Adrian held the queen at bay, Graves's unit made its move.

With all fiends mentally connected to some degree, every head turned when Adrian lunged, threatening to end her. The queen was irreplaceable. If killed by humans, there would be an unexpected power vacuum. No one knew what would happen then.

The city guards remained at the gate, but with their minds away, Graves's people easily picked them off. They stalked through the city, ending any beings they found and sliding their corpses into corners. Soon enough they were just outside, peering through cracks, listening to the standoff as it unfolded.

They waited.

And then, at the moment of maximal distraction — just as Graves had wanted from the start — they struck.

Commandos blew through two walls in unison, opposite one another. They'd known what was coming but the fiends inside had not. Fiend forces turned in two directions, split and improvising, diminishing their power.

Graves's people loosed their weapons. Some, Adrian had seen before. Others, he had not. It seemed that whoever stocked these missions (a shadow part of GEN, he imagined) had kept some of the best toys secret from all but this hit squad.

One of them had a thing like a laser, but with a beam like a broadsword. It sliced through an acre of milling soldiers of various classes, cutting them in half.

But they were full of Zen, unwilling to die ... and so they kept coming, kept clawing and climbing.

Graves himself led the charge on one side as he bellowed. His uniform was sleeveless; his arms were massive and bulging with veins. He came at them with mouth open, teeth exposed, both hands on a weapon that fired glowing rounds that swerved and circled like intelligent heat-seekers.

The rounds took their time to find targets, then attached to their bodies and burrowed their way inside like tiny, bladed digging machines. The invasion made the struck fiends wail — until the rounds found their insides, and exploded in azure fire.

But even those destroyed ones, full of Zen Element, kept right on coming.

Tethered, the Roughnecks could do little but stay where they were, duck their heads, and try to stay out of the way. Adrian kept his place by the queen, but that situation was moot and the queen seemed to know it, to know that's just what Adrian was thinking.

She cuffed him aside, heedless if he decided to press his button. Adrian didn't, though; his thumb was jarred from it — and when he fell back, the grenade itself was jostled, rolling away to fall into a hole on the floor.

Adrian fell to his knees and scampered after the grenade,

sliding beneath a rock formation along one side of the chamber. He reached, but could not see where he was reaching.

Then he had it. He gripped the thing triumphantly, and when he pulled the grenade free and held it up, he actually exclaimed a little in victory.

The feeling of victory lasted just seconds. The chamber was filling with reinforcements now — disposable soldiers and bosses as well.

Adrian lost count, seeing some fiends he knew and plenty of new ones. There was a whallop, a belarus, a ubiquitor. A towering macerator, a few more hellbringers. Untold numbers of Zen-blue halfskulls, which seemed to have become Hell's default soldier post-sundering-day.

Carl was nowhere to be seen. Was he a friend after all? Or an enemy? Alive or dead?

Adrian had no idea. The floor was a wash of bodies.

He felt a hand close on his ankle as he moved to stand. The hand pulled him hard; Adrian slipped and fell on hands and chest. Something smashed above him. He looked up to see the enormous spiked fist of a humbler — a Max-Juke-class boss — slam into the pillar he'd nearly risen in front of.

The humbler hadn't been swinging for Adrian. It had been swinging for one of Graves's men, who was now ribbon-thin, squeezed of its guts like toothpaste from a tube.

"Easy, pard," said Lee Barnes, who'd pulled him down. "It's a war out there."

Adrian looked back. The entire squad of Roughnecks was with Lee, still chained. Somehow, as an intact and interlinked group, they'd managed to crawl under a massive set of what looked like stalactites. They made a cave back here, away from the furor.

Rounds fired. Guts far too abundant to be human sprayed like comic slime. All around, small pieces of blue fiends of various castes and classes kept moving like zombie bits, alive in some way but unable to do much more than pat and poke. The entire battle royale was visible from here, filling the chamber. Slithereens had joined the party now, along with a few stilt-walkers. There were even a few of the small, fat fiends he and Ray had battled back before their kind was known: They looked like large yellow pugs without heads and attacked by firing a concussive wave.

Watching, Ray could only see a few of Graves's people remaining. How many had there been? Were more outside?

The queen had some sort of inborn energy weapon that created huge red electrical slashes with every swipe of her titanic claws. She seemed able to breathe fire, or something like fire: streams that looked like plasma and obliterated even stone and steel on impact. As Adrian watched, she took out three well-armed human commandos in a single breath — and this despite their lobbing several classes' worth of multi-weapon rounds at her at the same time. The commandos deployed classic weapons like Rattlers and Goms, but also new contraptions that maximized the cure-all that was brute force.

Graves stepped forward, yelled something that sounded macho, and unleashed a tree-trunk-thick round of something — light, maybe, plasma, maybe — at the queen's flank. It struck her, singed, but ultimately only made her angry.

She raked at Graves, throwing him against the wall. Even from his hiding place, Adrian could hear the man's Frog-reinforced spine snap.

The queen had been kneeling to fight. She brought herself to full stature and ducked to avoid the ceiling.

She peered around the room, which thanks to the abundant munitions brought by the attackers was three-feet-high in most places with bodies. Here and there among them were human fatalities as well. The queen paced the space, stepping on each to be sure.

She did Graves last. He exploded like a ketchup packet.

The remaining soldiers cleared the room as the queen hissed. After, only she and three still-alive hellbringers remained.

Then Adrian remembered Laurel. His head spun, panicked, sure he'd see her body among the dead. But he saw nothing. No trace of her at all.

Between them was the almost-rift that Adrian's own mind had begun to conjure. The one through which, he suspected, they might still be able to escape.

But how? It was right in the middle of the room, and once again the room was controlled by the queen and her minions.

The queen turned her great head toward Adrian. *You.*

She came forward while Adrian tried to stand his ground. He still had the grenade, but he'd never get close to the queen again. He couldn't just throw the thing. With the delay instead of instant-detonation, they'd know before he threw, and deflect it immediately.

The queen's crimson face was furious.

You did this.

"I didn't do anything!"

I could forgive your attempt to seize control. It is how I took power. But not this. She seemed to mean the destruction of her palace, the murder of so many chiefs. *You will not leave here. Your pain will be legendary.*

She showed her sharp teeth. Exhaled her breath like rotted meat.

"Fine. Kill me. Do what you have to. But we were not part of this."

You lie.

"We came in peace!"

With weapons. With a bomb in my middle.

"All I wanted was Laurel. That's all." His hands were still up, and one still held the grenade, so, being careful to keep the pin in place and re-closing the safety hasp, he let it drop.

LIES!

Adrian refused to back up, though the queen kept coming. "It's not a lie! I know you can hear my intentions! I couldn't have gotten this far if this was what I wanted from the start!"

The queen hesitated. That much was true.

Her head turned. She stared at the semi-rift: more like a window into the other world.

Your intention, the queen said, somehow meaning both Adrian and the rift at once.

She moved toward the rift as if fascinated. As if she hadn't seen thousands of rifts before.

You did this.

"I *think* I did it."

How?

"I don't know." He was shocked that she didn't; she always knew everything. "I wanted a way out. But look. It's just a window. You can't go through."

Adrian was looking into it now. On the other side, he could see bricks and a dark hallway: a facility with big spaces and high ceilings, but not Patel's HQ. It was sort of familiar. But from where?

You could not do this alone, the queen said, inspecting it. *This could only be done with our cooperation. Someone helped you.*

One of the hellbringers made a sound like a bark. The queen's head whipped toward it to find that it and another another behemoth were dragging something through the hole in the wall: a load on a wheeled sledge, partially covered by a tarp.

The hellbringer ripped the tarp away. The queen's face again registered instant fury.

It was a bomb. A massive, *massive* bomb, surely brought in by Graves's team. It was enough to level the city. Enough to undo everything in a hundred mile radius.

Carl's words came back to Adrian, now dripping with poison:

If our queen is struck, she will strike back.

The magnitude 35 rift was still wide open. The military thought they controlled it, but Adrian had seen with his own eyes that millions of fiend soldiers waited on its other side. Their function, when Adrian saw them, had seemed like defense. But Carl was right: If the balance was tipped, it could be offense just as easily.

And what would it mean, if millions of blue-filled fiends spilled into Fortune?

They were the tip of the iceberg.

Patel's words: *An act of war.*

By bringing this plane-ending bomb, Graves had committed an act of war.

31
LUKE

Hell's prison was much like one on Earth. There were walls, though they were made of rough red stone instead of iron or concrete, and there were doors made of seemingly the same metal as their shackles had been. Nobody was in shackles anymore, though.

Adrian had seen the Roughnecks placed in their cells before he was brought here, to his. Ray, Lee, Harrison, and Dee were in a two-by-two grid, Ray and Lee across from Harrison and Dee. They could talk, if they wanted. The fiends — "visitors," maybe — didn't seem to care. They wanted the humans confined, not denied everything. Commit crimes in Hell and you expect more than a slap on the wrist. Fishhooks and flaying sounded more like the ticket.

Adrian, placed in this abandoned block all by his lonesome, found Carl's words coming to mind:

To us, you are the demons.

And yeah, yeah, yeah. Taking pot shots at humanity was tired sport by now. Every movie and book and misanthropic movement had delighted so much in pointing out their own species's abominable nature over the past two hundred years that it was now boring. Humans were evil; maybe fiends weren't after all. It didn't make Adrian want to turn over a new leaf and start handing out daisies. He was the caged animal, and ready to embrace it.

He had no idea why he'd been separated from the others, left here in solitary. If Ray had been here, he might've had some theories about the Super Special Porter Boys.

He thought he heard water dripping. It was the only sound other than those he made himself.

It couldn't be water, though — not here where water boiled away. Could it be oil? Some other liquid able to withstand the heat? Why did he care?

He had to think about something. If he thought of nothing, fears came hard and fast. He had no idea why they were being held, or how long it would last. He had no idea why they had jails in the first place. Who else inhabited these cells, when no humans were here? Were they really like humans: despite the shared nature of so much of their consciousness, was it possible that some among them were good, and others bad?

Good and *bad* were slippery terms dependent on point of view, but "a wide range of temperament and diverging opinions" was definitely legit. The queen had plotted her coup. That supposed an individual mind who sought out other, like-minded individuals. It supposed opponents who felt differently. It supposed emotion: anger, indignation, hope, pride, jealousy, and some underworld desire for freedom.

Before the queen rose to power, she might have been put in this place — or a place like it, with much higher ceilings.

The thought was funny, but Adrian didn't smile. He was thinking of prisons. Of royalty kept behind bars to keep them from causing trouble. He thought of dark hallways built to accomodate the largest and most powerful of prisoners. He thought of a window into another world, and how, with enough Zen, he and Laurel might have escaped.

"I'm so sorry." He spoke to fill the silence, but all his voice in this empty place did was to remind him just how silent it was.

"About what?"

The door at the far end had opened without him noticing. Now a woman came toward him, down the cell row.

"Jesus. You're okay," he said.

"It's Laurel, not Jesus. Though I understand why you'd be confused."

They clasped hands through the bars. Strangely, despite the fact that both of their skins had been toughened by Frog or something like it, the warmth of her hands, to him, felt just the same.

"Is it really you?"

"Nobody asks 'Is it really you?'" Laurel answered. "Look at you. Maybe I could get you a tin cup. Let you run it back and forth across the bars."

"Are you hurt?"

Laurel shook her head. She didn't even look dirty. Adrian hadn't showered since he'd been here, for obvious reasons. Turned out dosing with Frog didn't keep a man's armpits from reeking. Laurel was pretty as a picture. Her skin was thick and dark, her hair in ropes that no longer held keratin.

She even smelled nice. Unlike him.

"I'm *fine*, baby," she said, petting his hand. "I want to know about *you.*"

Her tone unseated him. She was so casual. So blasé. Not only was she talking to him like he wasn't in jail — nor in Hell — but like she herself hadn't been snatched from the Earthly plane and brought here as slave labor. He'd already worked out that the screams he'd heard weren't Laurel's, and that he hadn't lost touch with her because she'd been in trouble. Those things were Graves's doing. He'd followed them like tracer rounds, and ended up exactly where he belonged.

But *this?* This calm and cool way she was talking to him? Even if she hadn't been mistreated or tortured, the no-big-deal of this was still a bridge too far. Laurel moved her hand from his hand to his face, cupping his cheek.

"When I saw you out there, I was so worried."

"You were worried?"

She said nothing.

"Laurel ..." Adrian remembered something. "We can get out of here. I know a way out."

"How?"

"I can make rifts. Somehow." Had she seen the window thing from earlier? He'd seen her for less than a minute before she disappeared, and he'd thought her dead. "I don't understand it, but a ... a sort of window opened. I think if I'd thrown my Zen grenade into it ..."

"You probably would have killed your brother. Or Harrison or Dee or Lee. Or Carl."

"You know Carl?"

She nodded. "I sent Carl."

"You ..." There was no end to that sentence. *"What?"*

"I sent Carl," she repeated, as if the problem was his hearing. "Well. I sent a halfskull with compartmentalized intelligence. *You* named him Carl. At least that's what he told me." She cocked her head a little and gave a half smile. *"Carl? Really?"*

She kept smiling at him. Despite being so happy, he almost wanted to smack her. This was not a place for jokes or smiles or being amused by human names given to demons. She should be morose. Dour. The best anyone should be here was "safe," "unhurt" ... maybe "just okay."

"What are you talking about?"

"It's complicated. I'll explain later." She said it like deferring inconsequential office gossip.

"Laurel ... What's been going on?"

She gave a very slight smile. "So much."

"Like what?"

She shook her head, and the smile finally vanished. A look of getting down to business crossed her features ... but he'd be damn curious about those smiles later.

"We don't have forever, despite what the Bible might say about this place. I told the queen that I needed to speak freely with you; that's why I didn't want you with the others."

"*You* put me here?"

"Not in the prison, but in this part of it. You're a criminal, A. You're lucky to be alive."

"I didn't bring the bomb! Graves—"

"I know. *Believe me* I know. She won't listen, but that's not a surprise. You have to know how to handle her, is all. The queen's weakness is pride. I've learned to flatter her. I told her I could get more information out of you if your friends couldn't overhear us, and that I wanted nothing more than to honor and serve her."

There were five thousand questions behind that. It sounded like Laurel somehow had the queen's trusting ear, but she also talked like someone who could give an in-depth tour of this place. There were so many assumptions. Trusting her that time was short, Adrian swallowed his queries to listen.

"They might be watching us right now, but they don't do audio bugging here. They have shared minds. Spying by listening-in isn't usually something they need. Officially I'm here to find out what greater plans you and those who sent you have behind that bomb."

"Dixon is behind me! Behind the military's back! I don't have any goddamn plans—"

"I know." She raised a pacifying hand. "But you have to understand how this looks. You were in the lead, knowing they read ill intent and guard against it. Your intent to find me made perfect camouflage for the others. They came in right behind you. We both know that happened because they used you, but from the queen's perspective, it was a plot. Because they struck last, you see? The sundering. They could have broken Earth's plane and let the monsters in. Their atmosphere would have soured Fortune before it equilibrated. But nobody here now wanted the sundering. It was too risky. Most believed it would kill this plane, not ours."

Adrian thought back. That's what Erika said, too. She'd spoken of the sundering as something necessary to regain all the Zen energy humanity had stolen, not something ideal, seeing as things would equal out to be like the human plane rather than theirs. They *had* to sunder; they'd thought that right up until Adrian had made his accidental deal to send Laurel to teach them how to refine Zen Element: a technology that, if it could be taught, would replace energy without needing to sunder.

"*Most* believed that," Laurel said. "But not all."

"Who didn't believe it?"

"The king said it would result in a battle, but that the victor would control both worlds. Any guesses as to who he thought would win? Any guesses at all, given how hard they sandbagged on you, and how easy you all knew it would be to lose if a lot of rifts — and a lot of fiends from all different classes — attacked at once?"

"We met the king. Soon after we left you. I didn't know he was the king. He called it off. He was the one who cancelled the sundering." Adrian didn't elaborate why.

Laurel either already knew Adrian had sent her here or didn't. If she didn't, now wasn't the time to open that wound. "I know that, too. What you don't know — what even *the queen* doesn't know — is why."

"But you know?"

She nodded. "Once I understood the science, the truth was hard to miss. The *conditions* here are very different from on Earth, but science is the same everywhere. I was able to work out a few things, then fortunately got an idea why certain things had been done *with full knowledge* of what I'd discovered before I said anything about my findings to the queen."

"What does that mean?" Adrian asked.

"It means the king was only half right. So I asked myself the same question: If he was right, and the sundering would have been good for them, why did he stop it?"

"And what was your answer?"

"He wanted a counter-reaction. He wanted all that's happened. They're incapable of opening targeted rifts, but our military-industrial complex is plenty capable. After the sundering almost — but not quite — happened, he correctly guessed that we would start doing exactly what we've done: preparing for next time. Doing whatever it took to make sure the fiend plane would never, *ever* get the upper hand again."

"But they caught him! He's in a holding facility right by the brigadehouse!"

"He sure is," Laurel said. "Right by the brigadehouse. Which meant most of the time, right by you and Ray. Or, as things turned out: Just by *you*."

"What about me?"

"You're Eldon's more insightful son. In touch with your emotions and *dreams*."

Adrian was beginning to understand. He'd dreamed of Laurel. That's why he was here.

"It was the dreadnought who got me to come in here after you."

She shook her head. "It was both of us. Me. *And* him."

Adrian's mouth fell open. He didn't speak.

"The queen seems powerful, but she's actually weak," Laurel said. "Eldon's intention to see the other world opened the first rift from our side — the first truly intended, truly targeted rift there was. It ... imprinted on the boundary somehow. That part's more pseudoscience, but I'd be a fool to deny what the hard science reinforces. Ever since that day, events have unfolded like an inevitable puzzle. Once this began, there was only one way it could end."

"How?"

"The way everything ends," Laurel said. "In equilibrium."

"What's that mean?"

"It means that all things tend toward entropy. Don't make me give you another lecture on thermodynamics, Adrian. The last time we tried that, we didn't have enough information and therefore thought breaches could be sealed."

"They can't?"

She shook her head. "Not in the largest picture. Two planes is a very strict form of order. So are two separate systems maintaining such different environments. You might say that when the universe was created with dual planes, we were always on a countdown to a sundering. It's a little more graspable to say instead that ever since they poked through to our side — and then much more when Eldon opened a hole back — that's when this really began. Nature abhors order. All things tend toward chaos."

"*All* things?" Adrian asked.

"The arrow of time is defined as an increase in entropy. An increase in chaos. In disorder. Things don't self-assemble in nature. Not in the long run. All things decay. Bodies. Stars. The planets." She paused for emphasis. "Our two very different planes."

"What are you saying, Laurel?"

"I'm saying that collapse is and always has been inevitable. They put me in with their version of scientists, who operate very differently from our scientists, though the principles are the same. Once I was in with them, I learned that the king knew everything I just told you. Adrian ... He *knew* that 'stopping the sundering' that day didn't change a thing. He knew we couldn't just patch the holes and go on living. Our life spans are short. Theirs are long. The threat of collapse isn't distant for them; it's inevitable within a few lifetimes. *Inevitable*, you hear me? It literally cannot be stopped on a long enough timeline. So if the king knew that, why would he agree to try to patch things up — to pretend vainly that things could go on as separate planes forever?"

It was all sinking in. Adrian thought he'd reached the end of the fiends' fifty-year con that day, but in truth the con kept going. The sundering was never meant to happen. Ray and Adrian, sons of Eldon and matches to the "intention energy of the rift" (whatever that meant), were always meant to arrive in time and do battle. Erika was always just a pawn, meant to drag Ray and Adrian to the fore. Same for Matt Baker. The military, Dixon, and even Laurel. The king's greatest scheme was still happening right now ... and from the sound of Laurel, she agreed with every bit of it.

"He needed you here," Laurel said, "and he needed himself in our plane. You *had* to come with positive intent or the queen, who he allowed to subvert him, would never have let you reach me. That's why I was taken — so you'd come and find me. I saw the window-rift you mentioned back in the throne room, Adrian. But you're wrong about what was necessary to complete it. If you'd thrown a Zen grenade at it, all you would have done was put our friends in danger."

"But if I only opened it halfway because I wanted a way for you to escape ..."

She was shaking her head. *"You* didn't open it halfway, Adrian. *He* did."

Adrian felt cold. She meant the dreadnought. She meant their deposed king. The tyrant who, from all Adrian had heard, was the most dangerous being the world had ever known.

"What you saw was the offer of his hand. All it would have taken to open the rift was for you to reach out and shake it."

Adrian understood. The dark hallways. The high ceilings. The vaguely familiar room he'd seen through that bright little window. It was the dreadnought's prison. There was no way for the dreadnought to escape in the human world because the walls and fortifications were too strong ... but there *was* a way for him to escape into *this* world, and Adrian held the key.

"Either way, there will be war. Either way, there will be suffering and death. The goal isn't prevention, because it can't be stopped. The goal is to *get through it.* To *survive.* And going as we are, Adrian — this bit-by-bit thing we're doing? Neither side will live for long if it keeps up. To put this in layman's terms, we need to *get it over with.* What the king has in mind is far bigger than the sundering. Far larger in magnitude, and only possible *now.* If the worlds had broken the first time, Fortune would have been contained. Walled off. Nuked, maybe. But now?"

She sighed. It was hard to guess her feelings on the issue, but Laurel was and had always been a scientist. She wouldn't be pleased or displeased by any of this. Instead, she'd be efficient. Facile. She'd already used the word that said all that needed saying: *Inevitable.*

Only a fool tried to fight what was impossible to stop.

"Now that our side has developed as much energetic rift-fare technology as we have, and they've developed to match it," Laurel continued, "now he can shatter the world."

Light caught Adrian's eye. He looked and saw the same bright spark he'd seen in the queen's throne room. The same drawing-down of light, the same opening, the same dark-hallway'd window into his own world.

"I can't be the man who shatters the world."

"*'Father, if You are willing, let this cup be taken from me,'*" Laurel quoted.

"What's that mean?"

"It's Luke 22:42. It means nobody wants to do the things that must be done, and you're not the first person to wish the duty didn't fall to you."

Adrian paused. He believed Laurel. He trusted not just her, but her judgement and her acumen. It was terrible, what she was saying ... but if she was saying it, he believed that it was true.

"Jesus, Laurel."

And she said, "Exactly."

They held hands. It was hard to breathe — and not for the heat, the lack of oxygen, or the sulfur.

"Son of Eldon, maker of the breach, I'm afraid it's up to you."

Adrian looked at their hands. At the way their fingers intertwined. All things were connected like those hands, were they not? That's what always came around, again and again.

He heard his father's voice, from a day long, long ago:

Always do the greatest good. Even if it means doing bad now. Even if it means everyone hates you and thinks you did something wrong.

He looked up. At the rift.

And then, without knowing how he was doing it, he opened wide and let the Devil in.

THE ZEN ELEMENT CHRONICLES WILL CONCLUDE IN 2025

The door has swung wide, and the king has returned to his throne in Hell.

Endgame, in the long con between the demon plane and ours, has begun.

If you'd like to be notified when the final book in the Zen Element Chronicles is available, make sure you're on my mailing list by visiting JohnnyBTruant.com/join.

THANKS TO MY SUPPORTERS!

122 amazing readers helped bring *City of Fire* to life as a beautiful limited edition through a 2024 Kickstarter campaign. **My extra-special thanks go to the following backers:**

SUPER SUPPORTERS

Jason Kelly

Thomas Bennett (AKA "Decoy Dave")

Anthony Erdmann

SUPPORTERS:

Athena

Deborah (Groff) Langarica

Ken Checinski

Jennifer Hetzel McBride

Jim White

Joe Golden

Patrick Riffe

Sheryl Kennedy Coe

E. Kim

Thank you from the bottom of my heart for supporting my work. You're the best!

ENTER THE TRUANTVERSE

When it comes to stories and the worlds they live in, books are only the beginning.

Visit JohnnyBTruant.com/join to get my best books sooner and cheaper than the other stores.

My list doesn't suck like so many author email lists. Seriously. It has unicorns.

ALSO BY JOHNNY B. TRUANT

Winter Break

Pattern Black

Pretty Killer

Cursed

The Bialy Pimps

Namaste

The Target

La Fleur de Blanc

Axis of Aaron

Devil May Care

Screenplay

The Island

Burnout

Sick and Wired

UNICORN WESTERN:

Unicorn Western

The Wanderers

A Fistful of Magic

Shimmer to Yuma

The Man Who Shot Alan Whitney

The Spectacular Seven

Open Meadows

The Unforgotten

The Magic Bunch

Unicorn Genesis

FAT VAMPIRE:

Fat Vampire

Fat Vampire 2: Tastes Like Chicken

Fat Vampire 3: All You Can Eat

Fat Vampire 4: Harder Better Fatter Stronger

Fat Vampire 5: Fatpocalypse

Fat Vampire 6: Survival of the Fattest

The Vampire Maurice

Anarchy and Blood

Vampires in the White City

Fangs and Fame

Game of Fangs

INVASION:

Invasion

Contact

Colonization

Annihilation

Judgment

Extinction

Resurrection

Save the City

Save the Girl

Save the World

Longshot

THE INEVITABLE:

Robot Proletariat

The Infinite Loop

The Hard Reset

Cascade Failure

Reboot

En3my

DEAD CITY:

Dead City

Dead Nation

Dead Planet

Dead Zero

Empty Nest

THE DREAM ENGINE:

The Dream Engine

The Nightmare Factory

The Ruby Room

The Pandora Core

The Engine Convergence

The Tinkerer's Mainspring

GORE POINT:

Gore Point

City of Fire

THE BEAM:

The Beam: Season One

The Beam: Season Two

The Beam: Season Three

The Beam Season Four

The Beam Season Five

Future Proof

Plugged

The Future of Sex

THE TOMORROW GENE:

The Tomorrow Gene

The Eden Experiment

The Tomorrow Clone

Null Identity

COMEDIES:

Everyone Gets Divorced

Greens

Fiends

Decoy Wallet

NONFICTION:

The Fiction Formula

Fiction Unboxed

Iterate & Optimize

The Story Solution

Write. Publish. Repeat.

The One With All the Writing Advice